# MAGGIE CHRISTENSEN

# Celebrations in Bellbird Bay

Cover and interior design: J D Smith Design
Editing: John Hudspith Editing Services

# Dedication

To my own wonderful soulmate, Jim.

# One

Sandy Elliot stared at the wreck of what was to have been her new business. *Celebrations* was a burnt-out shell, the newly painted sign now looking strangely forlorn above the blackened building.

Tears streamed down her cheeks as she watched the firefighters saving the neighbouring shops, glad they seemed to have only suffered minimal damage. But there was no way the shop into which she'd poured all her hopes and dreams could be saved.

When the call wakened her just as dawn was breaking, it had taken Sandy several moments to grasp what the caller was saying. But as soon as it sunk in, she sprung up and after checking her daughter was still sound asleep, pulled on the trackpants and tee-shirt she'd worn the evening before and drove as fast as she could, her stomach churning, hoping against hope they were wrong, and her new venture was safe.

Was the universe trying to tell her something? It was only three months since her partner of five years told her she was leaving the business they'd established together.

'You're what?' Sandy looked in horror at Rose, the other half of Sandy Rose, purveyor of desserts, cakes and pastries to Sydney's Lower North Shore. 'You can't.'

Rose looked uncomfortable. 'I know it's a shock, Sandy, but Bill has been offered this wonderful job… and it's in Cairns.'

'Cairns?' It might as well be on the other side of the world. Cairns was a long way from where their specialty business was located, the business they'd built together when they met working for the neighbourhood café in Neutral

1

*Bay. It had proved a lifeline to Sandy when her marriage ended when Fliss was only ten. Now her daughter was fifteen, just at the age where she needed stability… and Rose had dropped this bombshell.*

*'You'll find someone or something else,' Rose said, a toss of her head sending her hair over her shoulder. 'There'll always be a market for Sandy Rose cakes and pastries.'*

*But without Rose there would be no Sandy Rose, and Sandy's cakes and pastries didn't have the same ring about it, even if she could have managed the business on her own – the thought of working with anyone else was unbearable.*

*It was okay for Rose. She was ten years younger than Sandy's forty-five. She didn't have a child to consider.*

But Sandy was more resilient than she'd imagined and three months later, she had opened her new business. Knowing she couldn't compete with the pastries and macaroons which had been Rose's speciality, she'd decided to concentrate on the special occasion cakes for which she'd become well-known – cakes for weddings, birthdays and other special events, and to provide catering for the events, too. It was Fliss who'd come up with the name. 'It would be cool to call it *Celebrations*, Mum,' she said, when Sandy was searching around for a name for the new business. So, *Celebrations* it had become.

But now, there was little to celebrate.

'Sorry, miss. You can't stay here.' The voice pulled Sandy out of her thoughts. She stared at the police officer standing in front of her. 'It's my shop,' she said, holding back the next flood of tears.

'I'm sorry. If you give me your details, we'll be in touch. Looks like arson.'

*Arson? Who'd want to burn down her business?* Sandy felt a curl of fear. Her breath caught. She began to tremble, her knees buckling. She didn't have any enemies – none she knew of, anyway. She and, her ex, Grant, still argued about stuff, but he wouldn't be so vindictive as to do this, would he?

\*

When Sandy returned to the small Cremorne unit she called home, Fliss was in the kitchen making one of the smoothies she preferred for breakfast.

'You were out early. What's up?' she asked, pausing the blender to peer inside.

'Sit down, Fliss. I need to tell you something.' Sandy made an effort to stop her voice from shaking, but her daughter knew her too well.

'Mum, what's happened?'

'It's… there's been a fire…'

Fliss's eyes widened. 'Not…?'

When Sandy nodded tearfully, Fliss ran to her mother and wrapped her arms around her. 'What will you do?'

'We'll be all right,' Sandy said with more confidence than she felt. She still hadn't fully processed the extent of her loss. 'I'll find something. We can start again.' But even as she spoke, Sandy knew it wouldn't be easy. Her savings were all tied up in the burnt-out building. Jobs in her specialised field weren't easy to come by. She'd no doubt be forced to go back to the sort of waitressing position she'd had when she met Rose, a position which would barely pay the mortgage, never mind Fliss's school fees. At least there would be the insurance to collect. She thought longingly of the top-of-the-range commercial ovens she'd carefully chosen, the huge refrigerator, all the other pieces of equipment lovingly purchased. Then her heart sank remembering the list of clients whose cakes she could no longer provide. Her first task today must be to contact them. At least her laptop was here, at home.

'Oh, Mum!' Fliss hugged her mother tightly.

'It's okay, sweetheart, I was just thinking of all the people I'm going to be letting down.'

'It's not your fault.'

'No.' But was it? the police officer had mentioned arson, but what if Sandy had forgotten to turn something off, if she had inadvertently caused the fire herself? 'You should get off to school. What is it today?'

'Maths.' Fliss grimaced. 'Are you sure you'll be all right? I can…'

'I'll be fine. You go, sweetie. And good luck with the exam.' Sandy hugged her daughter.

Fliss went to the blender and poured her smoothie

'Remember I'm going over to Eva's to study after school. I'll be late home.'

'Sure.' Sandy's mind was already on what needed to be done that day.

But despite making one of her famous to-do lists, Sandy found herself gazing into space, still trying to come to terms with how everything had gone up in smoke – literally. She was still sitting at the kitchen table clutching a mug of cold coffee when there was a knock at the door. She opened it to admit two police officers.

By the time they left, Sandy was even more confused than ever. The officers, while taking her details, had been less than forthcoming about possible causes of the fire and cautioned her to keep them informed of her whereabouts until further notice. It also appeared that she was unable to contact her insurance company until they had completed their investigation, which could take some time. She had the uncomfortable feeling she was under suspicion.

When her phone rang, she was surprised to see Rose's number.

'Hello, Rose,' she said, her voice flat.

'Is it true? Was the fire in the new shop?'

'How did you hear?'

'It was on the news this morning – a new business in Neutral Bay went up in flames. I thought of you right away. Oh, Sandy, what a blow.'

At Rose's words, another tear trickled down Sandy's cheek.

'What will you do now?'

'I don't know, Rose, I really don't.'

*

It was another glorious day in Bellbird Bay, the sun shining, the sea sparkling and the air fresh with possibilities. Ruby Sullivan was riding her green bicycle into town, as she did every morning, the basket attached to the rear filled with cakes she had baked in the early hours of the morning ready for delivery to *The Pandanus Café*... when it happened. Out of the blue, a magpie swooped, causing her to swerve. It swooped again, this time she felt a piercing pain in her left eye, the shock forcing her to tumble off her bike onto the kerb at the edge of the road. The bike careered on for several metres, before hitting a wall, falling over and sending the boxes of cakes into the gutter. Almost blinded, she tried to struggle up, grateful when a car stopped and a familiar voice asked, 'Are you okay, Ruby?'

Trying to peer through her one good eye, Ruby saw the blurred image of Grace Winter, a woman she knew lived on the boardwalk at the top of which was Ruby's home. 'No,' she replied. 'The damn bird got my eye. It hurts like hell. I was on my way to *The Pandanus Café*. Looks like Cleo won't be getting any cakes today.'

'I'll give Cleo a call, and I'll get Ted to see to your bike. But forget about the cakes for now. It's more important I get you to the hospital.' Grace bundled the protesting Ruby into her car and drove off.

'I thought the magpies had stopped swooping by now,' Grace said, as they made their way to the Emergency department of the local hospital, where she helped Ruby out of the car.

'I can manage,' Ruby protested. She hated the feeling of being dependent on anyone, but was grateful for the support of Grace's arm, as the younger woman led her into the building. She suddenly felt old, forced to accept help, something she'd managed to avoid up till now. *Was this a sign it was time to slow down?* In an attempt to suppress her pain, she let her mind wander.

All her life, Ruby had been aware of signs and portents, able to see what others couldn't, to predict events before they happened. Some would say it was a gift, others a curse. But she'd always tried to use it for good, to help those she met, rather than frighten them with her predictions. She was well aware of the names she'd been called. Perhaps if she'd been born in a different time, she'd have been burned as the witch she was often labelled. But she'd tried to do her best... and everyone loved her cakes. Her skill in baking was something she'd learned from her mother, and it had stood her in good stead when she decided to turn the family home into a bed and breakfast. *Headland House* had developed quite a reputation over the years, and that and the cakes she provided to the café, helped supplement her pension and the small inheritance left by her mother.

'Ruby Sullivan?' the nurse called, and Grace helped her up again and through to where a doctor was waiting to examine her.

\*

'The eye will need surgery. The outer layer of the eyeball has been pierced by the bird, but we should be able to save your sight. We'll x-ray the wrist to determine if it's broken or merely sprained.'

Ruby listened in horror as the doctor outlined the procedure needed to save her eye, and the possible need for surgery on her wrist. Despite her ability to predict all manner of things for others, she hadn't predicted this. Who would imagine a magpie could inflict so much damage?

The doctor was still speaking. 'We've seen a few of these this year. The birds seem to be becoming more aggressive. Though it's late in the season.'

Before long, Ruby found herself tucked up in bed in a ward, Grace seated by the bedside.

'I called Cleo,' she said. 'She sends her love and says not to worry about the cakes. She'll make sure someone goes to pick them up, or what's left of them… and Ted will see to your bike,' she added, referring to her partner. 'Is there anyone I need to contact?'

'No, no one.' But even as she spoke, Ruby thought of the one person who could take her place, who could continue to provide the cakes for the café, including the two special ones she had promised – for two upcoming weddings. One was for Grace's daughter, the other for another resident of the boardwalk, Libby Walker.

If only she was free and willing to come to Bellbird Bay.

# Two

Rob was in the midst of another bout of fighting, surrounded by mortar blasts, the sound of the explosions deafening, shrapnel spraying everywhere in the barrage of artillery fire, as he tried to ensure the safety of his men. It was chaos. He gazed around at the bloodied bodies where his battalion had been. Where was Ned? He tried to peer through the fog of debris. Then another blast caught him unprepared. He felt himself fly through the air. He could hear a voice – was it his? – calling for Ned, before everything went black.

He felt something wet on his hand. His eyes flew open, and for a moment, he wondered where he was. He was lying in his own bed bathed in sweat, his heart pounding, his legs entangled in the bedclothes. The wetness on his hand was the nose of Bess, his trusty golden retriever, his therapy dog. It had been another nightmare. As his heartbeat gradually returned to normal, Rob let his hand drop to the dog's head, comforted by the feel of her soft coat.

Rob swung his legs off the bed, knowing the only solution was to rise, walk around and make himself a cup of tea. He'd discovered the benefits of camomile tea during his months in rehab when it had been the only refreshment on offer during the long nights of sleeplessness.

He pulled on a robe and made his way to the kitchen, Bess padding behind him like his shadow. He would be lost without his loyal companion. He fixed the tea, staring out of the window into the darkness while the water boiled. What a sad case he was, but at least there was no one to see him like this. He'd known from his first days back in Australia that he'd never be able to form any sort of relationship. In addition to the nightmares which robbed him of sleep, he was convinced he brought bad luck to anyone who got close to him.

Six hours later, having relegated his nightmare to the back of his mind, Rob whistled to himself as he rearranged the bicycles in the showroom, noting the repairs still needed to those he'd hired out two weekends ago for the triathlon, while Bess, his golden retriever lay contentedly at his feet. The October long weekend was the annual triathlon in Bellbird Bay, and a busy one for *Bay Bikes*, the business he'd set up here in his hometown after his discharge from the army. It had been a relief to escape the sights and sounds of the conflict in Afghanistan. He'd been invalided out, wounded both physically and mentally, and though still plagued by nightmares and bouts of depression, the peace of the small coastal town was helping him heal. He was one of the lucky ones.

Given cycling was one sport he was still able to participate in, it had been a stroke of genius to open a bike shop and provide bikes both for sale and hire. He also offered a repair service to those not skilled or willing to do it themselves. He had even taken on an assistant. Young Zack Crawford had started out as a customer and now worked for Rob weekends and two afternoons after school. He was a cheerful young guy and loved to hear Rob's stories of when he was a champion surfer. It was young Zack's goal to emulate him and his grandfather who had taken out the championship three years running, a feat only surpassed last year by another local, Owen Rankin.

'G'day, Rob.'

Rob looked up as the door opened to reveal young Zack's grandfather. Ted Crawford was a member of the surf lifesaving committee which Rob had recently joined, and he valued the older man's opinions. He was part of what Rob considered to be the old guard. Although the other men weren't really much older than Rob, they had been surfing champions when he was barely out of Nippers.

Ted was carrying in a green bicycle Rob didn't recognise. At first glance, it had been in an accident. One wheel was buckled, the mudguards dented, and the basket attached to the rear of the bike had been damaged and was hanging by one end. It looked like a woman's bike. 'What have you there?' he asked, pulling on the beard he'd grown to hide the scar on his chin. 'I didn't know Grace cycled.'

'She doesn't.' Ted chuckled. 'It belongs to Ruby Sullivan.'

Rob knew who Ted meant. Everyone in Bellbird Bay knew Ruby Sullivan, the old woman who lived at the top of the boardwalk, the one young kids liked to tease. Rob had been one of those kids, when he was too young to realise how hurtful it might be to a woman who'd never done anyone any harm. 'What happened?'

'Magpie. They've been bad this year. The poor woman was swooped upon when she was on her way to deliver cakes to *The Pandanus Café*. Luckily Grace was driving past and was able to help. Hence me having her bike.'

'Was she badly hurt?' Rob knew all about magpies swooping on unsuspecting walkers and cyclists. It was why many cyclists wore spikes on their helmets at this time of year... and walkers carried umbrellas.

'Grace said the magpie struck her eye. She's going to need surgery. And she has hurt her wrist and has abrasions from the fall. I'd guess she's suffering from shock, too. She's not a young woman.'

'No.' Rob pulled on his beard again. Ted was more than ten years older than Rob, so if he considered Ruby to be old, she must be... in her eighties? And she still lived alone in that big house, ran a B&B and delivered cakes to the café every day. He hoped he'd be as active at her age. Ruby was an institution in Bellbird Bay. He should have recognised the bike.

'Can you fix it? There's no telling when... *if* she'll be able to ride it again. But Grace promised Ruby she'd take care of it.'

'Leave it with me, Ted. Should be able to get it back into a workable state. Can't let the old woman down.' He had vague recollections of people calling Ruby a witch. He didn't want to risk her putting a spell on him. He smiled to himself at the thought.

'Good man.' Ted clapped him on the shoulder, then leant down to pat Bess, who barely moved.

'Now you're here, how about a coffee? I was about to take a break. Have you time or do you have to rush off somewhere?'

'Coffee sounds good. I have a few errands to run for Grace, but she's working at the library today, so there's no urgency.'

A few minutes later, the two men were seated in *The Greedy Gecko*, a café located along the road from *Bay Bikes*. One of the many things

Rob liked about being his own boss, was his ability to take a break when he felt like it, and the nearby café was a favourite of his. After a career in the army, it was good to have the freedom to make his own decisions, even if it had come at a price. The spinal cord injury which led to him being invalided out of the army had meant months in hospital and more months in rehab. Even now, he suffered pain when he tried to push himself, and he'd never be able to surf or take part in the triathlon again. But he had a good life and would never forget the camaraderie or the mates he'd left behind.

'How is young Zack working out?' Ted asked, when they had been served large mugs of the black coffee both favoured. 'He seems to be enjoying working with you.'

'He's a good worker, willing to turn his hand to even the most menial task – and there are a lot of them.'

'He speaks highly of you, too. Tells me you've been giving him a few surfing tips.'

'You're in a better position to do that than me,' Rob laughed, 'but he enjoys hearing my stories. Looks like you may have a future champion in the family.'

'You may be right.' Ted grinned. 'It would be good to see another Crawford on the honour board in the club.'

'He did well at the triathlon.'

'You were watching?'

'I only saw the beginning and the end, but Zack was up there with the best of them. He's a chip off the old block.'

'Not so old,' Ted chuckled. 'But you're right. It's good to see him. I was disappointed when his dad didn't have any ambition in that regard.'

'We can't all be surfing champions.'

'No.' Ted sighed. 'But at least Aaron's sorted himself out now. He and Mel are getting married next month, and there's a baby on the way. And there's Zack.'

The two were silent for a few moments.

'How about you?'

'Me?' *What did Ted mean?*

'Isn't it time you found someone? You're what... fifty? Never married?'

Rob shook his head. The army had been his life… till it wasn't. There had been no time for a relationship. And now… there was no way he could subject anyone to his recurrent nightmares, his occasional depression and the guilt that still plagued him. Bess was the only female in his life, and he intended it to stay that way.

# Three

Almost a week had passed since the fire, and Sandy was no further forward in deciding what to do. It was as if with the loss of her business, she'd lost all motivation and was going around in a dream. She managed to act normally when Fliss was around, assuring her daughter everything would be okay. It was only when she was alone that the insecurity of her position struck her, and she'd find herself resorting to tears.

She hadn't heard from the police again. So, when her phone rang and she saw an unfamiliar number, she assumed it was them. Hoping it was good news, and she'd be able to contact her insurance company, she pressed to accept the call. Surprised when a woman's voice asked, 'Is this Sandy Elliot?' she hesitated, before cautiously replying, 'Yes, who's calling?'

'You don't know me. My name's Grace Winter, and I'm calling from Bellbird Bay on behalf of Ruby Sullivan.'

'Ruby? Has something happened to her?' Sandy was flooded with guilt. She pictured the old woman who had been her grandmother's best friend. Sandy's parents had died when she was small, and her grandmother had brought her up. Every summer, from when she was six or seven until she was in her teens, she and her grandmother had made the trip to Bellbird Bay to spend a few weeks with Ruby, in her house overlooking the ocean. These had been halcyon days spent swimming, playing in the sand... and spending time in Ruby's kitchen. It was there Sandy's love for cooking had been developed as the old woman allowed her to help bake the most delicious cakes.

It had been five years since she'd seen Ruby, when she'd needed a shoulder to cry on in the days and weeks after her marriage collapsed, when she'd taken Fliss to Bellbird Bay. Since then, they'd only been in touch via Christmas cards, but Ruby would always hold a special place in Sandy's heart.

'I'm sorry to tell you...'

Sandy's stomach clenched. *Oh no, Ruby couldn't be dead.*

'... Ruby's had an accident.'

Sandy felt a wave of relief flow through her, but it did little to assuage her guilt.

'She was cycling along when she was swooped on by a magpie. It badly damaged one of her eyes and she has undergone surgery. I'm afraid she's broken her wrist, too.'

'Oh, poor Ruby. She'd hate that. She's such an independent person.' Ruby had always been a bit of a role model to Sandy – a woman who lived alone with no one to answer to, who needed no one, and who was self-sufficient. It was Ruby who Sandy had thought of when she decided to set up *Celebrations*, and she'd been looking forward to sharing the news of the business with her. 'But what... why...?'

'Why am I calling you? I don't know what your connection with Ruby is, but when I asked if there was anyone I should contact, she gave me your name. She seemed to think that perhaps you could come here and... fulfil several commitments she has.'

'She was my grandmother's best friend,' Sandy said, her eyes moistening at the memory of the woman who'd brought her up.

There was a pause, as if this woman – Grace – was unsure of what she was asking Sandy to do.

Then, 'You may be aware she provides cakes to one of our local cafés and has recently also provided wedding cakes to *Pandanus Weddings*.' Grace paused again. 'There are two weddings coming up.'

Sandy didn't immediately speak. She was too busy trying to absorb what Grace had said. Cakes to a café... two weddings. 'Does she...?'

'I'm sure Ruby will understand if it's not possible for you to come. You're probably busy and... I think she may have been confused when...'

But Sandy couldn't imagine Ruby being confused. She had been as sharp as a tack for as long as Sandy had known her, and she couldn't believe anything had changed in the past five years. If anything, she was more aware than the average person. A weird thought came to her. *Did Ruby know about the fire?* Then she gave herself a mental shake. Of course not. There was no way… but it was odd, this happening, just when… 'Can I think about it and call you back?'

'Of course. Ruby's still in hospital and likely to be there for a little longer. I'll tell her I've spoken to you.'

'Give her my love.'

'I will.'

Sandy sat staring at her phone. Poor Ruby. She could imagine how a period of inactivity would be anathema to the old woman – and what if her sight was affected? How would she cope all alone in that big house? But Sandy couldn't drop everything and go to Bellbird Bay, not even for Ruby.

She spent the day working through her list, refunding deposits to those clients whose orders she could no longer fulfill. The refunds left a hole in her bank account, and there was no prospect of filling it.

Next, she began to half-heartedly check out possible jobs, giving up in dejection at the sight of the wages offered. But she needed to do something.

By the time Fliss came home, the option of going to Bellbird Bay was looking more attractive.

'How did it go today?' she asked, as her daughter threw her bag on the floor behind the kitchen door.

'Don't ask!'

'That bad?'

'I hate chemistry. Don't know why we have to study it. Eva says…'

Sandy didn't wait to hear what Eva had to say. She was of the opinion Fliss was often too easily swayed by her friend whose parents were television celebrities and whose fame had affected their daughter's view of the world. 'Sit down, Fliss. I want to talk to you.'

Fliss opened the fridge and grabbed a sports drink before taking a seat. 'What is it now?' she asked belligerently.

Sandy sighed. *What had happened to the sweet little girl who was so eager to please her mother?* Everyone had warned her about the teenage years, but she hadn't believed it would happen to her daughter. It had. Seemingly overnight, her daughter had been transformed into a moody teenager who preferred to spend time in her room or with her friends to talking with her mother.

'I had a call today,' she said.

'Uh?' Fliss took a gulp of her drink, seemingly unconcerned.

'It was from Bellbird Bay. Remember Ruby Sullivan... the woman we visited there after Dad left?'

'The old lady in the big house near the beach?'

Sandy nodded. 'She's had an accident.'

'So? What's that got to do with us?'

Sandy took a deep breath. 'She wants me... us... to go there. She bakes for a local café... cakes... wedding cakes, too. She...'

'She doesn't want you to take over, does she?'

'Would that be so awful?'

'I have exams,' Fliss said, as if that ended the discussion.

'When do they finish?'

'In another week, but...'

'We could go then. It'll take me a week to get organised enough to leave. Just think, Fliss, we can spend summer by the beach and help Ruby at the same time.'

Fliss stared at her mother. 'You can't be serious,' she said, before storming out, running to her room and slamming the door behind her.

# Four

'Do I have to go? I could stay with Eva. I'm going to miss her birthday, the Year Ten formal, *and* all the Christmas parties. What will I do in Bellbird Bay?'

Sandy sighed and stopped in the middle of cleaning out the refrigerator. 'We've been through all this, Fliss. I'm sorry you're going to miss your formal. But it's only the Year Ten one. There'll be another in Year Twelve. Spending the summer at Ruby's will provide us with free accommodation, and I can keep what I earn from selling cakes. The income, plus the rent I get from the flat will just about see us through till after Christmas, by which time...' She paused. Hopefully, by then her insurance would have come through and she'd be able to find new premises, start again. The landlord of the burnt-out shop was unwilling to renew her lease, refusing to risk having cooking in his building. She knew he blamed her for the fire, even though the police were still investigating and seemed to have decided she wasn't at fault.

'But what'll *I* do?' Fliss asked.

'You'll go to school in Bellbird Bay. Most girls would give their eye teeth for the opportunity to spend the summer by the beach.'

Fliss groaned again and stomped off, slamming the door behind her.

Once she'd made the decision to agree to help Ruby out, Sandy had spent the past week in a frenzy of activity. She'd arranged with Fliss's school for her to miss the last couple of months of term, on the proviso she attended classes in Bellbird Bay, and had managed to rent out the flat for three months to friends of Rose's who were visiting from the UK. Everything had fallen into place. It was as if it had been meant… or some unseen hand was helping her. All she had to do was finish packing and do a final clean of the flat before they left.

Now things were moving forward, Sandy was looking forward to the change, to spending a few months in Bellbird Bay. The town held good memories for her, memories of her childhood visits and memories of holidays there with Fliss.

Wanting Fliss to experience the same holidays she'd had as a child, until her daughter was ten, they had made their way to Bellbird Bay every summer when Sandy could manage to take a week away from the business. Grant had never accompanied them, always too busy to take time away from the city and – as she later learned – from his mistress.

But that was in the past. This time she'd be working, though for Sandy, baking cakes was more pleasure than work, and she'd love being back there, spending time with Ruby. She was glad Fliss would be at school. The prospect of the fifteen-year-old moping around the house for two months would drive her crazy. And Fliss would be bound to make new friends.

*

Finally, they were on their way, and Sandy gave a sigh of relief as they left Sydney behind and were driving north in the van she'd bought and had painted specially for her business. It proved handy to carry all their belongings, but there hadn't been time to have it repainted. So it was still a vibrant pink colour, the name *Celebrations* painted on it in brilliant white along with a cartoon drawing of a wedding cake.

In an attempt to appease Fliss, the radio was tuned to a music channel which blared out a racket that made Sandy want to scream, but it was a small price to pay to silence her daughter's complaints – at least for a time.

When two days later, tired and exhausted, they reached the outskirts of Bellbird Bay, even Fliss seemed glad to get to their destination. 'Look, there's the sea!' she called out, gazing down at the ocean far below them. 'It looks cool.'

*Maybe it wouldn't be so bad.*

'Do you remember last time we were here?' Sandy asked, her heart lightening as it always did when she came to this magical place. *Why had she left it so long?*

'Vaguely. I remember playing in the sand, and you telling me to wear a hat.'

'You still need to do that. The sun here is much stronger than it is at home. It's easy to get skin damage. Maybe you can learn to surf,' she said optimistically.

'Maybe.' But Fliss didn't sound eager. 'What will the school be like? I won't know anyone.'

'We'll check it out on Monday. First, I need to go to see Ruby, check how she is and what she needs me to do.'

'Hmm.' Fliss lost interest.

'Is this it?' Fliss asked, grimacing when Sandy pulled up outside the shabby, white-painted, highset, weatherboard house, the front gate bearing the sign, *Headland House.*

'Don't you remember it?' The house looked shabbier than Sandy remembered, like an old lady who had seen better days. Ruby had let things go since Sandy had last been here, making her wonder if the old woman was still as sharp as she thought she was.

'Not really.' Fliss slid open the door and jumped out. 'Do you have a key?'

'Grace, the woman who rang me, said she'd pop it in the mailbox.' Sandy followed Fliss out of the van.

Fliss opened the white mailbox and held up an old-fashioned key. 'This it?'

'I guess so.' Taking the key, Sandy fitted it into the lock and entered the house. As soon as she walked in, the ambiance of the house surrounded her, enfolding her like a warm blanket the way it always had. The place seemed empty without Ruby's familiar presence, but it still felt to Sandy as if she'd come home, as memories of happy times spent here unravelled in her head.

'Earth calling Mum.'

Sandy was jolted back to the present. 'Sorry, sweetheart, but this place brings back so many happy memories of when I used to come here with my gran. Ruby was her best friend.'

'Is there anything to eat?'

Sandy chuckled at the mundane request. The place held no memories for Fliss... and it had been some time since they'd eaten. 'I'm sure there is. Ruby always made sure her fridge and pantry were full. She's only been gone just over a week. The kitchen's through here.'

Sandy walked into the kitchen and stopped. It was like stepping back in time. The room was exactly as she remembered. It probably hadn't changed in the past fifty years. It still had the cosy feel about it, as if the room was welcoming her back. There was the same scrubbed wood table, the ladder-backed chairs she remembered climbing up on to help Ruby stir the cake batter. In the centre of the table sat a large shallow pottery bowl, normally filled with fruit, but now empty. The old, oversized fridge hummed in one corner and the double-sized gas cooktop and oven she remembered stood against one wall, at right angles to the deep porcelain sink. The polished wood kitchen surfaces were home to a number of blue and white striped canisters, just like those her gran had on her dresser.

Sure enough, when Sandy opened the fridge, there was enough food to last them for another week, only the milk seeming to be past its use by date. She fixed ham and cheese sandwiches for them both, then called the hospital to be told Ruby was in fine shape and she could visit any time.

'Do you want to come with me?' she asked Fliss, who appeared to be in a better mood now she'd eaten.

'No, I might go for a walk.' Fliss peered out of the kitchen window to where there was a boardwalk, on the other side of which was a steep drop to the ocean, and a long flight of steps.

'You'll need a hat.' Sandy took a wide-brimmed straw hat which was hanging on a hook by the door and handed it to her daughter.

Fliss made a face but put on the hat.

'Be careful and don't get lost.'

'Mu...um! I'll see you later.' Fliss opened the door and disappeared through the gate.

Sighing, Sandy watched her go, then, deciding she was unlikely to come to any harm in this quiet spot, headed back to the van to drive to the hospital.

\*

'Thanks for coming, Sandy.' Ruby took Sandy's hand in her frail one, her one good eye misting. 'I knew you wouldn't let me down.'

Sandy was shocked to see how fragile Ruby looked. She was almost as white as the pillow on which she was lying, with a large white patch over one eye, and one arm strapped to her chest. *Was it the result of her encounter with the magpie, or had Ruby been failing for some time?* Sandy's guilt rose to the surface again, almost choking her. 'Of course I came. Gran would have wanted me to help out if I could and…' She bit her lip. There was no need to let Ruby to know about the fire.

But although the old woman might look frail, she hadn't lost her keen sense of perception. 'You've had a shock, too. I can tell. I'm guessing my accident came at the right time. Some things are meant to be.' She gave a hoarse chuckle, sending a shiver down Sandy's spine. *How did Ruby know?*

'It was a shock when your friend rang.' Sandy decided to ignore the implication of Ruby's words. 'I'm just glad I'm here. You need to concentrate on getting better soon. I can stay for as long as you need me.'

'You're a good girl, the only person I'd trust to fulfil my commitment to Pandanus.'

'Grace said something about a café and two weddings?'

'I provide cakes to *The Pandanus Café* each morning. It's part of *The Pandanus Garden Centre*. And Bev, who owns the centre also runs *Pandanus Weddings*… hence the wedding cakes. I know it's a big ask, but if you could…' Ruby's voice weakened, and her eye closed for a moment.

Sandy thought she had fallen asleep. So, the cakes and weddings were all connected to the same place. That would simplify things. She didn't remember a *Pandanus Garden Centre* or café when she visited as a child, or when she brought Fliss. But they hadn't spent much time away from the beach. It would be interesting to do more exploring this time.

Suddenly Ruby's eye snapped open again. 'You need to talk to Cleo,' she said, 'and you'll find all my recipes in a book in the drawer of the dresser. You're the only person I'd trust with them, and you must promise not to reveal them to anyone else. They were passed down to me by my mother who got them from *her* mother.'

Sandy felt the weight of the honour Ruby was giving her. 'I promise,' she said. 'Who's Cleo?'

'She manages *The Pandanus Café*. She'll be expecting you. I told Grace to let her know you were coming.'

'And Grace?'

'She's a neighbour. She'll probably...'

The door to the room opened and an elegant woman with silver hair peered in.

'Here she is. Speak of the devil.'

'Who are you calling the devil, Ruby?' the woman laughed. 'You must be Sandy. Welcome to Bellbird Bay. I know Ruby must be delighted to see you. Did you have a good trip?'

'Not too bad, thanks.' Sandy rose to shake hands. 'Lovely to meet you, Grace. Thanks for taking care of Ruby, and for contacting me.'

Grace smiled. 'It's what neighbours are for. We're not close neighbours but everyone knows Ruby. She's an institution in Bellbird Bay.'

'Hmph.' Ruby tried to push herself up on her pillow.

'Should you be doing that, Ruby?' Sandy asked, moving to assist her and adjust the bed, just as a nurse appeared.

'How is she?' Sandy asked the nurse.

'Improving, but she's not out of the woods yet. The doctor wants to see her again tomorrow. to check how the eye is healing. She may be allowed home next week.'

'Don't talk about me as if I wasn't here.' Ruby sounded stronger than she had when Sandy arrived. Surely a good sign?

Sandy and Grace grinned at each other.

'I'm afraid I'll have to ask you both to leave now,' the nurse said. 'You can come back to visit Ruby again tomorrow.'

Sandy leant over to give Ruby a kiss on the cheek. 'It's good to see you again, Ruby. I'll remember my promise, and I'll go and talk to Cleo tomorrow before I come to see you. How will I find her?'

'I can tell you how to get there,' Grace said, as Ruby seemed to tire again.

Sandy and Grace walked out together. 'I can't thank you enough for what you've done for Ruby,' Sandy said. 'I'm afraid I haven't kept in touch as much as I should have, but once she gets over this, I intend to rectify that.'

When they reached the car park, the women stopped. 'If you're not too tired from your trip, why don't you join us for dinner tonight?' Grace said. 'It'll just be Ted and me. We live a short way down the boardwalk.'

Sandy hesitated. 'I have my daughter with me.' *How would Fliss react to having dinner with a couple of strangers?*

'Her, too, of course. I'm sure you don't feel like cooking after your long drive.'

Grace was right. Much as she enjoyed cooking, it was the last thing she felt like doing tonight. 'Thanks, it's kind of you.'

'We're the house three doors down from the headland. You can't miss us,' Grace said. 'Around seven?'

'Thanks,' Sandy said again. Regardless of what Fliss might have to say about it, it would be nice to sit down to a meal prepared by someone else, and perhaps Grace could tell her a bit more about Bellbird Bay and this Pandanus place.

# Five

Fliss was curled up in a chair in the living room with her phone when Sandy arrived back from the hospital. She looked up and grunted when Sandy walked in.

'How was your walk?' Sandy asked.

'I met a woman with a dog and saw an old guy sitting painting. Is everyone here old?' The walk didn't seem to have done anything to improve Fliss's mood.

'It's a school day. All the younger people will be in school. It may be different tomorrow.'

'Hmm.' Fliss didn't seem convinced.

'I saw Ruby, and she told me about the café she bakes cakes for. I plan to go there tomorrow. We could go together and have coffee, then have a look around the town. What do you say?'

'I suppose,' Fliss responded ungraciously.

Sandy gave a relieved sigh. At least she hadn't refused.

'And we've been invited out to dinner tonight,' she said, trying to sound upbeat.

'I thought Ruby was the only person you knew here.'

'I met her friend, Grace, at the hospital – the lady who rang me. She lives on the boardwalk. It'll be nice not to have to cook on our first night here, don't you think?'

'Hmm.'

Frustrated, Sandy only said, 'We have to be there at seven. I'm going to take a look at Ruby's recipes, then I might have a short rest. Do you want anything?'

Fliss only shook her head and bent over her phone again, leaving Sandy to shake hers in frustration before heading to the kitchen, eager to find the recipe book Ruby had mentioned.

*

After a rest and shower, and dressed in a light summer dress, Sandy pushed open the door to Fliss's room to find her lying on the bed with her phone. Stifling the urge to yell at her daughter, she asked, 'Are you going to change for dinner?'

'I suppose.' Slowly, Fliss closed her phone and rose, then pulled a dress out of the wardrobe. 'Will this do?' she asked, holding up a short blue and white checked dress which Sandy had bought for her the previous summer, and which would now no doubt be too small.

'If you can still get into it.'

'Watch me.' Fliss grinned. She pulled off the shorts and tee shirt she was wearing and slipped the dress over her head. It fitted... just. 'See?' she said with a smirk.

'Okay but do something with your hair before we leave.'

Leaving Fliss to fix her hair which resembled a haystack, Sandy went to the kitchen to pick up a bottle of wine, promising herself to replace everything of Ruby's which they'd eaten and drunk, before the older woman came home.

'Will this do?' Fliss sauntered into the kitchen. She had pulled her long auburn hair into a ponytail and looked younger than her fifteen years.

'You look lovely, sweetheart.' Sandy hugged her. 'Let's go. It's only a short walk.'

'Will they be old people, too?' Fliss asked, as they walked down the boardwalk.

It was refreshing to breathe in the sea air after being used to the traffic fumes in the city, and the homes on the side opposite the ocean looked interesting. Many had been remodelled since Sandy used to visit. 'I expect they'll seem old to you,' Sandy said, 'but remember they are friends of Ruby's, so be polite.'

'Sure.' Fliss kicked at some stones on the path and stared at her feet.

Sandy sighed again. *Hopefully Fliss would make some friends at school next week and would change her attitude.*

'Welcome!' Grace came out to greet them at the gate. 'And this must be your daughter.'

'Fliss,' Sandy said. 'Fliss, this is Mrs Winter.'

'Call me Grace,'

'Hello,' Fliss said.

'Come on in and meet Ted. He's firing up the barbecue. Our grandson's coming to dinner, too. We thought Fliss might like some younger company.'

Sandy gave Fliss a quick glance, but the younger girl didn't seem impressed. She rolled her eyes at Grace who smiled in sympathy.

'I have three of my own,' Grace said, 'two girls and a boy. I remember what they were like as teenagers.'

When they reached the deck where a man of Grace's age was pottering around a barbecue, a large tortoiseshell cat appeared and began to wind itself around Fliss's ankles.

'Oh, what's his name?' she asked, showing her first sign of interest in some time.

'Tiger, and he'll let you do that for hours,' Grace said, as Fliss bent down to fondle the cat's ears.

'He's lovely,' Fliss said with a genuine smile.

Sandy began to relax.

'Come and meet Ted.' Leaving Fliss with the cat, Grace led Sandy across to the barbecue. 'Ted, this is Sandy. Sandy... Ted.'

'Hello, Ted. Pleased to meet you. It was kind of Grace to invite us to dinner.'

'You're most welcome. So, you're the person who's come to rescue us and keep us all in cakes while Ruby is laid up?'

'I don't know about that, but I'll do my best.'

'Ruby must trust you a lot to ask you to help out,' he said. 'We had no idea she had anyone...' He let his voice trail off, embarrassed.

'Oh, I'm not a relative. My gran and she were friends, and I spent my holidays here... at Ruby's... when I was little. It was she who taught me to bake and develop my love for it.'

'Well, we're grateful you were able to take time away from your no doubt busy life to come to Bellbird Bay,' Grace said.

Sandy flinched, reminded of how it had been a relief to leave the disaster behind her. But it was still there and would be waiting for her on her return. She had dutifully informed the police of her plans to leave town, and they had only asked for a contact address and phone number. Hopefully, they no longer suspected she was at fault.

The steaks were sizzling away, and Sandy and Grace were enjoying a glass of wine, when there was the sound of a door opening and closing and a young male voice called, 'Grandpa Teddy, I'm here!' followed by the arrival of a tall, lanky figure, a lock of his blond hair falling over his forehead.

Sandy heard Fliss's sudden intake of breath. She glanced at her daughter who was looking at the new arrival and blushing.

'Zack, you made it.'

'Sorry I'm late. I had trouble with my bike.' He gave Ted and Grace a hug, then stared awkwardly at Sandy and Fliss.

'Zack, these are our new neighbours, Sandy and Fliss. They've come to stay at *Headland House* while Ruby is in hospital. Sandy is going to take over Ruby's cake-making. My grandson, Zack,' he said to Sandy and Fliss.

'Hi,' Zack said.

'Lovely to meet you, Zack,' Sandy said.

Fliss didn't speak. She was too busy staring at Zack who appeared unperturbed by her scrutiny.

'What's up with your bike?' Ted asked, turning back to check on the steaks.

'Flat tyre. I fixed it. Where are you from?' he asked Fliss.

'Sydney.'

'I used to live in a city. It's a lot different here. Better.'

Fliss blushed again.

'What year are you in?'

'Ten. I've just finished my exams.'

'Fliss will be attending *Bellbird State College* while she's here,' Sandy said.

'It's a good school. A lot better than the one I went to in Brisbane when I lived with my mum,' Zack said. 'You'll like it. Do you surf?'

Suddenly shy, Fliss shook her head.

'Oh, you must. Everyone does here. Well, everyone except my dad.'

Zack chuckled. 'Grandpa is a surfing champion, and I'm aiming to match him. Isn't that right, Grandpa?'

'What's that?' Ted turned back from the steaks.

'Just telling Fliss she's talking to the future surfing champion of Bellbird Bay.'

Fliss giggled.

'No need to sound so sure of yourself, but you're probably right. Young Zack here is following in my footsteps,' Ted said proudly.

'There's no stopping these two when they start talking about surfing,' Grace said. 'But Zack's right about one thing, Fliss. All the young people do surf. You'll soon learn,' she said, as Fliss's lips drooped. 'I believe Will Rankin runs classes through the school. Zack?'

'That's right. He's a great teacher. You'll pick it up in no time, and I can give you extra lessons if you like.'

'Thanks,' Fliss whispered.

The rest of the evening went well. Sandy learned that *The Pandanus Garden Centre and Café* was owned by a local woman. It seemed Bev Cooper had started it almost from scratch and built it into a successful enterprise which now hosted *Pandanus Weddings* – hence the demand for wedding cakes. One of the weddings was that of Grace's daughter and Ted's son – Zack's dad. It took a bit of explaining on Grace's part as to how this came about, but it seemed to have been a bonus for both of them. Cleo, who Sandy was to meet next day, managed the café and had recently married the Will Rankin who taught surfing. It seemed everyone in Bellbird Bay was connected in some way or other.

'Did you enjoy the evening?' Sandy asked Fliss on the way home.

'It was okay.'

'What did you think of Zack?'

Fliss shrugged. 'Okay, I guess.'

It was too dark to see her face, but Sandy would be willing to bet she was blushing again. Maybe Fliss would change her mind about Bellbird Bay... maybe she already had.

# Six

Rob had promised to have dinner with his parents. They'd recently moved to a villa in *Bay Village Lifestyle Resort,* when the home they'd lived in all their married life had become unmanageable for them. They seemed happy enough there and were making friends with other residents, some of whom they already knew. It was a friendly over-fifties community rather than a retirement village, but Rob knew how difficult they'd found the decision to downsize. For this reason, he made the effort to dine with them on a regular basis.

He was later in leaving *Bay Bikes* than he'd intended, delayed by a group of cyclists keen to check out the latest line of road bikes which had recently been delivered. They were a group who cycled daily in a peloton, known as the local MAMIL – middle-aged men in lycra – and were preparing to participate in a charity ride in aid of the local Women's Centre, being organised by Will Rankin. While some wanted to enquire about hiring bikes for the event, others were interested in replacing their old ones. As a result, he barely had time to freshen up before heading off to see his parents.

When he did arrive at the modern villa in the over-fifties resort with Bess at his heels, he was surprised to hear the sound of voices coming from the rear of the building. He hadn't been expecting there would be other guests. Usually, when he acceded to his mother's demand he come to dinner, he was the only guest and he'd be subjected to an interrogation on his wellbeing, the state of his business and his lack of a partner.

'Hello!' he called, walking around the side of the villa to find his parents accompanied by another couple. All four held glasses of wine and there was a platter of nibbles on the table around which they were seated.

'Rob!' Rob's dad rose to clap him on the shoulder, while his mum gave him a hug. 'You haven't met our neighbours, Dot and Kev Butler. Guys, this is our son, Rob... and Bess.'

Both Dot and Kev nodded to Rob. 'Your dad talks about you a lot,' Kev said. 'I hear you were in the army – Afghanistan. Must have been rough.'

'Mmm.' Rob glared at his parents. He preferred to keep quiet about his time in the army. He'd made a new life for himself here in Bellbird Bay, and his own memories were enough to cope with, without others bringing up the war.

Seeming to sense his discomfort, Rob's mother said, 'Rob owns *Bay Bikes* now – provided a lot of the bikes for the triathlon the other weekend.'

'Really?' Kev seemed interested. 'It's been a few years since you and I took part,' he said to Rob's dad.

'You knew each other before you moved here?' Rob asked.

'Kev was a few years above us at school. He was a good athlete in those days.'

Rob looked at the older man and tried unsuccessfully to picture him when he was younger. It was sad what age did to a person. He supposed it would happen to him, too.

'A glass of wine, son?' his dad asked.

'I'll have a beer, Dad. No, I'll get it,' he added, as his dad made to rise again. 'Stay, Bess,' he said to the dog, who settled down to wait for him.

In the kitchen, Rob took a beer out of the fridge and popped the cap, taking a long slug to sustain him before he went back outside to join the others.

When he came back, they were talking about a trip Dot and Kev had made to the red centre, the name given to Australia's Northern Territory because of its vast red deserts.

'We've become grey nomads,' Dot said with a chuckle, 'and we're trying to persuade your folks to join us on our next trip. It's good to get away for a bit, and you meet such interesting people on the road.'

Rob looked at his parents in surprise. *Were they really considering this?*

'Well,' his dad said, shifting uneasily in his seat, 'we might take a look at hiring a van.'

'How long have you been thinking about this?'

'Your dad and I always enjoy watching *Creek to Coast* on a Saturday,' his mother said, referring to a programme on Channel Seven, devoted to camping and fishing, 'and when we discovered Dot and Kev had already done a few trips, we invited them over. We've just about made up our mind to join them on a trip down the coast after Christmas.'

'Right.' This was an aspect of his parents Rob hadn't been aware of, but good luck to them, if it was what they wanted to do with their retirement.

'You wouldn't mind, son?' his mother asked. 'It'd mean we'd be gone for over a month.'

'Go for it. I'm good, now. No need for you to worry about me. I have Bess to keep me company.' Hearing her name, the dog looked up, then settled down again. Rob knew how his parents had worried about him all the time he was in hospital and rehab. Even now he had recovered, he was aware of the glances his mother gave him when she thought she was unobserved.

'You heard about Ruby Sullivan?' he asked, to change the subject.

It was Dot who replied, 'Yes, it was my sister, Grace, who found her by the roadside and took her to Emergency.'

So, she was Grace Winter's sister. Not for the first time, Rob was reminded what a small place Bellbird Bay was. 'Ted brought her bike in to me for repair,' he said.

'I hope she makes a good recovery,' Rob's mum said. 'We'd all miss her cakes.'

'From what Grace said, she'll be in hospital for some time, but it seems a woman has arrived, who may be able to fill in till she's able to cope again.' Dot nodded, seemingly pleased to be the bearer of the news.

'A relative? I didn't know Ruby had any relatives, but then we never did know much about her, did we? I wonder...' his mother began.

Rob rolled his eyes. He hated this sort of gossip. No doubt the woman, whoever she was, would be subjected to all the usual tittle-tattle of the old biddies of Bellbird Bay. Even his own mother wasn't immune. If she was single, his mother would have them married off before the poor woman had been in town for ten minutes.

'Might be time to light the barbie, Dad,' he said.

'Good idea, son.' His dad seemed as pleased as he was to leave the group and move to where the *Weber* barbecue he'd bought his parents as a housewarming gift was sitting.

After a few minutes, Kev joined them, leaving the two women to speculate on who this woman was, where she had come from, and her connection with Ruby.

Rob was glad to reach home again. 'We're best when we're on our own, Bess,' he said to the dog, who seemed to nod in agreement, before giving a huge yawn. At first, Rob had objected when it was suggested he have a therapy dog, but Bess had proved to be a godsend and was now his constant companion, going almost everywhere with him. He'd be lost without her, and she did help comfort him when he was troubled by the recurrent bouts of depression, or wakened from yet another horrific nightmare.

# Seven

Sandy awoke to a glorious morning. The sun was shining, and it seemed a whole family

of kookaburras were sitting on the fence cackling loudly. She opened the window and breathed in the scent of the sea. It was good to be alive, she thought, then no, more than that; it was good to be here, in Bellbird Bay.

Even Fliss seemed more cheerful when she finally arrived at breakfast.

'Where did you say we're going today?' Fliss asked, taking a bite of the toast and vegemite which was all she wanted for breakfast. Despite her many pieces of kitchen equipment, Ruby didn't own a blender, so Fliss was unable to make her favourite smoothies. It was already a bone of contention, and Sandy had promised to purchase one for the sake of peace.

'*The Pandanus Café*. It's attached to a garden centre and it's the café which serves Ruby's cakes. I need to talk to the manager and explain I'll be providing the cakes instead of Ruby, until she recovers.' Seeing Fliss's belligerent expression, she added, 'Maybe we can go to the beach afterwards.'

'Can't I go to the beach and meet you later?'

Sandy hesitated, but only for a moment. 'I'd prefer if you came with me... just until we find our way around.'

'Okay.'

As soon as breakfast was over, Sandy herded a reluctant Fliss into the van and set off for the garden centre. When she arrived, she was surprised to discover how large it was and how many cars were in the car park so early on a Saturday morning. It was clearly a thriving business, and she remembered Grace telling her how the owner had built it up from practically nothing.

Finding a parking spot, they walked through the entrance, and after wandering through the garden centre, found the sign to the café, its entrance almost hidden by a tall hedge of blue flowers.

The café itself was another surprise. Built around a large pandanus tree from which the centre clearly got its name, it comprised a number of small tables artistically arranged among a series of low bushes and towering palm trees. Most of the tables were occupied, a sign the café was popular. Glancing around, Sandy spied the kitchen in the far corner, almost hidden from view by a screen of grevillea.

Glad she'd had the foresight to call ahead – the café was busier than she'd anticipated – Sandy made her way towards the kitchen, Fliss following more slowly. Just outside the kitchen, a woman with fading blonde hair scraped back in a ponytail who looked to be in her late fifties, was seated at a small table. She rose, hand outstretched as Sandy approached. Sandy sensed Fliss's irritation – another old person.

'You must be Sandy, Ruby's replacement,' she said. 'I'm Bev. Cleo will be out in a moment. Can I get you a coffee?'

'Thanks.' Sandy shook her hand. 'Pleased to meet you, Bev. This is my daughter, Fliss.'

'Coffee for you, too, Fliss?'

'Could I have a smoothie?'

'Sure. Here's Cleo now,' Bev said, as a woman closer to Sandy's age with a cloud of dark hair joined them.

'Sandy?' Cleo asked with a smile. 'You can't imagine how delighted I am to see you. We've been missing Ruby's cakes. I've tried to fill in, but I don't have her touch.'

A waitress appeared, and Bev ordered coffees and the smoothie for Fliss.

'First of all, how is Ruby?' Bev asked. 'We were devastated to hear about her accident. Everyone knows Ruby, and her cakes are legend.'

'She's recovering slowly,' Sandy said. 'I've arranged to be here till after Christmas, by which time I hope she'll be back to normal.' She bit her lip, wondering if it was true, or if the accident was a sign Ruby needed to take things easier. She couldn't keep baking and delivering cakes for ever. But she decided not to share those thoughts with the two women.

Their drinks arrived, and Sandy explained how she knew Ruby and gave them a rundown on her experience, avoiding any mention of the fire. 'I can provide references,' she finished.

'That won't be necessary. Ruby's word is good enough for us.' Bev said.

They chatted on, Sandy learning a little more about the operation of the café and the forthcoming weddings. She took note of the brides' details and promised to contact them to discuss what sort of cakes they wanted, an unexpected thrill of excitement coursing through her at the prospect.

After she'd been shown a back entrance to the café where she could make her deliveries, and arranged to make her first one on Tuesday, Sandy rose to leave.

'I'll walk you out,' Bev said. 'I need to get back to the garden centre, anyway.' At the entrance to the centre, they stopped. Bev stared at the pink van, which looked more out of place than ever there among the greenery of the garden centre. 'Your business?' she asked.

'It was. I haven't had time to change the van.' She'd be sorry to see it go. It was the culmination of months of work. But she had no need of it now; maybe she never would have again.

Seeming to sense Sandy's emotions, Bev didn't comment.

'Can we go now?' Fliss asked, clearly eager to get to the beach.

'Sorry,' Sandy said to Bev. 'Thanks for making time to meet with me. I look forward to working with you and Cleo.'

'We're looking forward to it, too. Will make a change. We love Ruby, but sometimes she can be...'

Sandy only smiled. She understood what Bev meant. Ruby was a law unto herself. She could be a great friend, but she didn't suffer fools gladly.

*

'Finally!' Fliss said, when Sandy pulled into a parking spot on the esplanade. Today the beach was busier, filled with families and groups of young people. Many were swimming, while others clearly preferred to lie on the sand, regardless of the danger of skin damage from the blazing sun. Groups of surfers were sitting out in the ocean on their boards waiting for a wave. On one corner of the beach was a van bearing the logo *Bay Surf School* along with a flag announcing the same. It was a typical Australian beach scene, reminiscent of Sandy's childhood. It had been too long since she spent time by the ocean. Once again, she breathed the ozone scent.

'Wow!' Fliss said, her eyes darting to and fro. 'This is more like it. Can I go in for a swim? I have my cossie on under my clothes.'

'Let's find a shady spot first.' Sandy unloaded the bag containing a rug, towels, water and a book, which she'd packed earlier, and they made their way to the beach.

As soon as they found a suitable spot, Fliss threw off her outer garments and headed into the ocean, while Sandy settled down with her book. But she found it difficult to concentrate, her mind filled with all the things she had to do before Tuesday... and she had to fit in another visit to Ruby.

'I'm hungry!' A wet Fliss flung herself down beside Sandy, spraying her with drops of saltwater.

'Dry yourself first, then we can look for somewhere to eat.' Sandy handed Fliss a towel. 'Did you have a good swim?'

'Mmm. It would have been better if I knew someone here.'

'I'm sure you'll soon make friends.' Sandy could see groups of teenagers around Fliss's age on the sand and playing beach volleyball. She mentally crossed her fingers. Life here would be difficult if Fliss continued to be moody.

After putting their beach gear back into the van, Sandy looked around. 'There's a café over there,' she said, pointing to a sign which said, *The Bay Café,* 'or the surf club. What do you think, Fliss?'

'Surf club,' Fliss decided.

When they walked into the club, after signing in, they were faced by a flight of stairs leading to the main part which housed the restaurant. On the wall was a large mural of a surfer on a giant wave, alongside an honour board listing the names of Bellbird Bay surfing champions over the past few decades. Pausing for a moment on the way up, Sandy was surprised to see Ted Crawford's name there, indicating he had been champion three years running.

At the top was a large restaurant with a bar on one side which opened out onto a wide deck.

'Oh, can we eat out there?' Fliss asked.

'I don't see why not.' Only a few tables were occupied, more people seeming to prefer to drink at the bar.

Once out on the deck and seated at a table overlooking the beach, Sandy studied the menu, while Fliss gazed down at the volleyball game which was still underway. 'That looks like fun,' she said wistfully.

'Maybe it will be included in the school sports program.'

'Do you think so?'

Pleased to hear a note of excitement in her daughter's voice, Sandy replied, 'Well, if they include surfing, they may well include beach volleyball, too.'

'That would be awesome. A lot better than hockey or netball,' Fliss said, referring to the only two sports offered by her Sydney school, neither of which appealed to her. 'Look, it's the woman we met earlier,' she added, gesturing towards the doorway.

Sandy looked round to see Grace Winter accompanied by another woman of around the same age or a few years younger. 'Her name's Grace,' she said.

'Look, they're coming over.' Fliss sounded as if she wanted to hide.

'Hello, Sandy... and Fliss. How lovely to see you again so soon. This is Libby Walker, soon to be Libby Holland. Hers is your other wedding. Libby, this is the lovely lady who is taking over from Ruby while she's incapacitated. May we join you?'

'Of course,' Sandy said, ignoring Fliss's barely concealed displeasure. 'Lovely to meet you, Libby.' She was surprised to learn one of the weddings was for a more mature couple.

After checking the menus, the three women ordered prawn salads, with Fliss opting for a pizza. Then, at Grace's insistence, the women shared a bottle of chardonnay, while Fliss chose a Coke.

'Did you manage to catch up with Bev and Cleo?' Grace asked, when they had progressed to coffee, and Fliss had left them to take a closer look at the game on the beach.

'Yes, thanks. They were lovely. I'm looking forward to working with them, though I hope Ruby will be back on board before too long.'

'How *is* Ruby?' Libby asked. 'It was a shock to hear about her accident. She's always seemed invincible to me… though, like Grace, I didn't grow up here. Nor did Adam.'

'She's recovering slowly,' Sandy said, then stared at her, suddenly making the connection. Adam Holland… was he the famous author? 'Adam?' she asked.

'My partner, husband-to-be.' Libby blushed. 'It may seem odd, to be getting married again at my age, but it will be the first time for Adam, and… yes, if you're wondering… he is the author.'

'I love his books… when I get a chance to sit down long enough to read one through.'

Libby chuckled. 'I'll tell him he needs to make them shorter.'

'No, I didn't mean…' Then she smiled, realising Libby was joking. 'I saw *your* partner's name on the honour board as I came up the stairs,' she said to Grace to change the subject. 'There's quite a mural there, too.'

'That's Ted, too… on the mural. Pity I didn't know him back then,' she chuckled, 'but he's worn pretty well.'

They all laughed.

'It's been lovely, ladies, but I should go and see what my daughter is up to,' Sandy said. 'I'll be in touch with you about your wedding cake once I get my head around Ruby's notes,' she said to Libby. 'And with your daughter, Grace,' she added. 'I'm planning to visit Ruby again this afternoon and hopefully she'll be more able to talk and let me know what she had in mind.'

'Sounds good,' Grace said. 'I'll tell Mel to expect to hear from you. She and Aaron are closer to your age, though probably a bit younger.'

'Thanks.' Bidding the two farewell, Sandy made her way out of the club. She was heading for the beach to pick up Fliss, when she saw her daughter. Fliss was leaning against the van, looking bored.

'What took you so long?' she asked.

'We were chatting. I thought you were watching the volleyball.'

'The game finished, and there was nothing else to do there. Can we go back to the house now?'

'I need to visit Ruby and I thought you might want to come too today. I'm sure she'd love to see you, and it would be good for you to meet her.'

'If I must. There doesn't seem to be anything else to do here,' Fliss complained.

Sandy sighed. She couldn't wait to get Fliss enrolled in school. Surely, once there, she'd make friends and find a social life? Otherwise, it was going to be a long, excruciating summer for Sandy.

# Eight

On Sunday morning, Rob wakened early from a particularly gruesome nightmare, his body beaded with sweat. After the usual calming ritual of a cold shower and a mug of camomile tea, while Bess ate her breakfast, he decided to take his loyal companion for a walk on the beach and pick up a bite to eat on the way. He didn't need to open the shop till later and had told Zack to come in at ten.

Delighted at the prospect of an outing, Bess leapt into the passenger seat of the van, reminding Rob it must be time to give the vehicle one of its occasional cleans. Then they were off, the dog seeming to smile, her tongue hanging out as they headed for the beach.

Rob parked at the esplanade and, picking up a takeaway coffee and a ham and cheese croissant from *The Bay Café*, he took Bess across to the beach. It was pretty quiet at this time in the morning, only a few dogwalkers like himself and the inevitable group of surfers sitting out on the ocean. Rob felt the familiar ache in his gut, the memory of how it felt to be out there with the salt on his face, breathing in the scent of the sea, waiting for the next wave to carry him in. How he'd love to experience it again, the freedom, the exhilaration, the rush of adrenaline. It was an addiction, one he'd been forced to give up. He'd been close to tears when his doctor had told him, refused to believe him at first. But once he'd come to understand the risk of neck injury by wipeout or being hit by a large wave, he'd accepted his surfing days were over. But it still hurt to see others out there doing what he couldn't.

This morning, he stopped for a few minutes, staring into the distance, to where a couple of the guys were already riding in on a wave. His skin tingled at the memory of how it felt.

Rob and Bess walked along the hardpacked sand at the edge of the water till they came to the dog-free section where, once off the lead, Bess bounded into the water. Then, having finished his breakfast, Rob stuffed the empty paper cup into his pocket and found a stick to throw for Bess. She loved this game and would be happy to spend hours dashing into the sea to fetch it, before laying it at Rob's feet panting and asking for more. This morning, her antics seemed more frantic than usual, and he laughed to see her enjoyment, the sight of the surfers almost forgotten in his delight at his pet's pleasure. It was as if the dog chose to deliberately distract him… perhaps she did.

When he reached the end of the beach, where a tall cliff with a set of steep steps rose to the headland, Rob gazed up at the white house on the point. He wondered about the woman who had come to stay there, who would bake the cakes for Ruby Sullivan. Then he thought about the old woman, hoping she'd make a good recovery. He'd suffered, but at least his eyes had been spared. He couldn't imagine how it must have felt to have a bird peck at your eye, perhaps blinding you. He shivered at the thought.

He had turned to walk back when he saw Bess run up to another dog and heard a voice yell, 'Milo!'

Running towards them was a woman, her white hair blowing in the breeze. 'He's friendly,' she said, her breath coming in pants when she reached Rob.

'I can see that. It's Libby, isn't it? Libby Walker.'

'I don't think…' She peered at him. 'Oh, I've seen you around. Don't you own *Bay Bikes*?'

'That's right… and this is Bess.'

'Hello, Bess,' Libby said to the dog who was now standing still to allow Milo to sniff her. 'She's a lovely animal. Golden Retriever?'

'Yeah. Yours?' Rob gazed at the large dog now circling around Bess, who wasn't objecting.

'Who knows?' she shrugged. 'I rescued him when he was only a pup. I never imagined he'd grow to this size. But I wouldn't be without him. He's been great company to me over the years.'

'Wait…' Rob clicked his fingers, suddenly recalling what he'd heard about Libby. 'Aren't you married to Adam Holland? I'm a big fan, and I love the TV series.'

'Not quite,' Libby laughed, 'but soon. Adam will be pleased to know he has another local fan.'

'Right,' Rob said, grimacing slightly.

'No worries,' Libby said, seeming to recognise his embarrassment. 'It's good to meet you. Perhaps we'll see you here again. We walk here most mornings.'

'I don't make it as often as that,' Rob said. Maybe he should make more of an effort. Bess loved it here. 'You live in one of those homes up there?' He gestured to the boardwalk.

'We do.'

'I've often envied the residents on the boardwalk. It must be wonderful to waken to the sound and smell of the sea.'

'Yes, it is. You grew up here… in Bellbird Bay?'

'Yeah.' Rob looked down at his feet, at his footprints in the sand. 'Never thought I'd come back, but here I am.'

'Want to talk about it?' Libby's voice was gentle.

'No… maybe… but not now. I need to open up the shop, and my young assistant will be arriving soon.'

'Okay, but any time you want to share…'

'Thanks.' Rob didn't know her, but he got the sense she meant it, and that she'd provide a non-judgemental ear – a bit like the counsellor the army had arranged for him, the guy he'd gone to twice before giving up, deciding he couldn't bear to rehash the whole experience.

After leaving Libby, Rob got home with just enough time to change into a more respectable pair of shorts and tee-shirt to arrive at *Bay Bikes* a few minutes ahead of Zack.

The young boy was full of chatter about his grandad, and a surfing video he'd been watching with him the previous evening. 'It was awesome,' he enthused.

Rob didn't respond, too overcome by the memory of the surfers he'd seen on his walk. It didn't always affect him this way… maybe it was the aftermath of his nightmare.

'You don't surf any longer,' Zack said, seemingly surprised at his silence.

'No. My injuries, in Afghanistan.' It wasn't something Rob wanted to discuss. Zack had never asked him about it before.

'I read something the other day...'

'Yeah?' Rob's heart sank, wondering what was coming next.

'... about adaptive surfboards.'

'Another time, Zack. There's a lot to do, today. I want you to help me fix up Ruby Sullivan's bike.' Rob felt guilty he hadn't worked on the bike till now. He'd made excuses to himself, reasoning the old woman was in hospital and wouldn't be needing it for some time, but he knew the job had to be done.

'Grandpa told me about her,' Zack said. 'He says she's a bit weird. He called her a witch.'

'She's all right, just a tad unconventional. When I was younger, we kids used to laugh at her and tease her a lot. It wasn't a kind thing to do. She's lived in the house on the headland for as long as I can remember.'

'Grandpa says she lived there when he was young, too,' Zack said, as if it had been in the Dark Ages.

Rob chuckled. 'Okay, let's get on with it, and see if we can make it as good as new again.'

They set to work, Bess lying in her usual corner and keeping an eye on them, until it was time for lunch.

'You've worked hard this morning,' Rob said. 'How about I treat you to a burger at *The Greedy Gecko* and we finish this in the afternoon?'

'Sounds good.'

\*

'I'm sorry I brought it up... about you not surfing,' Zack said, his mouth full of burger.

They were seated at an outside table so Bess could join them.

'It's okay. Sometimes it hits me more than others. You caught me at a bad time this morning. I'd been watching a group out there and wished I was with them.'

'Sorry,' Zack said again.

'No worries, mate. I'm alive. I can still swim and cycle. It's a lot more than many of the guys I served with can manage. There's no sense in focussing on what I can't do.'

'Is that why you opened *Bay Bikes*?'

'Part of the reason. After spending a long time in hospital and rehab, I wanted to do something for myself. When I came back home to Bellbird Bay, I couldn't face the thought of being dependent on my folks. I needed to get out… into the open air. I got out my old bike and started cycling around the coast, got talking to other cyclists and discovered a need for somewhere they could meet, talk bikes. *Bay Bikes* started out as a meeting place, somewhere we could enjoy a coffee or a beer and have a yarn, then it morphed into what it is now. Some of the guys still drop round for a chat and to share their latest rides on Strava.'

'But you're on the surf lifesaving committee.' Zack sounded puzzled.

'Yeah. That was Will Rankin's doing.' Rob recalled how he'd been stunned when the older man approached him to join the committee, had initially recoiled from the idea. But Will had been persistent, insisting Rob's experience would be invaluable to the group, so he'd given in. And, to Rob's surprise he'd enjoyed the camaraderie in the group, even enjoyed being part of the organising committee for the surfing carnival and the triathlon, though his responsibilities at *Bay Bikes* precluded him taking an active part on the day. 'Will Rankin can be very persuasive,' he said.

'He's helping me train. He's a good coach.'

'The best.'

The two were silent for a few moments, then Zack asked, 'Do you think I can do it… next year? Be champion?'

'Don't see why not. I was eighteen when I made it.' Rob could remember the day as if it was yesterday – the excitement, the fear, the worry, then the adrenalin rush when the result was announced, and he was carried shoulder high by his peers. He'd often thought of that day when he was facing death in Afghanistan, and again lying in the hospital bed wondering if he'd ever walk again. But he had, and being unable to surf was a small price to pay.

# Nine

After visiting Ruby on Saturday, Sandy had managed to track down a school uniform for Fliss in a charity shop in town. It meant the girl didn't have to feel out of place on her first day at *Bellbird State College* – one thing to feel thankful for. To Sandy's relief, the navy skirt and white blouse wasn't unlike the uniform at Fliss's Sydney school. She might even be able to wear the skirt again when they returned to Sydney.

Fliss didn't have much to say at breakfast on Monday morning. It was only natural for her to be nervous at the prospect of starting the new school so late in the year – and in Year Ten, by which time everyone else would have formed their friendship groups and cliques.

'You'll be fine, honey,' Sandy said, giving her a hug when they were ready to leave. 'I know it'll feel strange at first…'

'You're not the one who has to walk into a classroom full of strangers who'll look at you as if you came from outer space,' Fliss said.

'No, but…' Sandy tried to think of something which would make her feel better. 'Maybe you'll bump into Zack,' she suggested.

'He's in Year Twelve, Mum. I'm not likely to see him.'

'Oh.' Sandy had forgotten the huge divide between Year Ten and Year Twelve students. It was a long time since she'd attended high school. 'Well, at least there will be boys at this school. That will be different for you.'

'It'll be really weird. Eva said she wishes she was here, going to a co-ed school. I wish she was, too.'

Sandy bit her lip. One advantage of coming here was the distance between Fliss and Eva, who Sandy was sure was a bad influence. But what would the girls be like at *Bellbird State College*? And what would the boys be like? In Sydney, Fliss's only experience with boys had been the semi-regular get-togethers the school arranged with the neighbouring boys' college – and the surreptitious meetings in the shopping centre Sandy wasn't supposed to know about. She'd heard it said single sex schools made girls more aware of boys, and the close proximity in a co-ed environment took away the thrill of the unknown. She could only hope.

*

The school building itself looked no different from any other school Sandy had visited, the unrelenting red brick rising up from the expanse of grass and asphalt surrounding it. When they arrived, the playground was filled with students, the girls all dressed identically to Fliss, the boys in navy shorts and white shirts, ties askew. They received a few curious glances as they walked towards the main entrance, and Sandy was conscious of Fliss trying to make herself invisible.

The meeting with the principal went well. Luke Chisholm seemed a nice guy, welcoming Fliss and asking her a bit about herself and her old school. He only smiled when Fliss was quick to point out she was only here for the last two months of term, and said, 'Maybe we'll manage to change your mind. This is my first year here, and I have to say *Bellbird State College* is the best school I've taught in. We have a great bunch of kids here. I'm sure they'll make you very welcome. I've asked Jenny Stuart to be your buddy for your first few days. She can show you the ropes and introduce you around.' He turned to Sandy. 'As you know, the students aren't able to start on the Year Eleven syllabus, but we make sure they keep occupied. Being summer, we include a lot of outdoor activities. Are you interested in surfing, beach volleyball, Fliss?' he asked with a twinkle in his eye.

'Yes,' Fliss said, clearly beginning to relax.

There was a knock at the door, and a girl of Fliss's age, her short dark hair standing up in spikes, her skirt shorter than the regulation length, walked in, a wide grin on her face.

'Ah, here she is,' Luke said. 'Fliss, this is Jenny. Jenny, I'm relying on you to show Fliss around and to help her settle in.'

'Will do, sir. Can we go now?'

'Off you go. I'll just have a brief chat with your mum, Fliss. I'll no doubt see you about.'

The two girls left.

'Thanks,' Sandy said. 'It was a wrench for Fliss to leave Sydney, the school, her friends.'

'She'll be right with Jenny. Her mother's on staff here, and she's one of our rising sports stars. I understand you've come to the rescue.'

Sandy was puzzled.

'To take over Ruby's role.'

'Oh, yes.' *Did everyone know why she was here? Did they know about the fire, too? Surely not.* 'I'm going home to bake some cakes when I leave here.'

'Well, I'd better not keep you. I just wanted to assure you we'll do everything we can to help Fliss settle in here. It's not easy at this stage, and so late in the year. I understand her enrolment here was a condition of her current school – they forwarded all the necessary paperwork – so we'll aim to make the transition as painless as possible for her.'

'Thanks.'

Driving home, Sandy felt as if a weight had been lifted from her shoulders. Luke Chisholm was a completely different kettle of fish from Rhana Forsyth who ruled *Geraldine Spence College* with a rod of iron. She suspected Fliss might enjoy her brief respite here.

\*

After a busy morning, Sandy surveyed the selection of cakes and flans cooling on the kitchen bench with satisfaction. In future, she'd rise early to bake as Ruby had done, but she'd wanted to check the peculiarities of Ruby's oven for this first batch – and they had turned out perfectly.

She was enjoying a well-earned rest with a cup of tea and a sandwich when her phone rang.

'Hello?'

'Mrs Elliot?' It was a male voice she didn't recognise.

'Yes, who is this?' There were so many scams around these days, you had to be careful. She normally didn't answer her phone unless she recognised the number.

'Rob Andrews from *Bay Bikes*. We've been repairing Ruby's bike, and it's ready to be picked up… or I can deliver, if you'd prefer.'

Sandy had forgotten about the bike. Now she recalled Grace saying her partner was going to drop it off to be mended. She thought quickly. She was picking Fliss up after school – despite her insistence she'd be able to find her own way home. 'I can pick it up later this afternoon if that works for you.'

'No problem. Do you know where we are?'

'I can find you.' It was time Sandy found her way around the town, and this would be a good start. 'Around four?'

'See you then.'

Sandy finished her sandwich and packed away the results of her baking, before heading out to the van. She spent the next little while checking out Bellbird Bay, discovering several cafés, clothes shops, a bookshop and newsagent, plus the library and an art gallery, before sighting *Bay Bikes*. Now she knew where it was, she headed back in the direction of the school to pick up her daughter.

Her van was the only vehicle parked outside the school when the bell rang for end of classes. Maybe she should have agreed to Fliss's demand to make her own way home. But it was her first day, and Sandy was eager to find out how it had gone.

The students began to emerge in groups of twos and threes, many looking curiously at the bright pink van. Eventually, Sandy recognised Fliss. She was with two other girls, one of whom was the girl Luke Chisholm had designated as her buddy. They looked to be chatting amicably. Another weight lifted.

As Sandy watched, Fliss caught sight of the van and, saying something to her companions, left them to walk towards it.

'Hello, darling. Good day?'

'It was okay. You didn't need to pick me up. Jenny and Megan ride to school. No one's parents pick them up. It makes me look like a little kid.'

'Sorry. It's your first day. I wanted to…'

'Well, don't do it again. And the van looks silly. Who drives a pink van here?'

Sandy winced.

'Can we go home now?'

Realising they were still parked outside the school and attracting attention, Sandy started up the van. 'We need to make one stop on the way. I have to pick up Ruby's bike.'

'Ruby's bike? Where is it?'

'It's being repaired at *Bay Bikes*. I got a call to say it was ready to be picked up.'

'Oh!'

When they arrived at the bike shop, Fliss made no effort to move.

'Why don't you come in with me,' Sandy said. 'You might find it interesting.'

Fliss grunted but complied and entered the shop with her mother.

Inside, Sandy looked around at the vast array of bikes, some new, some clearly reconditioned and some in the process of being repaired. A tall, bearded man, wearing shorts and a tee-shirt revealing an arm decorated with a variety of tattoos came to greet them.

'Mrs Elliot?'

'Sandy,' she said automatically, flinching at his appearance. She wasn't a fan of men with beards, and the tattoos made her feel uncomfortable. She had a sudden image of the day when, as a teenager, she and a friend had been walking home from school, and been accosted by an older boy, his arms covered in tattoos. He had bailed them up against a wall, scaring them, only allowing them to pass when a group of boys from her school appeared on the scene. It was something Sandy had never forgotten, and for her, tattoos and the feeling of fear were inextricably linked. Although she knew it was foolish, that this man bore no resemblance to the boy she remembered, she had no intention of spending any more time there than necessary.

'Rob Andrews. You're the lady taking over baking Ruby's cakes.'

'Yes.' Sandy just wanted to get their business done and leave.

'We've done what we could with Ruby's bike. Managed to fix the buckled wheel and touched up the paintwork. But I'm afraid we couldn't do much for the rear basket – the one Ruby used to transport her cakes,' he said, clearly seeing Sandy's puzzled expression.

'Oh... I have a van to do that. But once Ruby is well again... I guess she'll work something out. The bike?'

'Zack,' Rob called through to the back of the shop.

Fliss's eyes widened, as Zack Crawford, still wearing his school uniform, wheeled a green bike into the shop.

'How much do I owe you?'

Rob shook his head. 'This one's on me, for Ruby,' he said.

'Thanks, that's very kind.'

Rob glanced through the window. 'Wow! That yours?' he asked catching sight of the van and clearly trying to stifle a grin.

'I had it done for my business... in Sydney.'

'Great name.'

'Thanks.' His remark surprised her. *She* thought it had been a great name for her business but hadn't expected this very macho man to agree with her.

'Mum, can I ride the bike home?' Fliss asked. 'Zack has asked me to...'

'I asked Fliss if I could buy her an ice cream, Mrs Elliot,' Zack said. 'I'm almost finished here, and you haven't tasted great ice cream till you've visited *Bay Gelato.*' He grinned, a lock of hair falling over one eye, making Sandy see what attracted Fliss.

'Can I, Mum?' Fliss hopped from one foot to the other, her face screwed up with the worry Sandy might refuse.

Well, at least he seemed to be a decent young boy, and Sandy had met his grandparents. 'I don't see why not,' she said, smiling. 'Don't be too late home.'

'I won't.'

As the two young people headed outside, Zack still wheeling the bike, Sandy couldn't help frowning.

'She can't come to any harm with Zack. He's a good kid.'

Sandy had almost forgotten Rob was standing there. 'I know... it's just... she's not used to being around boys.' *I'm not used to her being around boys.*

'Let me guess. Single sex school? Protective single mother?'

Sandy felt her cheeks warming. 'Am I so transparent?'

'No, I'm just perceptive. And I have to admit hearing a bit about you on the grapevine. Everyone was surprised when you arrived in town. No one knew Ruby had a relative.'

'Oh, I'm not a relative. My grandmother and she were friends – best friends. We used to come here for holidays when I was little. We always stayed with Ruby.'

Rob stared at her, seemingly lost in thought. 'Would I remember you?'

'I doubt it.' Sandy laughed. 'I was pretty young. But it was Ruby who inspired me to bake. She taught me a lot.'

'Well, if your cakes are as good as hers…'

'I try my best. Now, I should be going.' It was pleasant… talking to this guy who, despite the beard and tattoos seemed okay.

'Let me know how you go with the bike.'

'Will do.' Sandy opened the door to leave, but Rob followed her out, walking around the van to inspect it.

'Nice wheels,' he said at last. 'Should make people sit up and take notice.'

'Mmm.' Sandy wasn't sure she wanted that. Perhaps she should get it resprayed. But then what would she do when she returned to Sydney, when she wanted to re-establish her business?

'Well, see you around.' With a brief wave, Rob went back into his shop, leaving Sandy to get into the van. As she did, she felt a shiver of an emotion she hadn't experienced for years.

Funny, she thought, as she drove back to Ruby's, how their brief encounter had managed to change her mind about the owner of *Bay Bikes*. Maybe this sojourn in Bellbird Bay would prove more interesting than she'd anticipated.

# Ten

Rob stared out the window as the pink van disappeared from sight. There was a woman who could hold his interest for an entire afternoon… if he was looking for a woman, which he wasn't. For the first time since he came back to Bellbird Bay, he felt a stirring he'd thought dead for ever. But nothing had changed. He was still the physical and emotional wreck he'd been before Sandy Elliot walked into his shop. There was no sense in contemplating something that could never happen. As if sensing his mood, Bess padded up to him and pushed her nose into his hand. She had been lying in a corner throughout Sandy Elliott's visit. He doubted she had even noticed the dog. 'You understand, don't you, old girl,' he said to the dog, dropping his hand to her head and fondling her ears.

To take his mind off himself, he recalled the expression on Zack's face when he saw Sandy's daughter, and hoped the young pair were enjoying their ice creams. It was a long time since he'd been seventeen, but he could still remember the joys and pangs of first love. He wished them well, and hoped their friendship would last longer than his brief fling with… Annie Rice was her name. She'd left town even before he had, but it had been fun while it lasted, and he hoped she remembered him with the same affection he remembered her.

It was time to close up for the day, so Rob brought in the bikes which had been on display outside the shop and checked the day's takings, most of which had come from repairs. Then, he dropped Bess home and headed to the surf club. It was a pity the club didn't permit dogs, not even therapy dogs. He was hoping to run into Will Rankin there. Last time they spoke, the new mayor had floated an idea with Rob. In addition to the charity bike ride, he suggested they look at organising a special Christmas event for kids. It sounded as if it could be a lot of fun and bring in more business, so Rob was keen to pursue it, to discover exactly what Will had in mind.

'Hey Will!' Rob greeted the man standing at the bar. Despite being the new mayor of Bellbird Bay, Will Rankin hadn't changed his habits – or his appearance. The former surfing champion, owner of *Bay Surf School*, was still dressed in a pair of disreputable board shorts and a tee-shirt bearing his business logo, his faded blond hair still tied back in the ponytail he'd worn for as long as Rob could remember. It had been a sort of comfort when he returned to the town to discover how little had changed in the years he'd been gone; Will was one of those who had remained exactly the same.

'Rob. What'll you have?'

'Four X, thanks. I'll get it,' he said to the dark-haired barman, reaching for his credit card. 'Will?'

'The same, thanks.'

The men took their drinks out to the deck and chose a table apart from the groups which were already forming. The place was busy for a Monday evening.

'So, tell me more about this Christmas thing you mentioned,' Rob said.

'It's just a vague idea at this stage,' Will said, 'but it occurred to me we have a few events for adults, but not enough for the kids. And Christmas should be their time to celebrate. I've seen a lot of coverage of the Christmas parades they have in the US – floats, bands etc. I don't want to go that far. Don't think Bellbird Bay could cope with it.' He chuckled. 'But what about a bike parade?'

'How would it work?'

'We'd need to iron out the details, but I envisage a crowd of kids on their bikes riding through town, perhaps followed by a party on the esplanade. Maybe we could incorporate a visit from Santa... and gifts.'

'Sounds good.' Rob pulled on his beard. 'I'm guessing I could hire out bikes to those kids who don't have one – and maybe provide lessons leading up to the event.'

'Good man,' Will said, warming to the idea. 'What about some safety courses, too… and maybe include the scooters that are everywhere? I was nearly run over by one the other day.'

'What we need is a bike or skate park – maybe both,' Rob mused. 'I've seen kids on scooters in a skate park up the coast.'

'Hey, why didn't I think of that?' Will grinned. 'Leave it with me. I'll take it to the council and see if we can find a suitable location. Good to have you on board.' He reached out to shake Rob's hand.

Rob took the outstretched hand, not quite clear what he had agreed to, but willing to do anything to improve things for the youngsters of Bellbird Bay. It was different now, from when he was growing up. Back then, they were happy to ride along the empty streets, swim, surf or just hang around with their mates. These days it seemed everyone spent their time glued to a screen of one sort or another. Anything that would persuade them to spend more time out of doors was a bonus.

'Are you eating here?' Rob asked.

'No, Cleo is expecting me home for dinner.' Will checked his watch and drained his beer. 'Better go. It's been good to have this chat. I'll be in touch.'

When Will had gone, Rob wandered back into the main part of the club to order a meal, then returned to the table on the deck, wondering exactly what he'd got himself into. The Christmas parade idea seemed to have expanded into something bigger than Ben Hur, but if anyone could make it all happen, it was Will Rankin. Look what he'd managed to do for the town already with the various fundraisers he organised which had become popular annual events.

The burger and chips tasted as good as usual, making Rob wonder why he ever bothered to cook for himself when the kitchen here in the club produced such good food – much better than his own poor efforts.

He was rising to leave when a noisy group came through the door to the deck. Among them were Ted Crawford, his partner, Grace Winter, their children, Aaron and Mel, and Ted's grandson, Zack, along with Mel's young daughter, Isla.

'Hey, Rob.' Ted left the group to speak to Rob. 'Zack tells me you finished working on Ruby's bike, and Sandy Elliot picked it up. She seems a good sort. She and her daughter are a fine addition to Bellbird

Bay. I think Zack's smitten.' He glanced across to where Zack was helping his dad push a couple of tables together to seat them all. 'Single, too... Sandy, I mean.'

Rob winced. Surely Ted wasn't suggesting...? He got enough of that from his parents.

'Join us?'

'Thanks, but I've eaten. I was about to leave.'

'Oh, well, another time.' Ted looked across to where Grace was signalling to him. 'I'd better join the others. Take care... and think about what I said. It's no fun to grow old on your own.'

Rob was glad to leave the club, to be out in the fresh air again, to breathe in the scent of the sea.

It was only when he was back in the house he'd bought and renovated when he returned to Bellbird Bay, determined not to be a burden to his parents, that Rob remembered the faint stirring of desire he'd felt when Sandy Elliot walked into *Bay Bikes*.

# Eleven

A few days had passed since Sandy's visit to *Bay Bikes*, and Fliss had persuaded her mum to allow her to ride to and from school on Ruby's bike. The older woman had been happy to give permission on one of Sandy's visits to the hospital, on the understanding it was only till she needed it again. And both Cleo and Bev were happy with Sandy's cakes, reporting to Sandy's delight, that their customers said they tasted just as good as Ruby's.

Today, Ruby was to be allowed home so, after delivering today's batch of cakes to the café, Sandy headed to the hospital. Once there, she parked and made her way to the ward with which she was now familiar, to be greeted by the nurse on duty.

'Morning, Sandy,' she said. 'Ruby's raring to leave. We just have some paperwork to complete before you take her off.'

'Thanks.' Sandy smiled. 'Morning Ruby,' she said, peering around the door.

'About time,' Ruby said. 'I've been waiting for you.' She was dressed and sitting in the high-backed chair by the bed. There was still an eyepatch over the eye which had been damaged, and her wrist was still bound up, but Ruby seemed a lot brighter than she had when Sandy first saw her after the accident.

'The nurse said we have to wait for some paperwork.'

'Hmm. Sit over there where I can see you,' she said. 'I hope that daughter of yours is taking care of my bike.'

'She is, and she loves it. It's so good of you to allow her to ride it.' It had only been a few days, but Fliss was enjoying the freedom it gave her. Sandy didn't know what they'd do when Ruby needed it again, but of course, they'd be returning to Sydney – and all the problems that awaited her there. But there was no need to worry about that at the moment.

'I'm glad. It's served me well over the years. I hope…' Ruby's voice trembled. 'They've said my sight will be as good as new, but what if…' Then she peered at Sandy.

'What?' Sandy said, feeling a little unnerved by Ruby's one staring eye.

The old woman nodded 'There's a light at the end of the tunnel for you, my dear. You just have to be prepared to grasp happiness.'

Sandy shivered, a faint memory resurfacing of her grandmother telling her how Ruby had the gift of seeing things others couldn't. If she could see a light at the end of Sandy's current problems, Sandy wanted to believe her. But how could this old woman in Bellbird Bay know anything about the fire investigations which were still ongoing, Sandy's issue with her landlord, or the worry about her insurance?

She was saved from making any comment by the entrance of a nurse, a different nurse from the one who'd greeted her. This one carried a sheaf of papers and a bag containing what looked like medications.

'I understand you'll be staying with Ruby,' she said to Sandy, ignoring the older woman.

'That's right.'

She then began to explain to Sandy how to treat Ruby's eye, and when to administer the various eye drops in the package.

'Hello, I'm here,' Ruby said. 'I'm not deaf and I still have all my marbles.'

Sandy stifled a grin. Ruby hadn't lost her feistiness. She coughed. 'You should be speaking to Ruby,' she said.

'Oh, I thought…' the nurse said. 'Sorry, Ruby.' She began to explain the process again, this time speaking directly to Ruby.

When the nurse had finished, and both Ruby and Sandy acknowledged their understanding, they were free to leave.

Ruby's good eye widened when she saw the van. '*Celebrations*. Is that what you called yourself? I love the pink. You can't miss it.'

'It is, and no, you certainly can't.' Sandy thought of the stares that followed her as she drove around Bellbird Bay. It had been a good advertisement for her business in Sydney. It was a pity there was nothing to advertise here.

Sandy helped Ruby into the van, and they set off.

Ruby gave a sigh of pleasure when they drew up outside her house. 'It's good to be back,' she said. 'Who'd have thought a magpie could cause so much damage. They said I was lucky they were able to save my eye. And this…' she lifted the arm which was still in a sling, 'will stop me baking for a bit. You found my recipes?'

'I did, thanks. And Cleo and Bev seem satisfied with what I've produced.'

'I taught you well, and I'm sure that fancy college you insisted on going to helped a bit, too.'

Sandy hid a smile at the thought of the prestigious commercial cookery school she'd attended being referred to in this way. She was proud of the certificates she'd earned in commercial cookery and patisserie.

'Shall I help you out, Ruby?'

'No, I can manage. I'm not in my dotage yet, whatever that nurse might have thought.' She struggled with the seatbelt for a few moments before falling back against the seat. 'Well, maybe I'm not as strong as I thought. It's all that lying in bed. Once I'm back to my usual, I'll be fine.'

Sandy unfastened the seatbelt, helped Ruby out of the car and supported her as they made their way into the house where Ruby collapsed onto the sofa.

'Now, how about a cup of tea?' Sandy asked.

'That would be good, and maybe I can sample what you've been baking for Pandanus?'

'Sure.'

Sandy boiled the kettle and made Ruby a cup of tea – just the way she remembered she liked it. Then she went to the pantry and opened the tin containing the chocolate brownies she'd saved from her last batch, hoping Ruby would approve. Serving samples of her baking to the old woman was more nerve-racking than any examiner she'd faced in college.

Sandy waited with bated breath while Ruby bit into the brownie.

The older woman chewed for a moment, then took a sip of tea. 'Not bad,' she said. 'Not bad at all. Seems I did some good all those years ago.' She chuckled.

Sandy smiled at the old woman. Ruby's praise meant more to her than all the certificates she'd worked so hard for. 'Thanks, Ruby,' she said.

'Now, about the wedding cakes.'

'They're under control. I'm meeting with Grace's daughter, Mel, later today, and having coffee with Libby tomorrow to discuss what she has in mind. We should be right, but I'd love to share my ideas with you after I've talked with them both.'

'Good.' Ruby nodded. She put her cup and saucer carefully on the coffee table. 'I may have overestimated how well I felt,' she said in a shaky voice. 'I think I'd like to rest for a bit.'

'Of course.' Sandy was shocked at how the colour had suddenly drained from Ruby's face. Maybe she should have insisted she rest immediately they came back. But she knew Ruby would have refused. 'Let me help you up.'

It was a sign of how fragile Ruby felt, when she allowed Sandy to take her arm and help her into the bedroom. 'I'll look in before I leave,' Sandy said, frowning. She hoped it would be okay to leave Ruby alone. 'Fliss may get back before me, so don't worry if you hear her banging about.' There was no reply. Ruby's good eye was already closed. Sandy carefully tucked the light doona over her and gently shut the door behind her.

\*

Sandy had arranged to meet Mel at *The Pandanus Café* where Cleo would be available to answer any questions either of them had. It was Sandy's understanding Cleo would be providing the rest of the food for the wedding reception but didn't feel competent when it came to cakes. 'They're really not my thing,' she'd said to Sandy, 'and Ruby always did such a wonderful job.'

As she wandered through the garden centre, Sandy marvelled again at what Bev Cooper had created here in Bellbird Bay. It was a centre to rival any she'd seen in the city and appeared to be as busy as any of them, too. This time, since she wasn't delivering cakes, she'd parked at the main entrance, deciding to get more of a feel for the place.

When she walked through the archway into the café, it was already busy. Spotting a woman with a small child seated near the kitchen area talking to Cleo, Sandy made her way towards them. 'Hi, Cleo. You must be Mel.' She smiled and held out her hand.

'Hi, Sandy. Excuse me if I don't get up. I need to keep a hold of this one.' She nodded to where the little girl was trying to escape her clutches. 'This little trouble-maker is Isla.'

'Hello, Isla,' Sandy said, crouching down beside the little girl.

'I'll get her a babyccino and a colouring in sheet to keep her busy. Coffee for you two?' Cleo asked, disappearing into the kitchen as Sandy and Mel nodded.

'Good to meet you at last,' Sandy said. 'Excited about the wedding?'

'There's so much to organise. I didn't realise… But Mum's been great, and she tells me your cakes are just as good as Ruby's.'

'Thanks. It's kind of her.' Sandy glowed at the praise.

Cleo delivered the coffees and, once she had hers and the colouring sheet, along with some crayons, Isla settled down and allowed the two women to discuss the wedding cake.

To Sandy's relief, Mel wasn't like some of the demanding brides she'd had to deal with in Sydney. She was happy to listen to Sandy's ideas and go along with the suggestion of a simple two-tiered cake surrounded by decorative iced flowers. It was similar to one Sandy had baked for a small intimate wedding several months earlier.

'It looks wonderful,' Mel said when she saw the photograph. 'I didn't want anything too elaborate, though what started out as only family and a few close friends seems to have grown. But Mum wants it to be special. This will be perfect.'

'All done?' Cleo reappeared carrying a cup of coffee and joined them.

'Sandy is wonderful,' Mel said. 'She seemed to know exactly what I wanted. That's one less thing to worry about.'

Sandy beamed. After all the hassle in Sydney, it was so nice to be appreciated. She was enjoying dealing with everyone she'd met here in Bellbird Bay. 'And you'll be providing the rest of the catering,' Sandy said to Cleo.

'About that.' Cleo gave Mel an apologetic look. 'I have been doing the catering for *Pandanus Weddings*, but…' she glanced at Sandy, '… I googled your business, *Celebrations*…'

'Oh,' Sandy blushed. 'I meant to close the webpage until I was able to start up again.'

'No worries, but I noted you not only offered cakes, but also event catering.'

'Yes, there wasn't enough profit in the cakes alone, and I have experience in all types of cooking. I enjoy catering for special functions.'

'So, how would you feel about catering for the weddings here at *Pandanus Weddings?*'

'Oh!' This was the last thing Sandy had expected.

Without giving her time to reply, Cleo continued. 'I agreed to take it on when Bev initially set up *Pandanus Weddings*, and I enjoy doing it. But I'd much prefer spending my evenings with Will. And, now he's mayor, there are a number of official events where he'd like me to attend. It makes it difficult if the event coincides with a wedding.' She looked at Sandy. 'It was seeing your van that gave me the idea, then when I googled you…'

'I'd love to, if you're sure…'

'You could resurrect your business while you're in Bellbird Bay,' Mel, who had been silent till now, said. 'I'm sure there are other events which would be glad of your services.'

Sandy was stunned. It had never occurred to her to do any more than stand in for Ruby while she was here. But the thought of utilising more of her skills, of offering the full range of *Celebrations* here in Bellbird Bay, did have some appeal. She did have the van, after all, and she was pretty sure Ruby wouldn't object to her using her kitchen for preparations. 'Let me think about it,' she said.

'Don't take too long,' Cleo said, picking up the empty cups.

'I won't.'

After making arrangements with Mel to get back in touch and to provide some tasters if she did agree to provide the catering for the wedding, Sandy made her way back to her van which was causing quite a bit of interest in the car park. One woman approached her to ask, 'Do you cater for children's parties? I couldn't help noticing the sign on the van.'

Surprised, and still somewhat dazed from her conversation with Chloe and Mel, Sandy hesitated for a few moments before replying, 'I may be able to help you,' and giving her one of the business cards she still carried in her handbag. Fortunately, she had always used her mobile number as the contact for the business.

Driving back to Ruby's she felt a surge of enlivenment for the first time since she stood staring at the ruins of her business in Sydney. She'd ask Ruby for her opinion – and permission – and all going well, *Celebrations* would be back in business.

# Twelve

Rob set off early with Bess for a walk along the beach. Being Saturday, he knew he was in for a busy day. Recently, the peloton group of cyclists had taken to congregating outside *Bay Bikes* before and after their Saturday ride and had persuaded him to provide coffee. To this end he'd invested in a more elaborate coffee maker than the one he'd been using to brew his own and was dreading the day they upped their demands to the provision of tables and chairs. He had no intention of turning his shop into a café. There were plenty of those already in Bellbird Bay and he was in no position to compete with any of them, even if he wanted to. But, for now, the group seemed content to stand around chatting and drinking from the environmentally friendly disposable cups he'd sourced online.

He had to admit he enjoyed the company and as long as it didn't upset the local café owners, it was good for his business for customers to see a group of serious cyclists outside the shop.

Rob was so busy thinking about this and about young Zack's suggestion he branch out into cycling clothing and bike apparel, he failed to notice Bess had run off.

'Bess,' he called, and began to run, stopping when he caught sight of her making friends with a woman who was coming in the opposite direction, a woman he recognised as Sandy Elliot who had picked up Ruby Sullivan's bicycle, the woman who owned the bright pink van, the woman who had stirred those feelings in him.

'Hello, again. Your dog must have recognised me.' She smiled up at him.

'Hello, it's Sandy, isn't it?' he asked, as Bess returned to his side looking apologetic.

'And you're Rob.'

'How is the bike? Zack tells me your daughter has been riding it to school.' Zack still seemed to be enamoured with the girl he'd taken for ice cream, often bringing her name into his conversation.

'It's good, thanks. You did a good job. Fliss is loving riding it.'

'How is Ruby?'

'She's home now and itching to get back to normal. But it's going to take her some time, I'm afraid. I...' She hesitated, clearly with something on her mind.

Rob waited.

'It's nothing.'

Something was clearly bothering her, but if she didn't want to talk about it, he wasn't going to insist. He, of all people, knew how difficult it could be to share one's feelings. And they were practically strangers. 'Okay, have a good one.' He raised one hand in the semblance of a wave and moved aside to let her pass.

He and Bess continued to the section of beach below the headland, where he remembered how, last time they were there, he'd been wondering about the woman who was living in Ruby's house. Now they'd met, he was no further forward, but he did know her name and that she was the owner of a bright pink van. He grinned to himself, wondering about the van and the business it advertised. Then his expression became more serious as he remembered the shadow he'd seen in her eyes. He'd noticed it the first time they'd met, and again this morning. She had suffered. Rob knew all about suffering. The shadow in her eyes was the one he saw in the mirror most mornings, before he donned the cheerful expression he chose to show to the world, before he became Rob Andrews, owner of *Bay Bikes*, friend to all.

He sensed she'd been on the verge of saying more, perhaps confiding in him, before thinking better of it. Maybe he shouldn't have been in such a rush to get away from her, should have talked for longer. Maybe they'd meet again when he and Bess walked back. But there was no sign of her on their return journey.

\*

Sandy bit her lip as she left Rob Andrews and his dog behind. What had possessed her? She'd been close to telling him about what Cleo and Mel suggested, to asking his opinion. As if a man who owned a bike shop, whose arms were covered in tattoos, could offer her any advice about starting up a catering business in Bellbird Bay. But there was something about him that seemed to encourage her confidences; could she be attracted to the man? It had been a long time since she'd felt like this, since she'd met a man who made her insides melt. She stifled the feeling. She wasn't going to be in Bellbird Bay long enough to form a relationship. She would be returning to Sydney in the new year. There was no sense in becoming involved with anyone here.

She had lain awake half the night thinking about her business, about starting a version of *Celebrations* here in Bellbird Bay as Mel suggested, wondering how to approach Ruby, what Fliss would think, if there was any point given they were only in Bellbird Bay for a few months. But the idea attracted her, and it did have its merits. It would keep her busy, and it would bring in much needed income while she waited for the insurance to come through, and... But if there was a third reason, she had still to think of it.

When she reached the esplanade, Sandy turned to walk back, no further forward in her thinking, distracted by the brief conversation with the man from the bike shop. Then, catching sight of him and his dog in the distance and, realising they'd be bound to meet again, she climbed up onto the boardwalk for her return trip.

On her way up the boardwalk, she was fascinated by the row of what were clearly renovated beach shacks. Unlike Ruby's high-set home on the headland at the top of the boardwalk, these were single level houses, each with a large deck overlooking the boardwalk and the ocean. She'd already visited the one in which Grace and Ted lived. Libby Walker lived in another, and Sandy would be visiting her later in the morning. But before that, she needed to talk to Ruby.

'Is that you back, Sandy?' Ruby called from her bedroom when Sandy pushed open the door.

Sandy headed upstairs to the older woman's bedroom – she had been unable to persuade her to use one of the downstairs rooms, saying she had slept in the same bed for most of her life and didn't intend to change now.

Half an hour later, Sandy had helped Ruby shower and dress – with much grumbling on Ruby's part, and the pair were seated in the comfortable kitchen with cups of tea, a plate of freshly made toast and jars of marmalade and vegemite. Sandy was telling Ruby about her encounter with Rob and his dog on the beach when Fliss appeared, her hair falling over eyes bleary with sleep.

'Why are you up so early, Mum? It's Saturday. I heard you go out at the crack of dawn.'

'I went for a walk along the beach. It's beautiful in the early morning.'

'The best time of the day,' Ruby agreed.

Fliss opened the fridge, poured herself a glass of orange juice and joined them at the table, reaching for a slice of toast and the jar of vegemite, giving her mother a pointed look, reminding Sandy of her promise to purchase a blender.

'I have something to ask you,' Sandy said.

Both Ruby and Fliss stared at her.

'Me or Ruby?' Fliss asked, taking a bite of toast.

'Both of you.' Now she had their attention, Sandy hesitated. *Was this a mad idea?* 'It was something Cleo said, when I was discussing wedding cakes with Mel. She suggested I do the catering for the wedding instead of her and...' she took a deep breath, '... Mel suggested I start up *Celebrations* again... here in Bellbird Bay.'

'Your business.' Ruby nodded. 'It's a good idea.'

'You wouldn't mind? It would mean I'd have to use this kitchen to do all my preparations.'

'Not at all. It would be good to see the place get more use.'

'Thanks, Ruby.' Sandy turned to look at Fliss who hadn't spoken. 'Fliss?'

'Would it mean we'd be staying here?' Fliss frowned.

'No, it would only be until after Christmas, till Ruby's able to cope again.'

'Okay by me, then, I guess.'

Sandy felt a bubble of excitement fizz up, but she tried to remain calm. 'It'll only be for the two weddings to start with, but Cleo thinks...'

'Once people hear about you, you'll be in demand. A couple of the cafés do takeaway, but there's no one provides catering for parties etc. I predict you'll be turning away business,' Ruby said. 'So, *Celebrations* is coming to Bellbird Bay.' She nodded again in approval. 'What's your first step?'

Sandy checked her watch. 'First, I need to shower and change. I'm meeting Libby Walker to discuss her wedding cake – and presumably the catering – in just over an hour. And I need to let Cleo know I plan to go ahead with *Celebrations,* now that you've kindly agreed.' Sandy's head was in a whirl. There was so much to do if she was going to actually set up her business here.

'You need to get a move on,' Ruby said, seeming to read her mind. 'People will be planning their Christmas parties and other events for the festive season. You don't want to miss out. I can help.'

Sandy stared at her. How could Ruby help? She could barely see and had one arm in a sling.

'I'm not completely useless. I can still use the phone. I know everyone in Bellbird Bay... and they know me – and my cakes. My recommendation will count for a lot. I'll start with *The Bellbird Bugle,* our local newspaper. Now, you go and get ready to meet Libby, and I'll work on things here. It'll give me something to do when I'm stuck inside.'

'Thanks, Ruby.' Trust Ruby to want to have a hand in things, but it would be a big help. 'What do you plan to do today, Fliss?' Sandy asked.

'I'm catching up with Jenny and Megan. They said I can join them on the beach. They're going to be playing volleyball and I may be able to try it.'

'Oh, I'm glad you're making friends, honey. That sounds like fun.'

After a shower, and wearing a summer dress, her hair – the rich shade of auburn of her daughter's having faded slightly over the years – neatly tied back, Sandy called Cleo who was delighted to hear from her.

'I'm so pleased,' she said. 'You're exactly what Bellbird Bay needs. I can see you being very busy in the lead up to Christmas. Then there will be...'

'Steady on,' Sandy laughed. 'I won't be staying in Bellbird Bay. But Ruby agrees with you. I think she's on the phone to the local paper right now,' she said, hearing Ruby's voice in the other room. 'Goodness knows what she's asking of them.'

'Whatever it is, Finn will be too afraid to refuse. Will says they were all scared of her when they were growing up, thought she was a witch. And she still seems to have almost supernatural powers of perception.'

'I know what you mean.' Sandy laughed again, remembering Ruby's words in the hospital. It had been as if she'd known all about what had happened to her. But she really couldn't imagine how anyone could be afraid of Ruby. The old woman had been almost a second grandmother to her.

'Be sure to tell Libby it was my suggestion about the catering. I don't want her to think you're trying to cut me out.'

'Will do... and thanks, Cleo.'

'You're most welcome. Thank *you*. Will will be delighted. Now I'll be able to attend all those boring events with him.' She chuckled.

Ruby was still on the phone when Sandy looked into the kitchen before leaving. The old woman merely waved her away.

Sandy smiled and, ensuring she had her iPad and phone, checked Libby's address and set off, deciding to walk down the boardwalk. Libby had told her which house was hers, and said to look out for a large dog, so it shouldn't be too difficult to find.

It was such a glorious morning yet again, the sun sparkling on the ocean, a flock of seagulls flying overhead, the sort of morning that made one glad to be alive, that made Sandy's problems in Sydney almost disappear – almost but not quite. She knew she'd have to contact the insurance company soon, discover if the police investigation had concluded, if it really had been foul play, and what was to happen next.

But on a morning like this, in these peaceful surrounds, it was easy to pretend, even if only for a few moments, that all was right with the world. What it must be like to live here in one of these renovated beach shacks, Sandy thought, as she passed one after the other of the colourful dwellings she'd admired earlier.

Sandy stopped at the gate of the one which must be Libby's, opposite the viewing platform. A large dog of indeterminate breed came running to greet her, followed by Libby herself.

'I hope you don't mind dogs,' Libby said. 'He's friendlier than he looks.' She opened the gate, and the dog followed them inside and onto a wide deck on which was a table flanked by several comfortable looking cane chairs. 'I thought we could sit out here,' she said, before Sandy had time to reply.

'Lovely,' Sandy said, fondling the ears of the dog who was now pushing his head into her hand. 'I love dogs. What's his name?'

'This is Milo.'

At the sound of his name, the dog looked up, then his attention returned to Sandy.

'I think you've made a friend for life,' Libby chuckled. 'I'll just fetch us coffee... or would you prefer tea? I usually have herbal tea.'

'Herbal tea would be lovely,' Sandy said, taking a seat, the dog following her to drop to the deck at her feet. 'Oh, you are a lovely creature,' she said, scratching the dog's head. Fliss had often asked for a dog when she was younger, but it would have been impossible to keep one in their small apartment. A little voice in her head suggested they could have one if they lived here.

'Here we are.'

Sandy started at Libby's voice. She'd been lost in thought, in a daydream in which she and Fliss had moved here to Bellbird Bay and... But it was all a fantasy. Their life was in Sydney, it was where Fliss's school was, her friends... and Sandy's business. Though there was no business right now, she reminded herself, her heart dropping.

'Thanks. That looks lovely,' she said, seeing the mugs of tea along with the plate of scones Libby had set down on the table.

'Not up to yours or Ruby's standard, I'm sure, but do try one.'

'Thanks.' Sandy helped herself to one of the scones which was liberally spread with jam and cream. 'Delicious,' she said, after one bite.

'Adam may join us,' Libby said. 'He's caught up in his study at the moment, writing. He tends to become lost in the adventures of his latest hero. But he does surface from time to time. I let him know you were coming, so don't be surprised if he suddenly appears. He did say wedding cakes were more my thing than his.' She smiled, as if remembering a more intimate conversation.

'Shall we start?' Sandy had finished the scone. She took one more sip of the lemon and ginger tea and took her iPad out of her bag.

'Oh, yes, please!'

For the next half hour, Sandy showed Libby photographs of wedding cakes she had made in the past and discussed various recipes. They had just decided on a two-tier cake, similar to the one Mel had chosen but with different ingredients, when a tall figure carrying a mug of coffee appeared in the doorway. Milo immediately rose from where he had been lying to greet him, nuzzling his feet.

'You timed it well,' Libby said, looking up at him affectionately. 'Sandy, this is Adam. Adam this is Sandy, the lovely lady who has stepped in to help Ruby, and who'll be making our wedding cake.'

'I'm thrilled to meet you,' Sandy said, shaking his outstretched hand and feeling like a starstruck schoolgirl. 'I've read several of your books and I love the television series.'

Adam's ears turned red. 'Thanks. Have you ladies settled on the cake?'

'We have.' Libby looked at Sandy. 'Is there anything else?'

'Well…' Sandy took a deep breath, '… actually, there is. In Sydney I ran a catering business, *Celebrations*, and Cleo has suggested I do the catering for *Pandanus Weddings*, too. If it's all right with you,' she added, when Libby didn't immediately respond.

'What a brilliant idea,' Libby said. 'I was wondering how Cleo was going to manage all her lady mayoress duties and cater for the weddings, too. Will you be offering catering for other events in addition to the weddings?'

Sandy shifted uneasily in her seat. 'That's the idea, but only until after Christmas, until Ruby's well enough to take over cake making again.'

'Will she be?' Libby asked the very question which had been bothering Sandy since she had seen Ruby in her hospital bed. The old woman might pretend to be as hale and hearty as ever, might even sound like it, but would she be able to ride around town on her bike delivering cakes ever again?

# Thirteen

When Sandy left Libby and Adam, after a second cup of the lemon and ginger tea, they had finalised the catering for their wedding and were well on the way to becoming friends. Sandy couldn't believe how easy it was to make friends here in Bellbird Bay. Everyone was so welcoming. It was so different to the city where people preferred to keep to themselves. Libby had already spoken of several people who'd want to book Sandy and *Celebrations* for family events. It looked as if Cleo was right in thinking there would be a demand for *Celebrations* right here in Bellbird Bay. It would set Sandy up for her return to Sydney when she'd have to start all over again.

It was such a lovely day that Sandy, after a quick call to Ruby to make sure she was okay, decided to walk down the boardwalk towards the esplanade. Perhaps she'd catch a glimpse of Fliss on the beach, see if she had managed to get into a game of volleyball.

When she reached the esplanade, Sandy shaded her eyes to gaze across the beach, noting the surf school banner, before moving on to where a game of volleyball was in progress. She recognised Fliss among the onlookers, part of what appeared to be a cheerful group of girls. When she came to the surf club, she hesitated, drawn by the memory of how pleasant it had been on the deck, but lacked the confidence to go in on her own and was unwilling to pull Fliss away from her new friends.

Crossing the road, Sandy wandered along the line of shops, pausing to gaze into the window of a boutique called *Birds of a Feather* and admiring the brightly coloured garments on display, before peering into *Bay Books*, and promising herself a visit to both of these some other time. Right now, despite the scone she'd consumed with Libby, she was hungry. Ruby had told her the phone calls had tired her out and she was going to have a rest and, while Sandy was concerned that the older woman still hadn't regained her full strength, it freed her up to have lunch here.

Spying the sign for *The Bay Café*, outside of which sat a group of sun-bleached tables and a large menu board listing some enticing dishes, she took a seat.

It was pleasant, sitting there watching the world go by, a far cry from the buzz of Sydney's lower north shore where she'd lived for as long as she could remember. It would be all too easy to stay, to forget about the problems awaiting her on her return, and make a life here, in this peaceful coastal town. Sandy sighed, imagining Fliss's reaction.

Thinking of Sydney reminded Sandy that she had heard nothing from either the police or the insurance company since she left the city. She opened her phone and pressed the number given to her by the police.

A frustrating ten minutes later, she closed the phone again. There was no news, and it had taken for ever to get through to the correct department. It seemed they were still waiting for the report from the fire assessor. Deciding there was no point in contacting the insurance company as they'd be waiting for the report, too, Sandy signalled to the waitress and ordered a chicken and salad wrap and a latte.

The chicken wrap, when it arrived, proved delicious, and a question to the waitress revealed the café only provided food during opening hours. It was as Cleo had said, *Celebrations* wouldn't be in competition with local cafés. She was trying to decide whether to order a piece of apple tart and another coffee when a shadow fell across the table. 'We meet again,' a voice said. Sandy looked up quickly to see Rob Andrews' bearded face.

*

Rob had to pick up a book he'd ordered from *Bay Books*, so instead of eating lunch in the shop, or the nearby *Greedy Gecko*, he'd decided to stop at *The Bay Café*. It was surprisingly busy, but he supposed it might be usual on Saturdays. He normally didn't come here on the weekend. Searching for a free table, his eyes fell on the woman he'd met earlier on the beach. It appeared she'd decided to lunch here, too. Without taking time to think, he approached the table where she was studying a menu.

At the sound of his voice, Sandy looked up. 'Oh, hello.'

It wasn't the friendliest of greetings, and Rob had really no desire to join her, but some perverse streak found him saying, 'Mind if I join you?' and, without waiting for her reply, he sat down opposite her, Bess dropping to lie at his feet.

For a moment, he thought she was going to leave, then she sighed, and Rob detected a slight thawing of her manner. 'Not working today?' she asked.

'Taking a lunch break. I had a book to pick up.' Rob held up the bag emblazoned with the name *Bay Books* and gestured to the bookshop. 'I don't normally lunch here. You?'

'My first time. My daughter's on the beach hoping to get a game of beach volleyball and I'm…' She spread her hands.

'How are you finding Bellbird Bay,' he asked, when he had placed his order for a slice of pizza and a mug of black coffee, and asked if he could have a bowl of water for Bess.

'Peaceful,' she replied. 'After Sydney, it's like a dream.'

Rob knew what she meant. Coming home to Bellbird Bay after all his wartime experiences, after the months in hospital and rehab, had been more than a breath of fresh air. 'Intend to stay around, then?' He wondered why he was bothering to make small talk. It wasn't like him. He normally avoided talking to strangers – and she was practically a stranger.

'Only till Ruby's back on her feet.' Her forehead creased.

Rob experienced the strangest emotion, a desire to smooth away her worries. He looked away, dropped his gaze to Bess and stroked the dog's head.

Neither spoke, the silence lengthening and threatening to become awkward. Rob tried to think of something to say which would break the silence. He remembered her van, the brightly coloured van with the drawing of what looked like a wedding cake and the word... He couldn't remember the word.

'Your pink van... it makes quite a statement. A bit bright for Bellbird Bay.'

When Sandy didn't immediately reply, Rob wondered if he'd offended her. He was out of practice in talking to strange women, to any women other than customers. It might have been better if he hadn't sat down at all but had bought his lunch and taken it across to eat by the beach. Bess would have liked that. She loved pretending to chase the seagulls.

He was about to apologise when she smiled. 'It is pretty bright, isn't it, deliberately so. I had it sprayed to advertise my business in Sydney, and now... it seems I'm about to run a version of *Celebrations* here in Bellbird Bay... while I'm here, anyway.'

*Celebrations* – that was the word he'd been trying to remember. 'Let me guess, it's some sort of party thing, right?'

'Almost,' she chuckled. '*Celebrations* is a catering business – events such as parties, weddings, any sort of celebration, really. I've had to take over making a couple of wedding cakes for Ruby – for *Pandanus Weddings* – and Cleo – do you know her? – suggested I do the catering, too. It's all led to the idea that I offer catering services while I'm here, so...' Her voice trailed off.

'What's happening to your business in Sydney while you're here?' Rob didn't know much about the catering business, but he did know that if he left town for any length of time there wouldn't be much business to come back to.

The shadow Rob had sensed in Sandy's eyes when they first met, and again on the beach, was suddenly more apparent than ever.

'It burnt down,' she said.

# Fourteen

What had possessed her to tell Rob Andrews her business had burnt down? It wasn't a secret – it had been in the Sydney papers – but it wasn't something she wanted to broadcast, especially here in Bellbird Bay when she was about to set up *Celebrations* again.

Sandy had left the café soon afterwards, opting not to order the apple tart or the second cup of coffee, pretending she had an appointment, conscious of Rob's amused glance following her as she hurried across the esplanade and up the boardwalk as if she was being chased by a pack of mad dogs.

She couldn't pinpoint it, but there was something about the man that disturbed her, made her forget herself and, in this instance, reveal more than she intended. Maybe it was because of the same expression in his eyes she'd seen in her own when she looked in the mirror. What had happened to put it there?

Their conversation had been awkward; he had asked all the questions. As a result, he'd discovered more about her, while she still knew nothing about him, other than the fact he owned the bike shop, and his arms were covered in tattoos. That should be enough. In Sandy's eyes, it made him someone beyond the pale, someone she had no desire to know better. So why was she feeling so... so...?

Sandy was out of breath when she reached *Headland House*, relieved to hear Ruby's voice coming from the kitchen. 'Is that you, Sandy?'

'You're awake?' Sandy asked, walking in to see Ruby ensconced in a cane chair in the corner. 'Did you have a nice rest?'

'I did. How was your meeting with Libby?'

'Oh!' In her haste to leave Rob Andrews, Sandy had almost forgotten the meeting with Libby. Now she took a seat and told Ruby what they had discussed.

'Good, good,' Ruby said when she stopped to draw breath. 'The weddings will help get your work known. And I had a good conversation with Finn at *The Bugle*. He's sending one of his reporters and a photographer over on Monday. There'll be an article about you in next week's paper. Also, I've been in touch with a few other people who owe me favours. It won't be long before you're the talk of the town.' She grinned wickedly.

Suddenly, Sandy had an inkling of why people called Ruby a witch. She'd achieved more in one morning than Sandy could have in months in Sydney. 'Thanks, Ruby,' she said weakly, wondering how she was going to handle the interview with the paper. She wasn't accustomed to this sort of publicity, though it was something she'd often hoped for.

'Did something else happen?' Ruby peered at her.

Sandy felt herself redden. 'I bumped into Rob Andrews while I was having lunch.' She decided to say nothing about meeting him on the beach too. 'He… he makes me feel uncomfortable. He asked me about *Celebrations*, and I ended up telling him about the fire.'

'Rob's a good guy. He's had a lot to cope with. He was invalided out of the army, you know. Afghanistan. Used to be one of our surfing heroes, one of the local champions. I understand he's no longer able to surf. It's a great pity. Must be difficult for him. But he came home, set up the bike shop, got on with his life. Good to his parents, too, I hear. They live in *Bay Village Lifestyle Resort*.' Ruby shuddered. 'You wouldn't catch me in a place like that.'

Sandy smiled automatically. She couldn't imagine Ruby living anywhere other than this old house. But the information about Rob Andrews was interesting. It explained a lot – the shadow in his eyes, his awkwardness, maybe even the beard and the tattoos. She was flooded by a wave of compassion for him. She'd read about much of the conflict in Afghanistan, how many returning soldiers suffered from both emotional and physical wounds, from PTSD. Her troubles were insignificant in comparison. She was ashamed how she'd misjudged him, based on his appearance. Not everyone with tattoos was like the boy from her past; she knew she shouldn't have judged him based on them. In fact, today she barely noticed them, they were so much part of him.

'And Fliss?' Ruby asked, for once apparently oblivious to Sandy's mixed emotions.

'I saw her on the beach with her friends.'

'Jenny Stuart and Megan Watson. They're good girls from good families, though Megan's father was a tad wild when he was younger.'

'Do you know everyone in Bellbird Bay, Ruby?'

'When you've lived here as long as I have, you will, too.'

Sandy was tempted to say she wouldn't be living in Bellbird Bay, and that Sydney was a very different place. You could live there for years and never speak to your neighbours. But she decided to remain silent and allow the older woman to have her pipe dream.

*

Rob was sitting in his courtyard enjoying a beer, relieved to have been spared an invitation to dinner at his parents. It wasn't that he didn't love them. He did, but often felt claustrophobic in their presence, aware that, while they were proud of his army service, he was a disappointment to them in many other ways, having reached fifty with no sign or inclination to marry and produce the grandchildren they would dearly love.

His thoughts turned to his encounters with Sandy Elliot earlier in the day. It had been a surprise to meet her on the beach, then again at the café, and an even greater one when she had suddenly rushed off. But their conversation had been revealing. She was to set up business here in Bellbird Bay – a catering business which he was sure would do well. It was her final remark – that her business in Sydney had burnt down – that seemed to have prompted her to leave so abruptly. It was also no doubt the reason for the shadow he'd noted in her eyes.

His hand automatically dropped to Bess's head as the dog nuzzled his ankles, seeming to sense his thoughts. 'You liked her, too, Bess, didn't you?' he said to the animal who gave a low growl of agreement. *In another life...* he thought with a sigh. But there was no way he could inflict the wreck he had become on any woman, especially one as lovely as she was. He wondered what had happened to her husband, why she was still single. No doubt she wouldn't be for long. In his experience, women like her rarely were. He took a gulp of beer. *Why did that thought send a jolt of unease through him?*

# Fifteen

Sandy was glad it was over. The reporter from the local paper had been pleasant enough, but her questions made Sandy feel uncomfortable. She was unused to drawing attention to herself and hadn't expected the questions about how *Celebrations* had come about or what had happened to her Sydney business. She was more comfortable when they moved on to discuss Ruby and her relationship with the old woman who had taught her so much.

The photographer added to her discomfort as he took shots of her in Ruby's kitchen, both with Ruby and on her own, and by her van. The van seemed to fascinate both him and the reporter, making Sandy realise Ruby was right when she said it was the best advertisement she could have for her business.

Fliss, on the other hand, was embarrassed by the bright pink van, refusing to be seen in it if she could avoid it. But vans were commonplace, even in Bellbird Bay. Sandy was already familiar with the green van bearing the Pandanus logo. Then there was Will Rankin's blue Surf School van, his son's which promoted his surfboards, and Rob Andrews' white van for *Bay Bikes* – all apparently more acceptable to Fliss's fifteen-year-old eyes.

Thinking of *Bay Bikes*, reminded Sandy of its owner, and how she'd practically run away from him. Now she knew more about his background, she wished she'd been more communicative, asked him about himself. But, she consoled herself, Bellbird Bay was a small community, she'd no doubt meet him again, and be able to apologise.

'Have they gone?'

Sandy looked up to see Ruby walk out to where she was still standing by the van. 'Yes, thank goodness. It was good of you to arrange it, Ruby, but I hadn't expected it to be so full on.'

'You need to put yourself out there if you want to succeed. Did they say if it'll be in this week's paper? Finn promised.'

'They said it should be, as long as no major event happens in the meantime.'

'Poof. What's more important than the first Bellbird Bay catering service?'

'They wanted to know all about my Sydney business… and how I know you.'

'I hope you told them what they wanted to know. I rather fancy having my name in the paper – and my photo.' She preened.

'It's all due to you. I told them that. Without your encouragement when I was barely able to see over your kitchen benchtop, *Celebrations* would never exist.'

'But it does, and you're now part of other people's celebrations. What a wonderful gift to be able to offer.'

'Mmm.' Sandy had never thought about her business like that. When it had been *Sandy Rose*, it had just been a patisserie, serving cakes and pastries, then without Rose, *Celebrations* had come into being. But it had existed for such a short time, Sandy had never considered how she was part of other people's lives. Ruby, as always, was right, of course. Sandy was able to be part of their special days, be it a birthday, a wedding or some other celebration. *Celebrations* was more than just a catering business.

*

Rob chuckled when he picked up his copy of *The Bugle*. There, on the front page was a photo of Sandy Elliot standing beside her pink van. She was dressed in a businesslike apron, her hair blowing in the breeze, looking so… lovely. He felt the same twinge he remembered from their first meeting, the feeling that made him want to take a cold shower.

He scanned the article, interested to discover more about the woman, fascinated to learn the original *Celebrations* had only come about when Sandy's earlier business closed. So, she was resilient, too. And now she was about to start again in Bellbird Bay. What a woman!

He looked down at Bess who was lying in a pool of sunlight. His dog liked her. And Zack seemed enamoured with her daughter. He remembered how his young assistant blushed every time he said her name, and how he'd hared off after work on Saturday saying something about catching a game of volleyball on the beach. 'Time to go, Bess.' Rob folded the paper and stuck it into his pocket, planning to read it again later. Then he picked up his empty mug and went inside, the dog following him.

There weren't many customers in *Bay Bikes* that morning, allowing Rob to take care of several repairs which had come in earlier in the week. Over lunch in the back shop, he took the paper out again, this time studying the details in the article. In his earlier reading, he'd missed the part which stated she would be leaving again after Christmas when it was hoped Ruby would be well again and able to continue baking the cakes for which she was famous. Rob's stomach clenched at the news Sandy Elliot didn't intend to stay in Bellbird Bay. He knew there was no reason for him to feel disappointed. There was no place in his life for a woman, any woman, especially one who had her life sorted, who had a teenage daughter, who... But knowing all that didn't seem to change how he was feeling.

The bell on the shop door tinkled, and Rob folded the paper again and dropped it onto the desk as he walked through the shop.

It was a relief to see Mel Winter. He'd met Grace Winter's daughter in *The Greedy Gecko* soon after she started working in *The Bay Gallery* and they'd enjoyed the odd coffee together. He knew she and Aaron Crawford were to be married and he wished them well. She'd become Zack's stepmother. 'How can I help you, Mel? Are you about to join Aaron in the peloton?' Aaron was a member of the group which congregated outside the shop with their coffees, and Rob had become friends with the younger man.

'Not me,' Mel laughed. 'No, with Christmas coming up, and the new baby...' She glanced down at her stomach, '... we thought it was about time Isla had a bike. At least Aaron did, and Zack agreed.'

'Great idea. I'm surprised Aaron has waited so long.' Rob led her to the section of the shop where the children's bicycles were displayed. Mel immediately went towards a pink one with training wheels. It had a white basket and matching streamers on the handlebars. 'Oh, she'd love this one. She loves anything pink,' Mel said. 'Can you put it aside for me till Christmas?'

'Sure thing.'

'Also,' Mel dropped her voice as if her fiancé might hear her, 'I want to buy Aaron something special for his bike. I'm getting organised early for Christmas because when we get back from our honeymoon it will be almost here. What can you suggest?'

Rob pulled on his beard. 'Depends how much you want to spend. There's a bike phone mount bag for around $20, a trainer stand for $100, or, going on up, a reflective cycle belt or a new helmet. He and his mates have been looking at the new range I have in.'

'Ooh, a helmet sounds like the shot. And perhaps I can get the phone thing as a gift from Isla. She'd like that. Can I pay for all those now and pick them up closer to Christmas?'

'No problem.'

When the transaction was complete, Mel caught sight of the paper Rob had cast aside when she came in. 'Isn't it a great pic of Sandy, and an interesting article?' she asked.

Rob was about to ask how she knew Sandy when the penny dropped. 'Of course, you're one of the weddings,' he said.

'The first one. It's only a couple of weeks now. Sandy has been absolutely brilliant. Although I love Ruby's cakes and I'm sure any wedding cake she baked would be wonderful, it's been great to work with someone younger. And she's doing all the catering, too. It's going to be perfect.' She beamed. 'Sorry, you're a guy. You're probably not into all that. Aaron's leaving all the details to me and Mum, saying he and Zack will be there on the day.'

'Have a good one,' Rob said as he saw her out, not sure if he was referring to the rest of the day or the wedding. It didn't really matter. But it seemed Sandy Elliot had already begun to make her mark on Bellbird Bay.

# Sixteen

'Guess what, Mum?' Fliss let the front door bang behind her and raced into the kitchen just as Sandy was taking the layers of fruit cake out of the oven. Once they cooled and were iced, they'd form the sections for Mel's wedding cake.

'Shhh,' she said, putting a finger to her lips. 'Ruby's having a nap.'

'Sorry,' Fliss whispered.

'So, what's so important you needed to come home shouting about it?'

'I've been invited to the Year Twelve formal,' she said with a wide grin. 'Eva will be so envious.'

'Year Twelve? Who…? Oh, did Zack Crawford invite you?'

Fliss nodded. 'I'll need a dress, and my hair done, and makeup, and…'

'Steady on.' While pleased Fliss would be attending a formal after all – having been so disappointed to miss her Year Ten one in Sydney – Sandy was trying to process what this would mean. 'Year Twelve? They'll all be two years older than you. Do you really want to…?'

'Mum! I knew you'd want to spoil it. Jenny and Megan are green with envy… and everyone has the hots for Zack.'

Sandy swallowed, still trying to process Fliss's news, plus her daughter's summation of her friends' feelings towards Zack Crawford, who Sandy had found to be a nice, quiet boy. Was she wrong? But she was pleased for Fliss. She knew how difficult it had been for her to relocate. She should be pleased she'd made friends so easily, and she was aware Zack had been helping teach Fliss to surf, supplementing the lessons she was taking from Will Rankin as part of the school's sports program.

'I am pleased for you, Fliss. I do like Zack. It's just a surprise. When is the formal?'

'In three weeks' time, on Saturday twenty-fifth. I can't wait.'

'The twenty-fifth? The same day as Libby's wedding.'

'Does it matter?'

'No.' But Sandy's mind was working overtime. The wedding was at six, and she'd need to be there earlier. But she wanted to help Fliss get ready for the formal. And how would she get there?

'Don't fuss, Mum. I don't need you to hold my hand. I can have my hair and makeup done in the afternoon, and Ruby can make sure I look okay. I bet she'd love it. And Zack said he'll pick me up. He's got his license and can borrow his dad's car.'

Sandy felt her heart drop at the thought of Fliss and Zack driving to the formal, but she said, 'You're right. And we can have a girls' day out in Brisbane next weekend to find you a dress.' She did wish she was going to be the one to wave Fliss off on her first real date, but at least she could help her choose the dress.

'Awesome, Mum.' Fliss hugged her. 'Imagine me going to the Year Twelve formal. Wait till I tell Eva.' She disappeared, her fingers busily moving on her phone as she went.

Sandy sighed. Her little girl was growing up.

'What's happening?' Ruby appeared in the doorway. 'It's like central station around here, but I'm not complaining. I do enjoy the company.'

'Oh, I'm sorry, Ruby. Did Fliss waken you? She was so excited when she came in.'

'She did, but it's lovely to hear a young voice in the house, who's not one of the guests I've had over the years. She's a lovely girl. You've done well. She'll go far. So, she's taken up with young Zack Crawford, has she?' Ruby nodded. 'She could do worse.'

Sandy stared at the old woman. How did she know? But then, how did Ruby ever know? 'So it seems,' she said. 'He's invited her to the Year Twelve formal in three weeks' time, the twenty-fifth.'

'Isn't that the day of Libby Walker's wedding?'

'It is, but I'm sure we'll manage, and you'll be here to see she gets off okay.'

'I'd like that. You know, Sandy, you and Fliss... you're the family I never had. It's such a thrill to have you both here with me. Just a pity it took a murderous magpie for it to happen. But everything happens for a reason.'

'Hmm.' Ruby had said something similar before, when Sandy first arrived. But it was difficult for Sandy to imagine what reason fate had for her business burning down and Ruby's accident, even though both incidents had led to her coming to Bellbird Bay.

\*

'You're looking pleased with yourself, young Zack.' Rob paused what he was doing when the young boy walked in. He was grinning, and there was a spring in his step.

'Just organised my partner for the formal.'

'Let me guess...' Rob pretended to consider. 'Fliss Elliot.'

Zack reddened. 'Is it so obvious?'

'Probably not to anyone else. But I was here, remember, when she picked up Ruby's bike and you took her for an ice cream.'

'Oh, yeah.'

'What does her mother think?' Rob wondered how Sandy Elliot would feel about her fifteen-year-old dating the seventeen-year-old Zack. Strange how she'd been in his mind ever since that day on the beach... and in the café, he reminded himself.

'How should I know?' Zack shrugged. 'Fliss said "yes".'

But Rob couldn't help thinking about Fliss's mother. How would *he* feel if he had a fifteen-year-old daughter who'd been invited to a formal by a boy in Year Twelve? Sure, Zack wasn't any seventeen-year-old. He was more responsible than most and had been well brought up but... boys of seventeen... Rob remembered what he and his mates had been like at seventeen and wouldn't want any daughter of his to be in company like that.

'What?' Zack said, clearly seeing Rob's expression. 'Not you, too.'

'What do you mean?'

'Dad. Last night when I mentioned to him and Mel that I was planning to take Fliss to the formal, I got a real ear bashing – from

Mel, too. Seems she knows Fliss's mum. She's doing stuff for the wedding. No getting drunk. No drugs. No sex.' He reddened again. 'As if...' I don't know what they got up to at my age, but I'm not like that. Fliss and me...' he shuffled his feet, '... we're just mates.'

'Even mates kiss from time to time.'

The tips of Zack's ears turned pink. 'Well... maybe... but we wouldn't... I wouldn't... you know.' He shuffled his feet again.

'Okay, mate. Why don't you take a look at the trail bike in the far corner? It came in this morning, and I haven't had time to give it the onceover yet. Give me a shout if you need any help.'

'Right. Thanks.' Zack headed for the far corner, while Rob grinned to himself. The poor kid had already been through the mill with his folks. He didn't need Rob on his case, too.

His mind wandered to Aaron and Mel, to the wedding he'd been invited to at six on Friday in *The Pandanus Garden Centre*. He'd heard about *Pandanus Weddings*, the business set up by Bev Cooper in her garden centre a few years earlier when her brother and best friend married there, but this would be the first time he'd attended one. The first time he'd attended a wedding since he was best man at his mate's wedding in Canberra before their battalion was deployed to Afghanistan. Ned hadn't made it back.

It was one of the nightmares he had... of the time Ned died. They'd been together and Rob had almost copped it, too. At the time, he wished he'd been the one to die. Ned had a wife, a baby on the way. He should have been the one to survive. All those weeks in hospital, Rob had been consumed with guilt. When he was finally discharged from rehab, he'd gone to see Judith, to try in some small way to express his feelings. When he learned she'd lost the baby with the shock of hearing about Ned's death, he'd broken down and wept, and it had been she who comforted him instead of the other way around. He'd never forget the humiliation he'd felt.

It reminded him, too, that he'd need to buy a present for the couple and work out what to wear to the wedding. His normal attire of jeans or shorts and a tee-shirt wouldn't hack it. He guessed a visit to one of the men's outfitters he'd seen in the shopping centre was in order.

Then something Mel had said struck him. She said she was using Sandy Elliot's new business to do the catering. He thought Cleo

Johannsen provided catering for *Pandanus Weddings*. Maybe that had changed, and he'd see the pink van and its owner again as soon as Friday. The thought gave him a boost, and he started to whistle.

# Seventeen

By the time Friday came around, Rob had managed to purchase a gift for the happy couple – a sketch of Dolphin Beach which the owner of *The Bay Gallery* assured him Mel had often admired. He'd also found time to buy himself an outfit which even his mother approved of – a pair of black pants and a smart grey and white striped shirt. He'd drawn the line at a suit and tie, reasoning this was Bellbird Bay, and people tended to dress casually – even for a wedding, he hoped.

Closing *Bay Bikes* early, he headed home with time to have a shower and change before it was time to leave.

When Rob arrived at *The Pandanus Garden Centre*, there was no sign of the pink van and he decided perhaps he'd been wrong in thinking Sandy would be here. His slight tinge of disappointment was soon dispelled by the sight of Aaron and Zack arriving immediately after him. His friend was dressed immaculately, but casually, in a pair of cream pants and a blue cotton shirt printed with some sort of flower pattern. Zack was similarly attired, though his shirt featured geometric designs. Rob's own outfit looked formal by comparison.

They disappeared through the entrance, followed by several other guests who Rob didn't recognise. Rob followed more slowly, unsure what to expect from a wedding in a garden centre. Any other wedding he'd attended had been held in a church.

*

After a busy day during which she veered between excitement and fear of failure, Sandy packed her van with the food for the wedding, ready to set off. She knew there was no need to worry. The cake had turned out perfectly, and the tasting session she'd had with Mel and Libby a week earlier had been both fun and productive. At Cleo's suggestion, it had been held at *The Pandanus Café* so both she and Bev could be present, too. With her heart in her mouth, Sandy had provided several tasters for their approval, and to her intense relief, all had deemed them perfect, with Mel and Libby selecting what they wanted for their special days. Now, all she had to do was make sure Mel's chosen dishes arrived safely, ready to be served after the ceremony. Aaron's dad had promised to supply the wine which would be served by Bev's nephew who had taken on the role for all the weddings conducted here. Everything was in place, and she had convinced herself to forget her worries, for tonight at least.

Parking in her usual delivery spot behind the café, Sandy proceeded to unload the van, glad Fliss had opted to help on this occasion. If the business took off as everyone suggested, she might need to look for a more permanent assistant. But, for now, Fliss was happy to provide the extra pair of hands she needed, glad of the promised cash payment.

'It looks lovely, Mum,' Fliss said. 'I took a peek through into the centre. It's so romantic. It's Zack's dad who's getting married. He says he's okay about it. He likes Mel and doesn't get on with his real mum. I don't know how I'd feel it if was you or dad getting married again.' She screwed up her face.

'Well, there's no chance of me marrying again, Fliss, though I can't speak for your dad.'

'He says he won't. "Once bitten twice shy", he said.'

'Hmm.' It wasn't something Sandy wanted to pursue.

'I don't think I'd mind if *you* did,' Fliss said, after a few moments, 'as long as it was someone cool… someone like the guy in *Bay Bikes*. Zack says he's a legend.'

Sandy felt herself blush and busied herself in unpacking the van and carrying the food into the café kitchen.

They heard the music start, then it stopped, and a hush fell over the centre.

'Can I take another peek?' Fliss asked.

'On you go.' It was good to see her so excited. Sandy had seen too many weddings – and the often unhappy aftermath – to want to observe another. From what she had seen, Aaron and Mel looked set to make a success of it, but who could tell what the future might bring? This was Aaron's second marriage, Mel's first. There were children involved and another on the way. Maybe Grace and Ted had it right, preferring to live together rather than make the public commitment.

While the ceremony took place, Sandy prepared the platters of food which were to be served cold. She had enjoyed preparing them, and now took delight in making them look as appetising as possible before setting them out on the café tables which had been rearranged for the event. She and Fliss would mingle with the guests, serving those who weren't close to the tables.

At the far end of the café, Nate McNeil was setting up the bar, pouring glasses of bubbly ready for the toasts. Everything was as it should be. Sandy heaved a sigh of satisfaction.

She heard a cheer, then the music started again, and Fliss reappeared.

'It was so beautiful and romantic, Mum,' she said. 'The bride's wearing a loose cheesecloth dress and the groom's shirt is really colourful. It wasn't formal at all. Zack looked great, too,' she grinned. 'Really hot.'

Sandy didn't have time to respond. The guests were already coming through the café entrance, making their way to the bar and milling around the tables. She recognised Grace and Ted, Libby and Adam, Mel and Aaron, of course, and Zack. But there, in the middle of a group of middle-aged men, was a face she hadn't expected to see.

The *legend* that was Rob Andrews looked across to meet her eyes and smiled.

*

The ceremony had gone off well, if different to what Rob had expected. The bridal couple stood underneath a flower covered arch and, after they made their vows, everyone cheered. Then the music which had been muted during the ceremony, blared out again from its hidden source, Taylor Swift's *Love Story* now replaced by *Can't Help Falling in Love* sung by Kina Grannis. It was all so different to the traditional weddings he had attended in the past.

The more formal part of the proceedings over, everyone moved into the café, at one end of which a bar was set up, behind which Nate was serving glasses of bubbly. Ted Crawford called for silence and made a speech in which he celebrated the magic of second chances, the serendipity of him meeting Grace, and Aaron finding love with her daughter, Mel, joking about keeping it in the family. Then, after Aaron's response, to Rob's surprise, it was Zack's turn. The young man astonished him with his heartfelt praise of his father and his delight that he'd met Mel. Even Isla, Mel's little daughter got a mention, as did his grandparents, Grace and Ted, who were standing arm-in-arm and smiling at the happy couple.

At first, he couldn't see Sandy Elliot, though he knew she must be there. He'd caught a glimpse of her daughter watching the ceremony from behind the hedge leading to the café. Then, as he was enjoying a glass of bubbly and talking with members of the peloton Aaron was part of, he caught sight of her carrying a platter of food. She looked very professional as she moved around offering delicious looking morsels with a practiced smile, very different from the windswept woman he'd met on the beach or the anxious one he'd shared lunch with.

Rob met her eyes and smiled, to see an expression of what appeared to be alarm flash across her face, before she resumed her earlier smile when she reached the next group of guests.

Her daughter was clearly enjoying herself. Although she was also engaged in serving food, Fliss made straight for Zack, who said something to her which made her blush.

For a moment, Rob wished he was Zack's age again, that he could ignore the bridal party and the other guests, ignore the fact Sandy was at work, go right up to her and… At this point, his thoughts came to a grinding halt, and he was forced back to the present, to a life in which there was no room for a woman, for any sort of entanglement.

'Can I tempt any of you gentleman to a canapé?' Sandy held out the platter containing a selection of bite sized offerings with various savoury toppings. She blushed when one of the group responded with a ribald comment, but seemed to take it in her stride. Rob supposed, in her line of work, she was used to this.

'Fair go, mate,' Rob said, embarrassed on her behalf. The man had the grace to look ashamed and apologise.

Rob bit into the morsel he'd selected, to discover it tasted delicious and melted in his mouth. 'Wow, this is amazing,' he said, to hear her say, 'Thanks,' and see her blush prettily. Before he could say more, she had moved on. His eyes followed her across the café, determined, despite his vow regarding women, to get to know this one better.

# Eighteen

After the wedding, Sandy found it difficult to sleep. She was pleased with the result of her efforts, and both Mel and Grace had made a point of coming into the kitchen to thank her personally. It was an excellent start to her business, but she couldn't help the sliver of fear that flitted through her at the prospect of having to start all over again when she returned to Sydney. There, she wouldn't have Ruby's help and encouragement. The old woman had been amazing. She had so many contacts, and the article in the paper – Sandy still couldn't believe the photo of her and her van had made the front page – had already brought in several bookings.

But it wasn't only thoughts about her business that kept her awake well past midnight. Seeing Rob Andrews at the wedding had disturbed her more than she cared to admit. Dressed more formally, he looked different, more attractive, more approachable, more... She had tossed and turned for what felt like hours, wondering what it might be like to feel his beard against her cheek, his lips on hers, before falling into a restless sleep.

But this morning, there was no time for such thoughts. She had promised Fliss a day in Brisbane shopping for her dress for the formal, plus a special lunch. They'd need to leave early to fit it all in. After a quick shower and dressed in one of her favourite summer dresses, Sandy made her way to the kitchen to find Fliss and Ruby already there eating breakfast.

'Mum, at last!' Fliss said. 'You said we should get started early.'

'It's still early.' Sandy checked her watch. 'The Myer Centre doesn't open till nine, and the other shops will be the same. Some may not open till ten.'

'She's been champing at the bit to get away for the last hour,' Ruby said, chuckling. 'I'm sure you're both going to have a lovely day.'

'I hope so.' Sandy couldn't remember the last time she and Fliss had spent a day together in the city shopping. She hoped they'd find a dress that met Fliss's high expectations early, so they could enjoy lunch and perhaps manage a movie or the ballet in the afternoon. 'It won't take me long to have breakfast, Fliss,' she said, helping herself to a slice of toast and pouring the already boiled water over a peppermint teabag. 'Why don't you check what's on at South Bank this afternoon while I do that? Find something you'd like.'

'Okay.' Fliss's head dropped over her phone.

'How did Mel's wedding go?' Ruby asked. 'I was asleep when the pair of you got home, and all Fliss could tell me was that the ceremony was super romantic, and Zack Crawford was hot.' She chuckled again. 'I presume the catering and cake were well received.'

'They were, Ruby. Everyone seemed to enjoy them, and Mel and Grace were particularly complimentary. It was a successful start to *Celebrations* in Bellbird Bay.'

'It has a nice ring about it… don't you think?'

'Yes, but remember it's only till you're able to take over again. Then we'll be going back home.'

'And Rob Andrews was there?'

'How did…? Oh, did Fliss mention him?' she asked, seeing a twinkle in Ruby's good eye.

'Of course she did. I'm not psychic.' The old woman chuckled.

*You could have fooled me… and most of Bellbird Bay.*

'He seemed to be with a group of Aaron's cycling friends.' Sandy had discovered this by listening to the chatter as she moved around. It was only natural for the man who owned the bike shop to be friendly with a group of cyclists. After their eyes met – and her stomach churned – she hadn't seen much of Rob, not that she'd expected to, she reminded herself. He was a guest at the wedding; she was the hired help. But she had felt a tightening in her stomach each time she passed him or saw him in the distance.

'Ready now?' Fliss closed her phone as Sandy drained her cup.

'I think so. You're sure you'll be right on your own all day, Ruby?'

'I'm not an invalid. And Grace Winter said she'd drop in to tell me about the wedding. She's been quite solicitous since she found me on the ground. I think she feels some responsibility, though I can't think why. She didn't send the magpie to peck out my eye.'

'It didn't peck it out, Ruby, did it?' Fliss's eyes widened.

'No, Fliss. Ruby's exaggerating,' Sandy said, seeing the wicked gleam in Ruby's good eye. 'But it does pay to be wary around the birds, especially in the nesting season. I'm ready to go now.' Sandy picked up her bag, and giving Ruby a peck on the cheek, she and Fliss went out to where the van was parked.

'We're not going into Brisbane in *that*.' Fliss stared at the pink van with its large white lettering.

'How else did you think we were going to get there?'

'I don't know. I guess it will be okay.'

Sandy rolled her eyes. The van had never seemed a problem before, but she'd only had it for a short time before they left Sydney, and Fliss had often chosen to travel by bus or train.

Once they set off, the radio tuned to a channel of Fliss's choosing, the teenager seemed to relax and accept their mode of transport. When she wasn't singing along to the radio, she chatted with Sandy. 'I'm sorry I was such a pain about leaving Sydney, Mum,' she said. 'Bellbird Bay is okay.'

'Your new friends seem nice.' Sandy had met Jenny and Megan one day when they called for Fliss.

'They are… and I'm learning to surf and play volleyball, and…'

'Zack?' Sandy raised an eyebrow. Out of the corner of her eye, she saw Fliss blush.

'It's a big deal to be invited to the formal,' she said. 'Eva didn't believe me, so I sent her a pic of Zack.' She smiled smugly.

Sandy shot a glance at her daughter. Was all this just about making her friend jealous?

'I told her we were just mates,' Fliss said, 'but she didn't believe that either. Why must everything be about sex?'

Sandy almost choked. 'Maybe you've changed, outgrown Eva and her clique?'

'It's different in Bellbird Bay,' Fliss said, after a long pause. 'The girls there aren't boy crazy, and the boys seem to accept us as equals. It may be the co-ed thing. I like it.'

'Better than Sydney?' Sandy held her breath.

'Maybe, but we *are* going back, aren't we?'

'That's the plan. As soon as Ruby's well again and the insurance comes through.'

'But we'll be here for Christmas? Jenny and Megan were talking about all the things that happen then. It sounds like a lot of fun.'

'You'd miss your Sydney parties.'

'Ye...es, but it would be different. There's the tree lighting and the Christmas fundraiser on Christmas Eve where people dress up as Santa, and Zack is talking about a bike parade I could help out with. It's being organised by the bike shop guy, and Will Rankin who teaches surfing is involved. Zack says he's the mayor. And there's a beach party all the kids are going to, and...'

'It sounds like a full calendar of events.'

'So, we will still be here?'

'I guess we'll have to be.' Sandy laughed, pleased Fliss seemed to be settling into Bellbird Bay, but wondering how she was going to feel when they went back to Sydney.

By this time, they had reached the outskirts of the city, and Sandy was forced to stop talking and concentrate on the traffic. She was unfamiliar with the city and didn't want to take a wrong turning.

Parking in the underground car park at the Myer Centre, Sandy could sense Fliss's growing excitement. She regretted not making time for a shopping expedition like this with her daughter before now and vowed to have another one soon – perhaps before Christmas.

'Have you any idea what sort of dress you'd like?' Sandy asked, as they walked into the large store and found their way to the dress department.

'Not really. Eva said I should get something long and strapless, but I don't know.' She shrugged. 'Jenny thinks it might be a bit more casual, but the boys will be wearing suits or tuxedos.'

'Well, let's see what they have.' Sandy winced at the image of her fifteen-year-old daughter dressed in an outfit more suited to a twenty-year-old, remembering seeing photos of girls dressed for their formal posted on Facebook. Many had been showing an inordinate amount of flesh.

After searching through racks of what were labelled as *dresses for the school formal*, Fliss emerged with an armful of garments and headed for the fitting room. Sandy took a seat outside the cubicle and waited. While Fliss was busy, she checked her phone, surprised and delighted to find several more enquiries for her catering service. Most were for children's birthday parties, but there were two fiftieth birthday celebrations and one silver wedding anniversary. The benefit of events like these was they'd be held either in the evening or on a weekend afternoon, neither of which would interfere with her cake making for *The Pandanus Café*.

Ruby was slowly improving. Her eyesight in the damaged eye was almost back to normal. The eyepatch was due to be removed soon and she was starting to get some movement back in her wrist. But she was still finding baking too painful to contemplate. To Sandy's surprise, after her initial complaining, she seemed to have accepted her infirmity and to be enjoying supervising Sandy's efforts.

'What do you think, Mum?' Fliss appeared in yet one more dress and twirled in front of Sandy.

This time the dress, though less revealing than the earlier ones Fliss had paraded in front of her, was clearly designed for someone with a fuller figure.

'Fliss, I...'

'You don't like it!' Fliss's lower lip drooped. 'I'm never going to find a dress you approve of. I'm not a kid, Mum. This is a *Year Twelve* formal. I need to fit in.' She was almost in tears.

'I know, sweetheart. I want you to look lovely, but I want you to look like yourself, not some...' She bit her lip, knowing the word she wanted to utter would shock her daughter and damage their relationship. 'Maybe we need to try somewhere else.'

'Okay.' Fliss flounced back into the fitting room to re-emerge a few minutes later dressed in the strappy sundress she'd arrived in, which suited her so much better.

After a short break in a nearby café, where Sandy ordered coffee, Fliss a milkshake and they both indulged in a decadent slice of chocolate Bavarian cake, Fliss was in a better mood.

Their next stop was more successful. Sandy had a good feeling when they entered the small boutique nestled in a quiet side street. Here, the dresses appeared to be more in keeping with what she had in mind. Even Fliss seemed pleased with the selection the assistant produced and went happily into the fitting room.

When she emerged, dressed in an ankle-length, high-necked, white dress, cut out in the shoulders, Sandy couldn't believe her eyes. Her daughter looked like a Grecian goddess. She only needed an upswept hairstyle to complete the picture. 'Oh, Fliss, you look beautiful!' Sandy's eyes moistened. Fliss looked so grownup, while still retaining her youth and innocence. 'It's perfect!'

'It makes me look different.' Fliss turned back and forth in front of the full-length mirror. 'Do you think Zack will like it?'

'He'll be blown away.'

'It's your dress,' the assistant said, coming forward to lift Fliss's hair, just as Sandy had imagined.

'We'll take it,' Sandy said, without asking the price. There was no way they'd find anything more suitable.

'Now, lunch,' Sandy said when they returned to the van to drive to South Bank.

Fliss was madly texting, sending photos of her dress to her friends. 'They love it,' she announced smugly, closing her phone again, after a number of pings signalled their replies.

Parking in yet another underground car park, Sandy and Fliss emerged into the bright sunshine of Southbank Parklands and made their way to a line of cafés on the cultural forecourt. Fliss hadn't decided how she wanted to spend the afternoon, and this would be handy for either the movies or the ballet, providing they could get tickets.

'Oh, look, Mum!' Fliss pointed to where an enormous wheel was slowly spinning, carrying groups of passengers. Sandy had read about it, but this was her first sight of the iconic landmark on the South Bank skyline. Looking up, she realised it must rise around sixty metres above the ground and be a breathtaking way to take in a 360-degree panoramic view of the city. 'Can we go on that after lunch?'

'Are you sure? Wouldn't you prefer a movie?' Sandy had never been comfortable with heights and the thought of being suspended up there, on what looked to her like a flimsy structure, filled her with dread.

'No, that would be perfect.'

Sandy swallowed. She'd told Fliss she could choose how they spent the afternoon. 'Okay.'

Deciding on a café with outdoor tables, they studied the menu before Sandy ordered a roast cauliflower salad, Fliss opting for a hot smoked salmon and prawn salad, and both choosing bottles of sparkling mineral water.

The food was delicious, but finished too soon for Sandy who was still plucking up the courage to step into one of the gondolas on the wheel.

'Come on, Mum,' Fliss said, clearly unaware of Sandy's hesitation.

Sandy winced. But once settled into the small carriage, when the wheel began to move, she discovered to her surprise that the view was indeed stupendous, as Fliss excitedly pointed out the landmarks she'd read about on her phone during lunch.

'That was amazing. Thanks, Mum.' Fliss hugged Sandy when they disembarked. 'Wish they had one of those in Sydney.'

Sandy felt a little wobbly and was glad to step onto firm ground again, but Fliss's delight made up for everything. 'What now?' she asked. 'There's still time to take in a movie if you want, but I think we've missed the ballet.'

'There's nothing I really want to see, but...' Fliss's eyes gleamed. '... Jenny told me about this fabulous chocolate place.'

'Chocolate? We've only just had lunch.'

'I can always find room for chocolate,' Fliss grinned. 'It's not far.'

A few minutes later they reached the Max Brenner chocolate bar. Fliss's eyes lit up as she perused the menu, the grown-up teenager who had modelled the formal gowns reverting to her younger self again at the prospect of a chocolate treat.

After much toing and froing, Fliss finally decided on a chocolate souffle – a rich dark chocolate cake with a molten chocolate centre. Sandy, having already splurged on the chocolate Bavarian cake earlier, settled for a mug of mocha while she watched her daughter demolish the rich cake.

'That was yum,' Fliss said, scraping the last vestiges of the cake from her plate. With her mouth rimmed with chocolate, she reminded Sandy of a day when she was six and they were a family of three, on a day out at the Royal Easter Show, before she and Grant had gone their separate ways. 'Can we go home now? Jenny said a crowd are going to the beach tonight.'

Suddenly the teenage Fliss was back. Sandy sighed. But it had been a good day, one which had cemented the relationship with her daughter, the relationship which had faltered when she made the decision to move from Sydney.

Sandy glanced across at Fliss on the drive home. She had fallen asleep and with her eyes closed, her mouth still rimmed with chocolate, it was easy to forget she was growing up.

'Are we back?' Fliss opened her eyes and stretched her arms above her head, just as Sandy turned off the engine. She leapt out of the van, through the gate and into the house, calling 'Guess what, Ruby?' and leaving Sandy to lock up and follow more slowly.

'Sounds like you had a good time,' Ruby said, rising from her chair. 'You found a dress?'

'The perfect dress, Ruby,' Fliss said. 'And Mum bought a blender.' She held up the package.

'You had a call, Sandy,' Ruby said, when Fliss had disappeared into her room with her purchase. 'Rob Andrews wanted to speak to you.'

Sandy's stomach churned the way it now did when Rob Andrews was present. *Why had he called? What did he want?*

'I told him to call back,' Ruby said, a twinkle in her eye.

# Nineteen

Sandy wished she could be there to see Fliss dressed for the formal, but Libby's wedding had to come first. However, before she left, she'd been able to see her daughter with her hair and makeup done, looking beautiful and older than her fifteen years. She supposed it was how all the girls of Fliss's age wanted to look.

She was still concerned about Zack driving Fliss to and from the formal, but everyone had assured her he was too sensible to let anything untoward happen. Nevertheless, Sandy couldn't dismiss all the stories she'd heard about alcohol at school functions and was aware of parents she knew in Sydney who had actually provided alcohol to their underage children at pre-formal parties. At least Fliss wasn't attending one of those, and with Mel and Aaron on their honeymoon, Zack was staying with his grandparents who, Sandy was sure, had fairly rigid standards. But she'd be glad when the evening was over, and her daughter was safely home in bed.

Forcing herself to concentrate on the task at hand, she drove to the café and began to unpack the food for Libby and Adam's wedding. She was able to manage without Fliss's help, as this was to be a more intimate wedding than Mel and Aaron's. Adam hated publicity, so there would only be a small gathering of close friends, which was much easier to cater for.

Being here, catering for another wedding, reminded Sandy of the previous Friday, of seeing Rob Andrews, and the mysterious call from him next day when she and Fliss were in Brisbane. He hadn't called back, so whatever he'd wanted had either been unimportant or he'd changed his mind. But there was a niggle at the back of her mind. It had been there all week as part of her waited for the call that never came.

At least he wouldn't be among the guests tonight. Libby had been very definite that it was to be family and close friends only. Sandy knew Grace and Ted would be among the guests again, as would Bev and her partner, Iain. There would also be Libby's daughter, Emma, with her partner, Nick, along with Emma's daughter, Clancy, who was to be flower girl, scattering rose petals as Libby walked up the aisle towards the wedding arch. Libby had also mentioned Adam's sister, Ali, and her partner, Neil, with his daughter Bronte and her partner, Will Rankin's son, Owen. Everyone here seemed to be connected in one way or another. It took a bit of getting used to after the relative anonymity of Sydney.

The music started up in the garden centre, a sign the guests had begun to arrive. Sandy could hear Nate opening bottles of champagne behind the bar as she worked in the kitchen ensuring everything was ready to take out. Unlike Mel, Libby had decided on a sit-down meal, saying she couldn't abide people standing around, so Sandy was serving poached salmon with various salads, followed by cinnamon-honey crème brûlée, and finishing with the wedding cake and coffee.

Everything was ready to be served, when the bridal couple and their guests filed through the entrance to the café. Libby was elegantly dressed in a pale turquoise outfit, while Adam had chosen to wear a grey pinstriped suit with a white shirt and grey tie – very different to the outfits worn by Mel and Aaron. Both Libby and Adam looked glad the ceremony was over as they accepted the hugs and congratulations of their guests.

Once everyone had been served, Sandy poured herself a small glass of wine and toasted the couple from her vantage point in the kitchen. It was lovely to see the couple, who must be more than ten years older than her, willing to take the plunge and marry. She remembered Fliss's words about her or Grant marrying again, blushing at the memory of Fliss's choice for her. Rob Andrews! As if…

She was pulled into the present by Libby's daughter popping her head into the kitchen. 'Mum would like you to join us for the toasts,' she said, handing Sandy a glass of champagne.

'Oh, I don't think...' But before she could say more, she found herself hustled out into the café to join the wedding guests.

When it was all over, with none of the usual risqué jokes which were common at weddings, Libby came over to Sandy. 'Thanks so much, Sandy. You helped make our day perfect. If there's anything I can do to help you, you have only to say. Adam and I...' she looked across at her new husband and blushed, '... I never thought I'd have a second chance at happiness. But there seems to be something in the air here in Bellbird Bay. Maybe the magic will work for you, too.'

Sandy stared at her in surprise. She might expect Ruby to make a comment like this, but Libby Walker, now Libby Holland, hadn't struck her as fanciful.

Before Libby could expand on her comment, Emma called, 'It's time, Mum,' Suddenly, everyone got to their feet to form a group in the centre of the café. Sandy joined them, but stood to the side, ready to return to the kitchen. Libby picked up her bouquet. It was a simple posy of rosebuds. Smiling widely, she threw it directly towards where Sandy was standing.

Sandy's eyes widened as the posy fell into her outstretched hands which had risen to catch it as if propelled by some hidden force.

It didn't mean anything, she told herself as she packed up and drove home. The house was in darkness, and she was too wide awake to go to bed. Besides, she wanted to be awake when Fliss returned. She tiptoed into the kitchen where she made herself a mug of hot chocolate before curling up on the sofa and switching on the television, determined to forget those final moments at the wedding. It didn't mean anything. It couldn't. To consider anything else would only lead to raising hopes which could never come to anything.

*

Rob was enjoying a beer while watching football on television, Bess lying contentedly at his feet, when his phone rang.

'Zack, what's up? I thought you were at the formal.'

'We were, but we had a bit of a prang on the way home, and... I... I'm at the hospital. I think Fliss is okay, but she's had a shock and is very upset. I don't want to worry Gramps and Grace, so I called you.'

'I'll be right there.' Glad he'd only been on his first beer, Rob turned off the television, slipped his feet into his sandals and told Bess to stay. The dog lazily raised her head, then dropped it again.

Rob reached the hospital in only a few minutes and parked close to the entrance to Emergency. When he pushed open the door, he found the waiting room busy, but there was no sign of either Zack or Fliss. He went up to the reception desk. 'I'm here to see Zack Crawford who I believe came in earlier after a car accident,' he said to the red-haired woman behind the desk.

'Just a moment, sir.'

Rob waited impatiently while she checked the screen. 'It appears he's been taken to the short-stay ward. If you go through the door to your left, you'll find a pair of swing doors. Just ask one of the staff there.'

'Thanks.' Rob headed off. Zack had mentioned Fliss. What had happened to her? Perhaps her mother had already been to pick her up. A fleeting image of Sandy Elliot appeared in his mind's eye, then he reached the swing doors, and pushed them open.

He was directed to a curtained-off bed on the far side of the ward and pushing aside the curtain found Zack lying in a bed, Fliss seated beside him, her eyes red and swollen, her cheeks blotchy with tears. Zack was pale but otherwise seemed okay. The boy was in his shirtsleeves, the ends of a bowtie loosely hanging from his shirt's open neck. Fliss had a jacket – presumably Zack's – around her shoulders and was shivering. Strands of her auburn curls were falling around her face.

Both looked up when Rob walked in.

'Hey,' he said. 'What happened?'

'It wasn't Zack's fault,' Fliss said quickly. 'The other car...' she burst into tears.

Rob looked at Zack.

'It's what she said. I was driving Fliss home when a car veered onto the wrong side of the road, and I had to swerve to miss it. We hit something. Dad's going to kill me. His car... Someone called the police, an ambulance and...' He closed his eyes, seeming to drift off.

'Zack hit his head on the steering wheel,' Fliss took up the explanation. 'The doctor is worried he might have concussion. I only scraped my arm on something.' She held up her arm which had a long scratch on it. 'He's going to be all right, isn't he?'

Rob didn't answer immediately. He knew concussion could be serious, and the fact Zack had suddenly closed his eyes didn't augur well.

'I need to call his grandparents,' he said, taking out his phone, before noticing a sign prohibiting mobile phones.

'Please don't.' Fliss held up her hand. 'They'll be mad. We weren't drinking or anything.'

'I'm sorry, Fliss. They'll be worried when Zack doesn't return home. What about *your* mum?'

Fliss started to sob again. 'She was worried about Zack driving tonight. Now she'll never let me see him again.'

'Not necessarily. Let me talk with the doctor, find out what he has to say about both of you. Then I must call Ted.' He left the pair to find the doctor, or someone who could tell him more, wondering how he was going to break the news to his friend.

Luckily, as soon as he walked through the curtain, he almost bumped into a young man in blue scrubs who was about to enter.

'Are you Zack's dad?' he asked.

'A friend. He rang me. His dad's on his honeymoon. How is Zack? His friend said you suspect concussion?'

'It's always a risk in situations like this. We'd like to keep him in overnight to conduct an MRI before making any decision.'

'Right. Thanks. I'll call his grandfather. He'll want to be here.'

'Didn't the nurse call him?'

'Zack didn't want to worry him. I doubt he gave her the details.'

The doctor rolled his eyes, clearly used to treating young people involved in car accidents, many of whom, no doubt, driving over-the-limit and often in stolen cars, even here in Bellbird Bay.

'I'll stay until he gets here. What about his friend?'

'She didn't sustain any major injury, but she's suffering from shock.'

'I can take her home.'

'Thanks. It's been a busy night. Those two were lucky, unlike some. This time of year...' The doctor shook his head.

The call to Ted was difficult, but as Rob expected, he said he'd be right there and, less than half an hour later, both Ted and Grace walked through the curtain.

'Gramps,' Zack said, rousing himself somewhat, and trying to push himself up in the bed. 'I'm sorry. Dad's car...'

'I'm just glad you're okay,' Ted said. 'You mentioned possible concussion?' He raised his eyes to meet Rob's.

'The doc said they want to do an MRI tomorrow.'

Ted nodded.

'And how are you?' Grace went over to Fliss. 'You're Sandy's girl, aren't you?'

Fliss nodded.

'The last time I was in here, it was to visit Ruby.'

Fliss didn't respond, then, 'It wasn't Zack's fault,' she repeated.

'No one's placing blame,' Ted said. 'The important thing is you're both alive. Your mum must be worried about you, too. It's almost midnight.'

'Oh!'

'Now you and Grace are here, Ted, you don't need me. I can drive Fliss home.'

'Would you? It would be a big help. And thanks for calling us. I'm guessing this fellow didn't want to worry us?'

'You'd be right, and I think he was worried how you'd react.'

'I've seen it all before, Zack. Don't imagine your dad was perfect. He's the cause of all my grey hairs. Rob was right to call us.'

'Dad?'

'We don't need to bother him just yet. We'll discover tomorrow if the MRI is clear. Let's wait till then before we decide whether or not to interrupt his honeymoon. I presume the police impounded the car?'

Zack nodded.

'Right then. You don't need me here,' Rob said. 'Take care, Zack. Hope everything goes well tomorrow. Can I call you, Ted?'

'Sure thing. Thanks again.'

'Now, let's get you home, Fliss.' As he spoke, Rob put his arm around Fliss's shoulders. She'd stopped crying by now, but was still shivering, still suffering from shock. She needed to be home with her mother, tucked up in bed. He hoped Sandy was still awake.

# Twenty

The movie Sandy had been watching finished. It was one she'd seen before and hadn't enjoyed it very much even then, but it passed the time. She stretched, turned off the television and checked her watch. She'd expected Fliss home before now but forced herself not to get upset or annoyed. She remembered how time flew when you were having fun. It was a long time since she'd had fun, she realised. Since she and Grant split, there hadn't been much time for fun. She'd been too busy building her business and taking care of Fliss to have any sort of social life. She'd probably made more new friends since coming to Bellbird Bay than she had in the past five years.

What a sad state of affairs, she thought, picking up her empty mug. Perhaps when they returned to Sydney, she should make more of an effort, join one of those groups she saw advertised – a book club, a Pilates group or something. Now Fliss was getting older, it was time she did something for herself – something that included a man? That may be going too far, but something that helped her make new friends. When she and Grant divorced, those couples they used to meet on a regular basis seemed to drift away. A divorced woman was viewed as a threat to the happily married couples – an indication their lives might fall apart, too. At least that was how it seemed.

She was yawning and wondering how much longer Fliss would be, when there was a knock at the door. Her heart immediately dropped, fearing the worst. Switching on the hall light, she opened the door to see Rob Andrews standing there with Fliss. Her daughter had a man's jacket around her shoulders, her face was streaked with tears, and her hair was falling about her face.

'Mum!' Fliss rushed into her arms.

Sandy's arms automatically wrapped around her daughter. She stared at Rob over Fliss's head. 'What?' she mouthed.

'She's fine, just suffering from shock. There was an accident.'

'You'd better come in.'

Once inside, they stood indecisively in the hall for a moment, then Sandy gestured to the open door to the room she'd just left. 'Take a seat in there while I sort this one out.' Her arms still around Fliss, she led the girl upstairs, helped her out of her dress and into bed, piling extra blankets on her. Then she went back downstairs to make her a cup of sweet tea. But, by the time she took it upstairs, Fliss was fast asleep. 'Talk in the morning,' she whispered, dropping a kiss on her daughter's forehead, before going back downstairs to face the last person she'd expected to see that night.

When she walked in, Rob was staring out of the window to where the moon was just visible in the blackness of the night. He turned at her step.

'Thanks for bringing Fliss home. What on earth happened? You mentioned an accident?'

Rob pushed a hand thorough his thick hair.

Looking at him closely, Sandy could see he appeared drained. What had happened?

'Zack called me from the hospital,' he said at last.

Sandy flinched.

'They had a prang on the way back from the formal. They both assured me they hadn't been drinking, and Fliss insisted Zack wasn't to blame,' he added, clearly seeing her mortified expression. He recounted his conversation with the doctor, and Ted and Grace's arrival at the hospital. 'So then I drove Fliss back here,' he finished. 'I hope Zack's okay. It's a sad end to their evening.'

'Oh!' Sandy's hand went to her throat. She thought she was going to choke. She felt the colour drain from her face. What if…? She swallowed hard.

'You'd better sit down.' Rob helped her into a chair. 'Are you all right? Are you going to faint?' His eyes were filled with concern, his touch gentle.

'I think so. I'm not going to faint. It's just…' She tried to ignore the images flashing through her head.

'You need something to drink. Tea, coffee, something stronger?'

She definitely needed something stronger after learning how he had come to be bringing her daughter home at almost one in the morning, how Fliss could have died. It didn't bear thinking about. She should never have let Zack drive her to the formal. 'Whisky,' she said in a shaky voice. 'I can…'

'Let me get it. Just tell me where.'

'Kitchen.' She pointed. 'There's s bottle in the pantry and glasses in the top cupboard.'

'I'm driving, but I'd welcome a small glass of something, too.' He pulled on his beard. 'Won't be long.'

Sandy was trembling as she waited for him to return. Her stomach was churning. She wished she hadn't invited Rob in. But what else could she have done? She needed to find out what had happened at the formal for Fliss to come home with him, so dishevelled and distressed. Various possibilities each more horrendous than the last, flashed through her mind. But at least she was safe.

Rob returned with two glasses and handed one to her.

'Thanks.' She cupped the glass in both hands and took a sip, shivering as the fiery liquid burned down her throat and hit her stomach.

Rob sat silently for a few moments holding his glass in his hands between his knees.

Sandy ran a finger round the edge of her glass. She wasn't sure why she'd suggested whisky. She didn't like spirits. She supposed she must have suffered a shock when she saw Fliss at the door with him and imagined the worst. 'I expect Fliss will be okay in the morning. When will they know about Zack?'

'Tomorrow, I understand, though it's today now, isn't it? You must be tired. I should go.'

'Yes.' Sandy wasn't sure what she was saying yes to. She was grateful to him for bringing Fliss home. She should… 'I'd like to repay you in some way. It was good of you to bring Fliss back.'

'No need. It's what anyone would have done.'

Sandy wasn't sure about that, but let it ride. 'I'll show you out.'

'Thanks.' Rob rose and followed her to the door.

'Thanks again,' Sandy said and watched as he got into the van with the *Bay Bikes* logo and drove off into the darkness.

*

Despite her late evening – or early morning – and the images of Rob Andrews which filled her dreams, Sandy woke at her usual time, ready to bake for her daily delivery to the café. When she looked in on Fliss before going downstairs, her daughter was still fast asleep.

'What was all the rumpus last night?' Ruby made her way into the kitchen and sat down at the table.

'Oh, I'm sorry if it woke you.'

'I'm a light sleeper.' Ruby brushed away Sandy's apology. 'Did Fliss get home all right?'

'Yes, but…' Sandy proceeded to repeat what Rob had told her. 'Rob Andrews brought her home. It seems he was the one Zack called. I guess he was afraid to call his grandparents.'

'Young people! How's Fliss this morning?'

'She was asleep when I looked in.'

'Best thing for her. At that age they bounce back quickly. She'll be fine, be wanting to see the boy again, I'll bet.'

'Mmm.' Sandy wasn't sure she could trust Fliss with Zack again, certainly not in a car. 'Tea?'

'Yes, please. And a slice of toast if you're making it.'

Sandy smiled. Ruby was enjoying having breakfast made for her. She'd no doubt miss them when they left.

'So,' Ruby said, when they were both eating toast and marmalade accompanied by cups of peppermint tea, 'Rob Andrews was here, too, last night.'

'I told you. He brought Fliss home.'

'And you invited him in. I heard the door open and shut a second time.'

*There was nothing wrong with the old woman's hearing.*

'I couldn't just let him drive off again.'

'Some might have. And…'

Sandy stared at Ruby in surprise. 'There's nothing more.'

'But you did thank him?'

'Of course and… I did wonder…' While she was baking for the café, it had occurred to Sandy to make another cake as a thank you gift for Rob.

'You should bake him a cake,' Ruby said, taking the words out of Sandy's mouth. 'The way to a man's heart is through his stomach.'

'What a cliché, Ruby. I'm not interested in the way to Rob Andrew's heart. But I was considering baking him a cake. I dread to think what might have happened to Fliss if he hadn't been there.'

'Oh, someone else would have driven her home. This is Bellbird Bay, remember. You're not in the big city now. We care about each other here. But it was good of him.' There was a mischievous twinkle in her eyes, as if she knew more than Sandy. Now the eyepatch had been removed, Ruby was as feisty as ever.

By the time Sandy returned from delivering her cakes, Fliss had emerged and was sitting in the kitchen with toast and a boiled egg. As Ruby had predicted, she looked none the worse for her experience but was concerned about Zack.

'Can you take me to the hospital, Mum?' she asked, as soon as Sandy walked in. 'I need to know he's okay. It was such a wonderful night right up to… We danced and danced. He looked so grown up in a dark blue suit.'

'I know. The jacket is here. It was around your shoulders when…' she swallowed, '… Rob brought you home.'

'Oh, I remember. I was pretty spaced out. So, the hospital?'

'You can call now, but I can't take you in till later, and I'll want to talk with that young man. There's something I have to do first.'

Ruby shot Sandy a gloating look.

'Okay, yes, Ruby. I'm going to bake the man a cake. But don't read any more into it.'

Ruby chuckled.

'A cake? Who for?' Fliss asked.

'Ask your mother,' Ruby said.

'I am.'

'For Rob Andrews, as a thank you for bringing you home.'

'Oh! Well, he was there… at the hospital.' Fliss thought for a few moments. 'Zack's grandparents were there, too. Rob called them. Zack didn't want him to. I hope he doesn't get into trouble. His dad's car was pretty smashed up.' Her forehead creased.

Sandy dropped Fliss at the hospital, promising to pick her up in an hour, and drove on to park outside *Bay Bikes*. At the last minute, she had second thoughts. She knew nothing about the man. What if he didn't have a sweet tooth? What if he was diabetic? She looked at the box containing the Black Forest gateau sitting on the passenger seat. It had turned out perfectly, the two layers oozing the cream which also provided the topping. It was a gesture, nothing more. It didn't matter if he didn't eat it. He could throw it into the bin, for all she cared. But that wasn't true. Sandy took pride in her work. She like to think, with every cake she baked, she was providing someone with a taste of happiness. What was it about Rob that made her think these crazy thoughts? Why had he got under her skin? She couldn't be attracted to him, could she?

Well, too late now, she sighed, picking up the cake box and getting out of the car.

The shop was empty when Sandy pushed open the door, the bell sounding louder than she remembered from her previous visit.

'Be with you in a tick.' Rob's voice came from somewhere in the back of the shop. Then he appeared, wiping his hands on a dirty rag. 'Sorry, I was busy with a repair,' he began, stopping when he saw her. 'Well, hello.' His face broke into a welcoming smile. 'How can I help you today? Come to buy a bike?'

'I… this is to say thank you for last night.' Sandy held out the cake box. 'I hope you like cakes.' She felt herself blush.

'A cake?' He took the box, holding it carefully. 'I love cakes, but there was no need.'

'I wanted… it's what I do,' she said, wishing she'd never come. *What was she doing here?*

She turned to leave and bumped into a bike, sending it flying across to where Rob was standing.

Ignoring the bike, he gripped Sandy's arm. 'Don't go. Not yet.'

She stared down at the hand on her arm, trying to ignore the tingle of his touch.

Rob removed his hand and gave a wry smile. 'I think we got off on the wrong foot. I'm not the ogre you seem to think I am. Last night, I just happened to be in the right place at the right time. You wouldn't have expected me to leave your daughter there. And Ted and Grace were busy with their concern about Zack – who appears to be much better this morning. Can we start again – as friends? We have to live in this town – even if you're only here for a short time – and it seems your daughter and my assistant will be seeing more of each other. What would you say to dinner?'

'Dinner?' Sandy knew her voice came out in a squeak. *Rob Andrews was inviting her to dinner?*

'Nothing flash. I thought perhaps *The Firenze*. Do you like Italian food?'

'I… yes.'

'Good. Friday? I'll pick you up at seven. Oh, thanks for the cake.' He peeked into the box. 'Wow! Black Forest gateau. My favourite.'

# Twenty-one

The week went by quickly. Although he was suffering no aftereffects from the accident, and the MRI had been clear, Grace had persuaded Zack to take the week off from working in *Bay Bikes*. But the boy had dropped in after school on Wednesday to thank Rob for coming to the hospital, for taking Fliss home, even for calling Ted.

'He was more worried than angry,' he said. 'And I managed to persuade him not to call Dad. He and Mel will be back tonight, and I'll have to face him then.'

'How is the car?'

'It's still with the police, and I have only a hazy memory of it. But I guess the bonnet is stoved in and there's probably other damage. I think we hit one of the posts at the side of the road and I remember Fliss screaming, but after that everything is a bit hazy. I called you as soon as I could.'

'I'm sure your dad will understand. It could happen to anyone.'

'I hope you're right.' Zack didn't sound convinced.

'Anyway, how was the formal? I'm assuming you and Fliss are still an item.'

'Yeah, if her mum doesn't hate me.'

'Want me to put a good word in for you?' As soon as he spoke, Rob wished he'd kept his mouth shut.

Zack's eyes widened. 'You and Fliss's mum?'

'No,' Rob said quickly, lest Zack got the wrong idea. 'But she doesn't know many people here, so I invited her to dinner.'

'Wow! I've never known you to go on a date... with a woman.'

'Can't I have a woman friend?'

'I guess.' Zack was silent for a few moments, then, 'Does Fliss know? What does she think?'

'I have no idea of the answer to either of those questions. You might have to ask her.'

'Hmm. Maybe not. Well, I guess I'll find out. I should be able to get back to work again after school next week, if Grace says it's okay.'

'Whenever you're ready. There's no rush. But I do miss your cheerful presence.'

Zack chuckled and headed off, leaving Rob to contemplate the evening ahead and wonder if inviting Sandy Elliot to dinner had been a mistake. He'd done it on the spur of the moment, overcome by the gift of the cake. But now he thought of the possible fallout of them being seen together. If his mother found out, she'd be bound to read more into it than dinner with a friend, and the Bellbird Bay gossip mill being what it was, she'd be sure to find out. He sighed. It was one of the problems inherent in having come home.

'What do you think, Bess?' he asked his faithful companion. But Bess only yawned. She had no advice to offer. Rob sighed. While it was good to be back in the place where he'd grown up, to enjoy the peace of Bellbird Bay after what he'd been through, it was impossible to lead any sort of private life.

A sudden rush of customers wanting to check out his latest stock of bikes kept Rob busy till closing time. The unpredictability of his work was one of the things he enjoyed. Some days no one came into the shop, while on others, he could be rushed off his feet. Today, he was glad to lock up and head home. There was just time for him to shower and change and make sure Bess was fed, before he had to pick Sandy up.

At two minutes to seven, Rob drew up outside *Headland House*. The house seemed lonely, sitting all by itself on the headland, the paint on the weatherboard cladding beginning to flake, and the front yard overgrown. It looked as if it needed a makeover. He seemed to recall Ruby had been running it as a B&B and wondered how she was handling guests while Sandy and Fliss were there. Maybe she'd had to put that part of her business on hold as a result of her accident.

It was Fliss who opened the door. 'Hello, Rob. Mum said you two were going out to dinner. Thanks for bringing me home.'

'You've recovered?'

'I wasn't hurt. It was Zack who got the worst of it. So, thanks.'

'You're welcome.'

'Rob!' Sandy appeared behind her daughter, looking lovely in a blue dress the colour of her eyes – he didn't recall noticing them before – and wearing more makeup than he remembered. She was blushing.

'Hey. Ready to go?'

'Yes.' She turned to Fliss who was still in the doorway. 'Don't be out too late tonight, Fliss. You know how I worry.'

'No, Mum. Yes, Mum.' Fliss sounded bored, but she was smiling. 'It's Friday night. No school tomorrow.'

'I'm just remembering last Saturday night, when...'

Fliss rolled her eyes.

'Okay, I know you're not being driven anywhere tonight. But be careful on the beach. No swimming after dark, no alcohol, no....'

'Mum!'

'Okay. I trust you, Fliss, but I know what it's like when a crowd of young people get together.' Sandy bit her lip. 'Sorry to subject you to this, Rob,' she said. 'I am ready to go.'

'You have a good time, too,' Fliss said, waving them off.

*

The local Italian restaurant, *The Firenze*, had become a favourite of Rob's since he'd been back. It was run by the third generation of a local family, and he remembered Paul from school. He was one of those who'd stayed in Bellbird Bay, like Will Rankin and a few others, while some, like Rob, had left as soon as they could, only to return years, even decades later. There was something about the place that drew you back. He'd never worked out exactly what it was. It seemed to have the same effect on many newcomers to the town, too. Rob wondered if Sandy would find herself deciding to stay.

The restaurant was crowded, making Rob glad he'd booked a table. He had always come alone before, taking the chance he'd find a spot.

Tonight, the waiter greeted him like an old friend and showed them to a table in the far corner of the restaurant, handing them menus and asking if they'd like anything to drink while they decided on their order.

'Wine?' Rob raised an eyebrow towards Sandy.

'Yes, please. White.'

'A bottle of the house chardonnay, please,' he said, glancing around the restaurant, relieved he couldn't see any of his mother's friends.

'Looking for someone?'

'Not exactly. My mother... she knows half the town and...'

'You don't want her to find out we're having dinner together?' Sandy seemed amused.

'It's just... she'd get the wrong impression. Ever since I got back, she's been trying to marry me off. Oh, it's not that I don't... You're a very attractive woman. But I'm not in the market for a relationship.' Rob felt embarrassed to lay it out so bluntly.

'Neither am I.' Sandy smiled at him.

*Why did he feel a prickle of disappointment?*

By the time they'd ordered, both choosing the oysters followed by tagliatelle with local tiger prawns, rocket pesto, cherry tomato, chilli oil, and basil, the moment was forgotten, and they were chatting about Italy, which both had visited.

'Mmm, this place is really authentic,' Sandy said, after her first mouthful of tagliatelle.

'Don't sound so surprised. The present owner is the third generation of Italians. Paul's grandparents came to Australia after the Second World War. They settled in Bellbird Bay and opened a restaurant. *The Firenze* has been going ever since.'

'Sorry. It's... I hadn't expected... Oh, dear, I'm making it worse. Can we change the subject?'

'Of course. What would you like to talk about?'

To Rob's surprise, Sandy pointed at him with her fork. 'You. I know very little about you, but you've managed to find out a lot about me.'

'Not much to tell.' Rob shifted awkwardly in his seat. He didn't like talking about himself; it made him feel uncomfortable. But Sandy was right. He did know a lot about her, some of which she'd told him, the rest he'd managed to glean from Zack or by other means – not all of them legitimate. He knew how to manipulate the gossip mill for his own ends. 'I left Bellbird Bay as soon as I could to join the army. That was my life till I was invalided out and came back here. I opened *Bay Bikes* and the rest is history.'

'I did hear you'd been injured. Afghanistan, wasn't it? Want to talk about it?'

'No!' He took a gulp of the wine which had just been poured. 'Sorry, I didn't mean to sound rude, but I don't talk about it… not ever.'

'I'm sorry. I shouldn't have asked.' Sandy looked so penitent, Rob felt guilty. It had been a simple question.

'Not your fault.' He drew a hand through his hair. 'It was hell out there. I don't like remembering. Some of my best mates were killed. I should have been, too.' He gazed down at the white linen tablecloth picturing the blood and devastation that haunted him. He shook his head. *Would the images never leave him?*

'It must be hard.' Sandy put her hand gently on his.

The sympathy in her words and the softness of her skin was almost enough to undo him. He swallowed. *She had no idea.*

Over coffee and dessert, Sandy asked, 'Why a bike shop?'

This was something he was more comfortable talking about. 'It seemed like a good idea. I've always enjoyed outdoor sports and when I discovered surfing was no longer an option, I decided to concentrate on swimming and cycling. There are a lot of cyclists in Bellbird Bay. I saw a need and filled it. Simple as that.'

'Mel told me that Aaron and his mates often congregate there after their rides.'

'That's right.' Rob chuckled, on firmer ground now. 'There's quite a group of them who try to outdo each other. Although I enjoy the sport, I've never been competitive. I guess the army would have knocked that out of me if I had been. We needed to have each other's backs. And I didn't,' he muttered under his breath.

'What?'

'Nothing. I was thinking aloud.'

'That was a delicious meal, thank you. I'm glad this place doesn't offer catering, or I'd be out of a job.'

'Your business, it's going well?'

'So far. I have as many bookings as I can handle. I'm actually thinking of taking on an assistant. Fliss is willing to help on the odd occasion, but only when it doesn't interfere with her social life.'

'She's enjoying life in Bellbird Bay?'

'She is.' Sandy leant back in her chair. 'It's such a relief. She didn't want to come here, but Ruby's request came at exactly the right time for me. I'm delighted how well she's managed to fit in and make friends. Then, there's Zack…'

'He seems smitten. He's a good kid.'

'So everyone tells me, but he is two years older than her, and we won't be staying in Bellbird Bay.' She frowned. 'It's not good for her to become too involved… and look what happened last Saturday.'

'It was an accident… no one's fault. Zack's pretty broken up about it.'

'As he should be. I want to have a word with him before…'

'Don't be too hard on him. The poor kid is already beating himself up, and I expect he'll get a tongue-lashing from Aaron when he gets back… about the car. It's probably a write-off.'

'Hmm.' She pursed her lips.

Rob decided to change the subject. 'So, you mentioned your Sydney business burnt down. What will you do?'

'I'll start again. Just as soon as Ruby's well enough for us to leave, and the insurance comes through…' Her forehead creased.

'Is there a problem with it?'

'I'm not sure. The police are still waiting to hear from the fire assessor, and I presume the insurance company is too. There was some talk of arson at the time and my landlord has refused to renew my lease, so I'll have to make a fresh start. But I've done that once already, twice if you count here.'

'You wouldn't consider staying, now things are going well for you, and your daughter seems happy here?'

Sandy stared at him as if he had suddenly grown two heads. 'Stay? In Bellbird Bay? Our lives are in Sydney – our home's there, Fliss's school, all our friends. It's where I grew up, where Fliss's dad lives…' She paused.

This was the first time he'd heard mention of Sandy's husband – presumably her ex-husband. 'You're divorced, I take it.'

Sandy nodded. 'Five years ago. It was all very amicable. We've remained friends and, until we came here, Fliss spent a lot of time with him.'

'He was happy for you to leave Sydney?' Rob was curious about her former relationship.

'The timing worked there too. Grant is currently overseas on a sabbatical. He teaches at the university. What about you? No former wives or partners?'

'Not me. I saw what the forces did to marriages, though perhaps I just never met the right woman, and now...' He spread his hands.

'Now?' Sandy took a sip of her coffee which had been served while they were speaking.

Damn the woman! She'd slipped this one in when he was unaware.

'Now, there's no point. I'm not the man I was. I can't...'

Luckily, Sandy didn't pursue the matter, merely giving him a strange look. But he could see her curiosity was aroused. Damn her, he thought again. He'd told her he wasn't looking for a relationship. Wasn't that enough? She'd said she wasn't either, but when did women ever mean what they said?

'Friends?' she asked.

'Friends,' he agreed. After all, wasn't this what he'd told Zack?

When they reached *Headland House*, Rob said, 'Thanks for coming to dinner. It was good to get to know you a little better.'

'Thank you. I enjoyed it.' Then, in a quick movement, before Rob had realised her intention, Sandy reached across to give him a peck on the cheek and was out of the van in a flash.

Rob stared after her, his hand going up to the spot where her lips had touched, cursing himself for letting down his guard, for opening up to her. Now she might think... might imagine... but there could never be anything between them. He hadn't suffered from nightmares for almost a week now, but he knew they'd return, and he could never take the risk of exposing anyone else to seeing him in the throes of one of them.

# Twenty-two

Sandy was smiling when she walked back into *Headland House*. Rob Andrews wasn't the sort of man she'd thought he was when they first met. She'd enjoyed the evening, the meal, his company. He was a bit of an enigma, this man who had spent so many years in the army before coming back to the peace of Bellbird Bay.

'Good night?' Ruby was sitting in a corner of the living room, almost invisible in the large armchair. She was slowly improving, and it wouldn't be long before Sandy's help was no longer needed.

'Yes, it was.' Sandy continued to smile.

'Rob Andrews is one of the best.' Ruby nodded. 'There's something I need to talk with you about.'

'Okay.' Sandy took a seat on the sofa. *Was Ruby going to tell her she was ready to take her business back? What would that mean for Sandy's party bookings?*

'As you know, I've been running *Headland House* as a B&B.'

'Yes, you said you'd cancelled any bookings when you were in hospital.'

'I did... or Grace did. But with Christmas coming up, I feel bad about letting my regular clients down.' She peered at Sandy. 'I wondered...'

'Do you want Fliss and I to vacate our rooms?'

'No, not at all. There's plenty of room for everyone. I wondered if you'd agree to help me with them. It's only a matter of changing the bed linen, making sure the rooms are clean and tidy and making breakfasts.'

'Oh!' Only? How had Ruby managed that on top of her baking? Sandy took a deep breath. 'I'm sure between us, Fliss and I could do that, and…'

'And?'

'I've been thinking of taking on an assistant to help out with *Celebrations*. Maybe she could help, too.'

'Sounds like a good idea. Talk with Cleo. She has a list of people she can call on when needed. Perhaps one of them might suit.'

'Thanks, I'll check with her tomorrow. When do you anticipate the first B&B guests arriving?'

'In a couple of weeks. The first will be a couple who've been coming here for years. I'd hate to disappoint them.'

'Right. Is Fliss home?'

'Got back a few minutes before you and went straight to her room.'

'I think I'll follow her to bed. How about you, Ruby?'

'I'll stay here for a little longer. I'll see you in the morning.'

'Goodnight, then.' She gave Ruby a peck on the cheek, noticing how fragile the old woman still was, her skin as thin as tissue paper.

'Goodnight, dear.'

At the top of the stairs, Sandy hesitated for a moment before gently tapping on Fliss's door. When there was no reply, she pushed it open. Her daughter was sitting up in bed, her eyes on her phone. At the sight of her mother, she turned it face down.

'Everything okay, Fliss? Did you have a good time?'

'It was okay. Zack wasn't there.'

As she spoke, Sandy noticed the girl's eyes were red. *Had she been crying?*

'Did you say something to him?' she asked. 'You said you were going to.'

'Not yet.' It was on Sandy's growing list of things to do. 'Were you expecting to see him? Had you made an arrangement?'

'Not exactly, but… it's Friday night, Mum. Everyone else was there. And Eva says…'

*Eva again!* 'What has Eva to do with it?'

'I texted her when I got back, told her about Zack… and she said…'

Sandy could see Fliss was close to tears. She sat down on the bed and took her daughter into her arms. 'What did Eva say?'

But Fliss only shook her head.

Realising her daughter wasn't going to reveal her friend's words, Sandy took a deep breath. 'Darling, Eva is in Sydney. She's not here in Bellbird Bay. She's never met Zack. You shouldn't take any notice of what she's saying.'

'But she's my friend!'

*Not a very good one.* But Sandy didn't dare say it aloud.

'Why don't you turn off your phone now and get a good night's sleep? I'm sure everything will look better in the morning.' Sandy stroked a strand of hair out of Fliss's eyes and kissed her on the forehead, wishing she could wave a magic wand and make everything better for her.

Fliss didn't reply but turned off her phone and slipped down under the covers.

'Goodnight, sweetheart. Sweet dreams.' Sandy left, turning off the light and closing the door behind her.

As she prepared for bed, Sandy couldn't get her daughter's woebegone expression out of her head. She tried to remember what it had been like to be fifteen, to have her life influenced by the whims of some boy. Zack seemed like a good kid, and everyone said he was. But even good kids had their moments. She should have spoken to him like she had intended, made her concerns clear, elicited some sort of promise, told him he'd have to win her trust back if he was going to continue to see Fliss. It was what any good mother would have done. Did that make her a bad mother... or just one who had a lot on her mind? Maybe Grace and Ted had had a word. No doubt they'd find out soon enough.

And Eva clearly hadn't helped; whatever she'd said to Fliss had made matters worse. She could wring that girl's neck. She'd thought, by coming to Bellbird Bay, she'd removed Fliss from what she viewed as the girl's toxic influence. She'd forgotten about their habitual texting.

When she closed her eyes and was drifting off to sleep, the image of Rob's face came into her mind, making her smile again at the memory of the pleasant evening they'd spent together. He had been more forthcoming about himself than before, but Sandy was sure there was still something, some secret he was keeping to himself.

*

Saturday's quota of cakes was baked and sitting on the bench ready to be packed up, the kitchen redolent with the smell of baking, when Fliss appeared for breakfast. One glance told Sandy the girl hadn't slept well. Her eyes were still red, her hair uncombed, and she was still wearing the old tee-shirt she had slept in.

'What's happened, Fliss?' Ruby spoke before Sandy could open her mouth.

'Nothing.' She opened the fridge, took out the orange juice and poured herself a glass, standing at the sink to drink it.

'Breakfast?' Sandy asked.

'I'm not hungry.'

'You need to...' Sandy began, only to see her daughter's mouth set in a mulish expression.

'What's on today?' she said instead.

'Nothing.' Fliss looked down at her feet.

'Why don't you come to *The Pandanus Café* with me? We can do something afterwards.'

Fliss didn't immediately respond, then grunted, 'Okay, I suppose.'

'You get yourself dressed while your mother and I pack the cakes,' Ruby said.

Fliss disappeared.

'It's a difficult age,' Ruby said. 'I see it all the time in the young ones who come to stay. Their moods swing from happy to sad in the time it takes for them to change their mind. I'm guessing last night was a disappointment?'

'Zack didn't turn up. Then her friend in Sydney texted something that upset her. Looks as if she hasn't slept either. I wish there was something I could do to help.'

Ruby seemed to think for a moment. 'It may not seem to be the end of the world to us if a seventeen-year-old doesn't turn up, but it is to the girl who's waiting for him. I'm sure Zack must have had a good reason. You didn't see his face last Friday when he set eyes on Fliss in her gown for the formal. It'll all come out right. She'll be fine.'

Sandy wished she could be as sure but decided to bow to Ruby's greater wisdom. The old woman did have a reputation for being able to predict the future and, even if Sandy had often doubted it, this time she wanted to be a believer.

Fliss was silent on the way to the café, checking her phone every few seconds, much to Sandy's annoyance, though she did remember what it had been like waiting for a boy to call – before the advent of mobile phones and texting.

'Can you give me a hand taking these in, then we can have a coffee? I need to have a chat with Cleo,' Sandy said when they parked behind the café.

'Okay.' With one last glance at the silent phone, Fliss stuffed it into her pocket.

Once the cakes had all been carried into the café's kitchen, Sandy said, 'If you've a minute, Cleo, I need a word. And can I order one cappuccino and a flat white?'

'Sure. We won't get busy till later, and they're on the house. You saved us a lot of worry by coming here and taking over from Ruby.'

'Thanks.'

'Take a seat. I'll be out in a minute.'

When Cleo appeared, she was carrying a tray containing not only three coffees, but a plate with three pieces of Sandy's banana bread. 'Bet you don't often take time to sample your own baking,' she said.

'You're right,' Sandy laughed, taking a piece even though she had just had breakfast. She was surprised and pleased to see Fliss pick up another piece and bite into it. Her appetite seemed to have returned.

'Now, what did you want to talk about? You're not planning to leave us?'

'Not yet.' But Sandy knew they would be leaving eventually. 'No, I have quite a few bookings between now and Christmas, and I need to take on an assistant. Ruby thought you might know of someone.'

'Oh, I'm so pleased for you. I was sure your business would do well here. I do have a list of people I can call on when I'm stuck. They're mostly students looking for a bit of extra cash. As long as you don't need trained cooks.'

'No. I can do all the cooking, but it would be good to have help in serving and food preparation.'

'I'll check my list and email you the contact details of those I think would be a good fit for you.'

'That would be great, thanks. Fliss is sometimes available, but I don't want to spoil her social life.' She glanced at her daughter who was staring moodily at her phone again. It buzzed and she rose and wandered off.

Sandy stared after her, her forehead creased.

'I understand. I remember what Han was like at that age.'

'Han?'

'Hannah, my daughter. She's in her twenties now and teaching at Bellbird Primary, living in a share house with her boyfriend and a few others. Not for much longer, though.' She smiled. 'She and Nate have just become engaged. They plan to marry next year.'

'Oh, congratulations. You sound happy about it.'

'I am. Very. Nate is Bev's brother's stepson. He's a lovely guy. You've met him. He's the one who's been serving alcohol at *Pandanus Weddings*, and he works behind the bar at the surf club – tall, dark-haired.'

'Of course.' Sandy remembered the dark-haired barman. She was pleased for Cleo, but it would be a long time before Fliss was at that stage.

'Sorry, I'm babbling on about my daughter. But what I wanted to say was that stage doesn't last.'

'Thank goodness,' Sandy said, as Fliss came back, stuffing her phone into her pocket. She was smiling.

\*

Rob was opening up when Zack wheeled his bike inside. 'Hey, good to see you. Feeling better?'

'Mmm. Dad and Mel are back.'

'Oh!'

'Dad insisted I stay home last night, and he took my phone. I couldn't let Fliss know. Can I borrow yours?' Zack gazed at Rob with a pleading expression.

'I don't want to go against your dad…' Aaron was a friend who deserved his loyalty, but he remembered all too well what it was like to be seventeen and in the throes of first love. 'Oh, okay.' He handed his phone to Zack. 'Just don't tell your dad.'

'Thanks, Rob.' He grinned and took the phone into the back shop. Rob could hear his voice, but not the words. He smiled. *Young love*!

'Thanks,' Zack repeated as he handed the phone back.

'Is your dad upset about the car?'

'Yeah, I… he didn't know I planned to use it.' Zack looked embarrassed. 'I wanted to impress Fliss. Guess it was a mistake.'

'You're not wrong.' But again, he could understand the boy's reasoning. Surely Aaron could, too?

'Want me to have a word with him?'

'Would you? Though I don't know if it would do any good. Mel tried to reason with him, but he was adamant I couldn't have my phone back, and I needed to contact Fliss.'

'What about your granddad?'

'He thought I had Dad's permission. I may have bent the truth a little.' Zack reddened again.

'So you lied to your grandad?'

Zack shuffled his feet. 'I'm sorry now; wish I hadn't, but…'

'You wanted to impress Fliss. Well, it's not the first time a guy got into trouble trying to impress a girl. But I've seen the way she looks at you. You didn't need a car.'

'You think so? You think she likes me?'

'I'm pretty sure she does. How did your call go?'

'We're going to the movies tonight.'

'You see? She was probably hanging out for your call. Girls worry about these things just as much as guys do.'

'I suppose.' There was a pause. 'What about you?'

'What about me?'

'You and Fliss's mother. She's pretty hot for a woman her age.'

Rob almost choked, but Zack was right. Sandy Elliot *was* pretty hot. It was what was making him hot under the collar every time he was in her presence.

'Nothing going on there, Zack.' Rob could feel his face burning and hoped Zack didn't notice.

# Twenty-three

'What would you like to do now?' Sandy asked Fliss when they were leaving the café.

Fliss was busy texting and didn't immediately answer. 'What?' she said, seemingly realising her mother had spoken to her.

Sandy stifled her impatience. 'I asked what you wanted to do now. I did promise we'd do something together.'

'Oh, yeah. Would you mind if we didn't? Jenny and Megan have invited me to a game of volleyball, and...' she blushed, '... Zack has invited me to the movies tonight.'

'So, you have heard from him?' Sandy had suspected the reason for Fliss's changed mood.

'Yeah.' She frowned. 'His dad didn't let him go out last night and took away his phone. All because of the stupid accident.'

Sandy silently counted to ten. 'The accident could have been a lot worse, and it was his car. How did he manage to call you?'

'He's at the bike shop and borrowed Rob Andrews' phone.' She grinned and glanced at Sandy out of the side of her eye. '*Your* friend, Mum.'

Sandy sighed. There was no sense denying it. It would only fuel Fliss's curiosity. 'So, do you want me to drop you off at the beach?'

'Please.'

'You'll be home for lunch?'

'I'm not sure. Depends what the others want to do.'

'Do you have enough money to buy lunch?'

'Yeah. Dad put some into my account.'

Sandy flinched. She knew Grant topped up Fliss's account from time to time. She wished he didn't. She guessed it was his way of dealing with his guilt at leaving the way he did.

'Let me know what you decide.'

After dropping Fliss off, Sandy decided to use her unexpectedly free morning exploring the shops on the esplanade. It was something she'd been meaning to do but hadn't yet made time for. Parking the van, she headed first to the boutique which had caught her eye on an earlier visit. *Birds of a Feather* looked like her sort of shop.

Peering into the window, Sandy admired the brightly coloured garments on display before pushing open the glass door.

'How can I help you?' An elegant blonde woman approached her with a smile. 'I'm Greta.'

'Sandy,' Sandy said, noticing the woman was wearing one of her own stock. 'I need a new outfit and love your window.'

'Thank you. I always feel there's something special about wearing bright colours. The correct outfit can change your mood.'

'I love the one you're wearing,' Sandy admired the blue dress patterned in tropical flowers, 'but it might be a bit much for me.'

Greta gazed at Sandy as if assessing her. 'Try this rack,' she said, pointing to one on the far side of the shop. 'I think you may find something to your liking there. Is it for a special occasion?'

'No, I tend to wear black for work and want something completely different for when I go out.' As she spoke, Sandy wondered exactly what occasion she was imagining. *Did she expect Rob Andrews to invite her to dinner again? Or was she preparing for her new life back in Sydney?*

Greta stared at her for a moment, then snapped her fingers. 'I know who you are. You're *Celebrations*! Sorry, that came out wrong. What I mean is, you're the woman who's helping Ruby out and who has set up a catering business. Your pink van has made quite an impression around town. I hope your business is doing well.'

'It is, thanks.'

'I'll leave you to browse.' Greta moved away and became busy behind the counter.

Sandy looked through the garments on display, spoiled for choice. They were all so lovely. Finally, she selected several garments and carried them across to Greta. 'Can I try these?'

'Of course you can.' Greta led her to the change room and held back the curtain. 'Just give me a call if you need any help.'

Alone in the tiny cubicle, Sandy wondered if she was being stupid, if she really needed more clothes. But it was ages since she bought anything for herself, and her current wardrobe was a bit old-fashioned – at least according to Fliss, it was.

She had just taken off the jeans and tee-shirt she was wearing and was reaching for the first dress – a bright red one with a border of white daisies – when her phone buzzed with an incoming text. She hesitated. *What should she do first?* The phone won.

*Enjoyed last night. RU up for a rematch? Tomorrow at the surf club? Rob.*

Sandy smiled and tucked her phone back into her bag. She'd reply later when she'd had time to think about it. *Why did her heart take a sudden leap?*

She was in a buoyant mood as she tried on the outfits she'd selected, finally deciding on the red dress, a pair of wide-legged royal blue pants and a tunic which featured a matching geometric pattern. 'I'll take these,' she said to Greta, placing them on the counter.

'Good choice. They'll suit you really well. Going somewhere special?' she asked again.

Sandy blushed. 'I've just been invited out to dinner at the surf club.'

'Oh, I love that place. Tonight?'

'Tomorrow.'

'I may see you there. Leo and I...' it was her turn to blush, '... we often eat there on Sundays.'

'Your husband?'

'Partner, fiancé, but it's still so new I get tremors each time I think of him,' Greta confided.

Was that how Sandy felt when she met Rob, the feeling in her gut? 'It's been a long time since I...' she said, suddenly feeling a connection with this woman she'd met for the first time.

'I can relate to that.' Greta laughed. 'But, believe me, it's worth it when everything falls into place.'

Suddenly Sandy felt uncomfortable. What was she doing confiding in this stranger? It wasn't even as if she and Rob were... They weren't, were they? There was still so much about him she didn't know, things she was sure he was hiding, secrets from his past. And he had said he wasn't looking for a relationship. Well, neither was she, but it was nice to be invited to dinner, to feel attractive, to...' She realised Greta was staring at her. 'Sorry?'

'I asked how you wanted to pay.'

'Oh, card.' Sandy took the visa card from her purse, feeling embarrassed to have been caught daydreaming. *What must Greta think of her?*

Sandy paid, took her purchases and left the shop. Greta hadn't seemed to notice how distracted she was. Perhaps she was used to customers daydreaming in the midst of a transaction. She seemed nice, as did everyone Sandy had met here. It would be so easy to fall into a sense of complacency and forget her life was in Sydney.

Making a quick trip to the nearby bookshop where she recognised the owner as one of the guests at Libby's wedding, she picked up the latest book by Adam Holland. Then, feeling peckish, she took a seat at one of the sun-bleached tables outside *The Bay Café* and ordered a coffee and a slice of carrot cake.

It was pleasant sitting there watching the world go by, happy sounds from the beach across the way reaching her. She wondered how the volleyball game was going but managed to refrain from walking over to check. That would really annoy Fliss. Opening her phone to check her emails, she found one from the insurance company stating the investigation was still ongoing, and no funds could be released until it was concluded. *Why were they taking so long? Surely it was an open and shut case?*

'May I join you?' Sandy looked up to see Grace Winter. The older woman looked as elegant as usual making Sandy feel drab in her jeans and tee-shirt. She was glad she'd made her purchases.

'Of course. It's lovely to see you, Grace. I was just enjoying the ambiance of Bellbird Bay.'

'A bit different to what you're used to.' Grace chuckled. 'Looks like you've been taking advantage of our local boutique.' She gestured to the bag at Sandy's feet bearing the logo of *Birds of a Feather*.

'Yes, I thought it was about time I replenished my wardrobe. I was surprised...'

Grace didn't allow her to finish. 'Most visitors to the town are surprised to find such an upmarket boutique here. Greta has done well. Life hasn't been easy for her,' Grace pursed her lips, but clearly didn't intend to elaborate, 'but she's always managed to remain cheerful. It's a gift.'

'Mmm.'

'What about you? Your daughter was with Zack when he had his accident. I saw her at the hospital looking distraught. How is she now?'

'Better. They seem to be able to recover quickly at her age. She was a bit low this morning, then she heard from Zack and bounced right back.'

Grace looked thoughtful. 'That would be partly Aaron's doing, I expect. He and Mel returned yesterday, and he was furious when he learned about his car. Understandably. It seems he wasn't aware Zack intended to drive it. When they left Ted and me, he was reading the riot act to Zack, and threatening all sorts. I suspect he overreacted and may have confiscated Zack's phone. If Zack managed to contact your daughter, my guess is he borrowed someone's, maybe Rob's.' She raised an eyebrow.

'Rob?' *Rob's phone? That's what Fliss had said. Was this why he'd contacted her – to discuss Zack and Fliss?* Her heart shrank.

'He takes a keen interest in the boy – both him and Will Rankin. Ted reckons between the two of them, they'll have Zack making surf champion and winning the triathlon.'

'Oh!'

'Is something the matter? You're not worried about Zack and your daughter?'

'I am... a bit.' Sandy bit her lip. 'I hadn't realised he took the car without his dad's permission.' Sandy wished again she'd made time to speak with him. But she was more worried about Rob's motive for inviting her to dinner again.

'It's been sorted. He was duly repentant and won't do it again. And there's no need to worry. Young Zack has his head screwed on the right way. He was in a bit of a mess when he came to live with Ted and his dad, but he soon sorted himself out. I think it was when Ted started teaching him to surf. Then he became involved with Will at the surf school, and when Rob offered him a part-time job... I'd be delighted if he was involved with a daughter or granddaughter of mine.'

Grace's tea arrived along with a slice of carrot cake. 'Testing out the opposition?' she asked, seeing the half-eaten piece on Sandy's plate. 'It's not a patch on yours or Ruby's. I had coffee in *The Pandanus Café* earlier in the week and had a slice of yours there.'

'Thanks.' Sandy took a sip of her coffee.

'How is Ruby, by the way? I haven't been to see her lately.'

'She's on the mend, but…' Sandy felt she could confide in Grace, '… I'm worried about her. Physically, she's improving but it's as if she's lost her confidence. I'm not sure how she's going to manage when Fliss and I go back to Sydney.'

'You do intend to go back?'

'Of course. As soon as things are settled there. I've promised to be here until after Christmas and to help out with a few of Ruby's B&B guests, but after that…'

'She's still taking in guests?'

'She says she has regulars she doesn't want to disappoint.'

'Of course, that's Ruby all over. I do hope she recovers fully.'

'So do I.'

'On another topic, I hear you had dinner with Rob. I know it's none of my business, but… his mother recently joined my book club. Gwen lives in the same community as my sister. She worries about him, about how insular he's been since coming back to Bellbird Bay. I think you may be the first person he's invited out or had a meal with.'

Sandy's stomach churned. She wasn't prepared for this conversation. It was just as Rob feared. Word had got around about their date – *was it a date?* And going to the surf club would only make matters worse. Perhaps she should refuse. But he was good company, and she didn't have anyone else to eat out with, and… she did find him attractive. But was she just setting herself up for a broken heart?

# Twenty-four

Rob still hadn't heard back from Sandy when he closed up for the day. Zack had gone off whistling, pleased to have arranged a trip to the movies with Fliss, while Rob was having dinner with his parents again.

He pondered Sandy's lack of response as he stood under the shower. She seemed to have enjoyed herself, but he was so out of practice with women, how would he know? Maybe he'd been too precipitous in inviting her out again so soon and scared her off. But if they were going to be seen together again, it was better to get it over with... and they'd certainly be seen at the surf club. He wasn't sure exactly when he'd decided to bite the bullet and to hell with what his mother thought – maybe it was seeing Zack so fired up at managing to contact Fliss. Whatever the reason, he knew he was looking forward to seeing Sandy Elliot again.

He was rubbing his hair dry when his phone buzzed. Dropping the towel, he picked it up to see a text from Sandy.

*Okay. S*

It wasn't much, but it was enough. He felt the beginning of what he recognised as a thrill of anticipation. It was a long time since he'd felt anything like it. It scared him. Maybe this was all a mistake, but it was too late to back out now. He sighed as he pulled on the blue chinos and blue and white striped shirt which would meet this mother's approval, and hoped there wouldn't be any others at dinner tonight.

By the time he drove through the entrance to *Bay Village Lifestyle Resort*, the sun was low in the sky. Rob could see a flock of black cockatoos flying overhead and the scent of jasmine from the hedge bordering the pathway filtered through the open window of the van, reminding him of his childhood. They had been happy, carefree days when he and his twin brother played soldiers in the large backyard of their parents' home, both determined to become real soldiers when they were grown up. But Brett hadn't lived to realise his dream, killed by meningococcal when they were only in primary school. Since then, Rob had been the main focus of his mother's attention. It had been a relief – as well as fulfilling a promise to his dead brother – to join the army as soon as he left school.

Seeing the delight on his mother's face as she hugged him, and feeling the strength of his dad's handshake, Rob felt guilty he didn't visit more often. It was one more weight in the burden of guilt which began with Brett's death, and he had carried ever since. Why hadn't he been the one to die? Ned's death had only exacerbated it.

'No guests tonight?' he asked, glancing around.

'Just us,' his dad replied. 'I managed to persuade your mum we needed some family time. She's joined a book club now, and with all her other commitments, *I* barely see her.'

'That's not true, Bob.' Rob's mother nudged him. 'Though I do find, since moving here, there are so many activities to get involved with. Your dad's happy to stay home pottering around the house and garden,' She smiled affectionately at her husband.

'I don't have your mother's dog spirit,' Bob said.

As if thinking she was being talked about, Bess barked, making them all laugh.

'I made your favourite,' his mother said as they walked through the house to the kitchen, where the aroma of the macaroni cheese which had been Rob's favourite meal when he was about twelve, filled the room.

'Beer, son?' Bob asked.

'Thanks, Dad.'

Rob's dad poured a beer for Rob and himself and a white wine for Rob's mother, and they took their drinks out to the courtyard.

'How are things?' Rob's dad asked, when his mother had disappeared into the house to check on the meal.

'Okay. Shop's busy as usual. A lot of the local children seem to be getting bikes for Christmas. I'm not complaining.'

'Your mum's been hearing things about you. I wanted to warn you. Don't be alarmed if she's getting herself all worked up about nothing. You know what she's like, Rob. I'd like a couple of grandchildren as much as she would, but I understand what you've been through, and I wouldn't blame you if...'

'Dinner's ready!' Gwen appeared in the doorway.

'Here we go,' Bob said, finishing his beer and rising.

Rob did the same, sighing at the prospect of being grilled by his mother about Sandy. Bess, who had been lying at Rob's feet, padded after them, to be rewarded by a bowl of leftovers in a corner of the kitchen.

Gwen managed to restrain herself until they had finished the apple tart she'd baked for dessert and had graduated to coffee, before she began the interrogation Rob was expecting.

'A little bird told me you took a woman to dinner at *The Firenze* last night,' she said.

'I presume the little bird was one of your cronies.'

Gwen bridled. 'One of my good friends who told me what my son didn't. I would have thought I'd be the first to know you had found someone. Who is she? Dot didn't recognise her.'

Rob sighed. He'd known it would be like this. Why had he invited Sandy to dinner in the first place? Because he liked her and felt sorry for her. She didn't know many people here in Bellbird Bay, and her daughter and Zack were seeing each other. It had seemed natural to invite her to dinner. But he did wish his mother wouldn't make such a big thing about it. He could already see the wedding bells in her eyes. And Dot? Wasn't she the woman who he'd met here last time he came to dinner? How could he have failed to notice her in *The Firenze*?

'Yes, I did take someone to dinner last night, but I didn't expect it to make the headlines. Sandy Elliot is new to town. She's helping out Ruby Sullivan by baking cakes for *The Pandanus Café* and is doing catering while she's here. You may have seen her pink van around town – *Celebrations*.'

'Oh, I've heard about her. No one knew Ruby had relatives. She has a daughter, too, doesn't she?' Gwen pursed her lips.

Rob could almost hear what she was thinking. 'She's not a relative, and yes, she has a daughter. Young Zack is enamoured with her; took her to his formal.'

'Oh! Dot mentioned that. Grace Winter is her sister. Didn't they have an accident? Young people these days!'

'I don't think they're any different to what we were,' Rob's dad said, chuckling. 'I hope no one was hurt.'

'Only Aaron's car.'

'This Sandy Elliot,' Rob's mum began.

'Leave it be, Gwen.' Bob put a restraining hand on her arm. 'If there's any more to know, Rob will tell us. Let him enjoy his coffee in peace. We don't need to know the ins and outs about everyone he chooses to have a meal with.'

'But...'

To Rob's relief, his mother seemed to recognise the expression on her husband's face and fell silent. Bess chose that moment to join them and, in the kerfuffle of fussing over her, the conversation turned to whether or not Rob's parents should get a dog. His dad thought it would be good company for them, while his mum worried about what would happen when they wanted to set out on their travels; they were still talking about getting a caravan.

'It can join me and Bess,' Rob said, effectively putting an end to the debate for now. But he knew they'd continue to argue about it until his dad, as usual, got his way. While it might seem to others that his mother ruled the roost – and she was the more outspoken of the two – his dad usually prevailed. It was he who had supported Rob entering the forces when his mother didn't want him to leave, and who had supported his desire to live by himself when he returned home. If his mum had her way, he'd have been holed up here with them in this over-fifties community.

Rob was glad when he could leave without offending his parents. He did love them both, but sometimes – like tonight – he found his mother difficult to cope with. He walked to the van, Bess lolloping at his heels, his mother's final words ringing in his ears.

'We'd love to meet your friend. Maybe next time you come to dinner?'

Take Sandy Elliot to dinner with his parents? Nothing was further from his mind.

# Twenty-five

Sandy spent a lazy afternoon on Sunday. After baking and delivering her batch of cakes to *The Pandanus Café*, and ensuring the bedroom was ready for Ruby's first guests, she curled up on the sofa with the latest Adam Holland book she'd purchased in *Bay Books*.

Fliss had gone to meet her friends on the beach, hoping for another game of volleyball which she seemed to have become obsessed with, and Ruby was having a nap. She was napping more frequently these days, but Sandy didn't think it was cause for concern, though she did have a moment of apprehension at Ruby's expression when she suggested Fliss might hand back her bike soon. It was this which led to her telling Grace she thought the older woman was losing her confidence.

But today she didn't want to worry about that, or about the delay in her insurance. The sun was shining, she had a good book, and she was going out to dinner with an attractive man. What more could she want? Quite a lot actually, but she didn't want to think about that now.

Sandy's relaxing afternoon was disturbed by the sound of the front door slamming and Fliss's footsteps coming along the hallway. She had been so engrossed in her book, she hadn't noticed time passing. Checking her watch, she realised it was almost time to start getting ready to go out.

'I won't be in for dinner,' Fliss called out, on her way upstairs. 'We're meeting on the esplanade for pizza.'

Sandy shook her head, but was pleased Fliss seemed happy again.

Peeking into the kitchen, she saw Ruby was awake and seated in her favourite chair. 'Will you be all right on your own tonight, Ruby?'

'I've been living here on my own for more years than you've had hot dinners. Why wouldn't I be?'

Sandy refrained from reminding the old woman of her recent accident, of her apparent lack of confidence on some occasions. She merely smiled.

In less time than it took for Sandy to speak to Ruby and pour herself a glass of water, Fliss came bounding downstairs again. She was wearing a miniscule pair of shorts Sandy didn't remember seeing before and a top which bared her midriff.

'You're going out like that?'

'Duh! It's what everyone is wearing, Mum. Don't be so old-fashioned.'

'Okay, honey. Have fun and don't be late.'

Fliss rolled her eyes.

*Was she being old-fashioned? Was she beginning to sound like her grandmother?*

'You look lovely, Fliss. I only wish I was your age again. We didn't seem to have as much fun in my day,' Ruby said, a twinkle in her eye. 'I assume Zack will be part of the group having pizza?'

Fliss didn't reply, her blush saying it all.

As the door slammed behind Fliss, Sandy turned to Ruby. 'Am I being too hard on her? Things are all so different here. In Sydney, I always knew where she was and who she was with. Here in Bellbird Bay, it's as if Fliss has become a different person.'

'She's growing up. It was always going to happen. Now she's discovered boys – one particular boy – there'll be no stopping her. Be grateful he comes from a decent family, one you know.'

'I suppose.' But Sandy wasn't convinced. She knew Fliss had to grow up sometime, but it had happened so suddenly. One day she was her little girl, and the next she had a life of her own, a boyfriend, and... who knew what she was getting up to? It was all very well for Ruby to remind her Zack came from a decent family, and for the school principal to say Jenny's mother was a teacher at the school, but even kids from decent families could get into trouble. She'd read so many stories about teenagers and alcohol, drugs, sex... Her stomach churned.

'She'll be fine. Why don't you go and get yourself ready? Your date will be here before you know it. I'm just going to make myself a plate of salad for my dinner and I think I feel like a small glass of wine with it.'

Glad that at least Ruby seemed to be on the mend, Sandy followed her advice and headed off to shower and change.

As the water cascaded over her in the shower, Sandy allowed her annoyance and worry about Fliss to wash off, a frisson of excitement taking their place as she thought about the evening ahead. After her initial doubts, she'd accepted Rob's invitation to have dinner at the surf club, aware it was tantamount to advertising to Bellbird Bay that they were… what, exactly? Friends, she told herself. That was all. Neither of them was interested in anything more than friendship. But it felt odd to have a male friend – an attractive male friend. She allowed herself a moment to imagine what Grant might think, before reminding herself, it was none of his business, just as the women he chose to see – and who Fliss enjoyed telling her about – were none of hers.

Sandy pulled on her new dress – the red one with the border of white daisies, carefully applied her makeup and made sure her hair was looking good. Then she examined herself in the full-length mirror, surprised to see a glow in her eyes that she hadn't seen for a long time. She heard a knock on the door, Ruby's voice and Rob's answering one. It was time. She took a deep breath, picked up her bag and made her way downstairs.

'Sorry this is my only form of transport,' Rob said as he settled her into the *Bay Bikes* van.

'I like vans.'

'Of course you do.' Rob grinned.

Inside the surf club, Sandy was again impressed by the size of the building. Walking up the stairs, Rob pointed out the mural of a surfer, which she'd seen on her previous visit. When Rob wanted to hurry her past the honour board, Sandy paused to read his name there among others she recognised. 'You won the championship?'

'It was a long time ago, before…' His lips tightened, warning her to drop the subject. But Sandy remained curious as to what had happened when he was in service to change him so much.

At the top of the stairs, they headed for the bar where Rob ordered a beer for himself and, with a raised eyebrow in Sandy's direction, a glass of white wine for her. Sandy recognised the dark-haired barman as the one who had served wine at the two weddings and nodded a greeting. Then Rob led her out onto the wide deck overlooking the beach.

'This is beautiful,' she said, her eyes taking in the wide expanse of sand, the ocean, dark and forbidding, seeming at one with the sky in which a myriad of stars were shining. Many of the tables were occupied, but the chatter was almost drowned out by the roar of the waves.

'Not bad, is it?'

They were silent for a few moments.

'Penny for them?' Rob said.

'Sorry, I was daydreaming. It's so lovely here. It's going to be difficult to go back to the city.'

'You've said that before.'

'Sorry, but…'

'What's the matter?'

'I worry about Fliss. Since coming here, she's changed. I can't seem to get through to her. She's not my little girl anymore. And now she has a boyfriend…'

'Don't you remember what it was like to be a teenager?'

'She's fifteen.'

'And Zack's seventeen, almost eighteen. I can remember when I was his age – raging hormones.'

'You don't think…? She's underage.'

'I don't think that matters too much to kids these days.'

Sandy felt her stomach clench. This was her daughter they were talking about. And she felt uncomfortable talking about sex with Rob sitting so close she could breathe in the scent of soap and something indefinable.

Seeming to sense her discomfort, Rob covered her hand with his. 'I don't think you have anything to worry about where Zack's concerned. He as much as told me they weren't…' He coughed.

'Oh!' Sandy was suddenly very aware of Rob's nearness, of his lips, the warmth of his hand. She withdrew hers. But it didn't stop the butterflies in her stomach. She took a gulp of wine, almost choking.

'We were spotted in *The Firenze*,' he said, his words breaking the tension she was experiencing. 'A neighbour of my mother's.'

'Does it bother you?'

'Not really. She was always bound to make something of nothing if she heard I was even talking to a woman.'

He might be trying to brush it off, but Sandy could tell he wasn't being completely honest. 'You haven't taken anyone to dinner before now?'

'Not in Bellbird Bay.'

And he'd been living here for years. She'd really like to know why… and why he'd broken what seemed to be a habit, to invite *her* out twice. She was about to ask him when he picked up one of the menus which were lying on the table.

'What do you fancy? I always have the burger and chips. Best in Australia.'

Sandy laughed. She scanned the laminated sheet. 'Grilled salmon with salad for me, please.'

'Another wine?'

Sandy looked at her glass to realise it was almost empty. She hadn't been aware of drinking so much of it. 'Please.'

'Won't be long.' Rob disappeared into the club, leaving Sandy staring after him.

*Had he realised she was about to ask a difficult question or was his sudden mention of the menu a coincidence?*

Before she could reach a conclusion, Rob was back with a beer and a glass of wine. 'We're all set,' he said.

Sandy picked up her almost empty glass and drained it, before saying, 'Before we decided on our order, I was about to ask you something.'

Rob stared down into his beer, as if he knew what she was about to say and didn't want to hear it.

'Why have you never taken anyone to dinner before me? It's not just to avoid the gossip, is it?' She tried to make her voice light, to pretend the answer wasn't really important to her. But it was. She wanted to know what made this man tick, what secret he was hiding from her.

Rob sighed. He took a gulp of his beer. Then he stared out into the darkness as if the answer was out there somewhere. When he turned back to face her, his face was different, his expression tortured.

\*

Rob flinched at Sandy's question. He should have known, anticipated it. But it had caught him unawares. What could he say? No one knew his agony, the horrors, the fear, the guilt he suffered every day. It had been like that for as long as he could remember. It had all started with Brett's illness. Watching his twin, his other half, the brother who was part of him, suffer, he'd wondered when it would be his turn, when the illness which had turned Brett into someone he didn't recognise would strike him, too. But it hadn't. Brett had died, and he had lived, lived on alone, beset with guilt. No one realised how much he missed his brother. His parents were so wrapped up in their own grief, they failed to notice their remaining son was grieving, too. It was only after the funeral that his mother turned to him with an outpouring of love and grief, smothering him with the affection she'd previously shared between him and his brother.

Then there was Ned.

At first, he couldn't speak, fearing how she'd change when she heard. Then, as if propelled by some unseen force, the words poured out of him, only interrupted by the arrival of their meals. He continued to speak, the food cooling on the plates as he told of the guilt he'd never been able to overcome, of mates dying, the weeks and months in hospital and rehab, the despair, the fear he'd never walk again, the depression, the nightmares that disturbed his sleep. 'So, now you see why I've avoided any sort of commitment,' he finished. 'How could I subject anyone to that?'

For several minutes neither of them spoke. Then Sandy said, 'I'm sorry, Rob. I had no idea. I'd read about the trauma suffered by return soldiers, but what you've suffered is beyond all that. Have you thought of getting help, counselling?'

'Tried that. Didn't do any good. Now you know, you may want to change your mind about me.' He grimaced.

'Why? None of what you've told me is your fault. It doesn't change the person you are, the person I met in your bike shop, the person Zack calls a legend, the person I agreed to have dinner with.' There was a pause. 'Do your parents know... what you've told me?'

Rob shook his head. 'No one knows.' Except now someone did. Sandy knew. What had possessed him to spill his guts to this woman who was practically a stranger? 'We should eat our dinner before it gets cold,' he said.

'I think it already is.' Sandy smiled and picked up her knife and fork.

# Twenty-six

The next week passed slowly for Sandy. The two children's birthday parties she catered for were a blur of noise and activity, fuelled by the excess of sugar ordered at the whim of indulgent parents. Through it all, she couldn't stop thinking about what Rob had told her. The poor man. How he must have suffered, still be suffering. She felt a spurt of anger towards his parents, towards the couple she'd never met. How could they be so unaware of their son's feelings, have ignored his horror at losing his twin, at being the one to survive. While she could understand his desire to get away, to fulfil the promise the two boys had made to each other when they were too young to know the consequences, the army had probably been the wrong career for the sensitive young man still grieving for his lost brother and filled with survivor guilt.

The rest of the evening had been awkward. They'd finished their meals and left the club with little more in the way of conversation and driven back to *Headland House* in almost complete silence. Before Sandy slipped out of the car, Rob's only show of affection had been to squeeze her hand. She hadn't dared give him the peck on the cheek she'd ventured on Friday.

Now a whole week had passed with no call or text from him, and Sandy was filled with a sense of sadness, mixed with sympathy for the boy Rob had been and the man he had become. She wished there was something she could do to ease his pain, but all she could do was wait and hope he'd get in touch again.

The weekend ahead promised to be busy. She had a fiftieth birthday celebration to prepare for, and Ruby's first guests were due to arrive. Both were to happen on Saturday. Fortunately, Fliss's life was on an even keel. She appeared happy with her new friends, her new skills in surfing and volleyball... and Zack, with whom she seemed to spend every spare minute. Also, Cleo's list of possible assistants had come up trumps, and now she had Liam helping out on a regular basis. The young man was in his final year of a bachelor's degree in hospitality management and nutrition at the local university and was thrilled to become involved with both *Celebrations* and *Headlands House* B&B. To Sandy's delight, Ruby immediately took a liking to the young man, treating him like the grandson she didn't have.

But first, there was a barbecue to attend. Grace Winter had invited her and Ruby to the event, which was to take place this evening, to celebrate Ruby's recovery. Fliss had said she'd be there, too, with Zack.

'I don't know what all the fuss is about,' Ruby complained, when Grace had called round to invite them, but Sandy knew the old woman was secretly thrilled to be the centre of attention.

At Grace's request, Sandy had baked a special cake, managing to make it late one night after Ruby had gone to bed, though she was sure Ruby was aware of it. Not much got past her, especially now she had her sight back in both eyes.

'Will this do, Mum?' Fliss came whirling into Sandy's room, dressed in a short polka dot pink and white dress with shoestring straps, her hair tied back in a neat ponytail.

'You look lovely, sweetheart.' Sandy was glad Fliss had decided to forgo her favourite shorts on this occasion.

'What are you going to wear?'

Sandy looked at the bed, covered in discarded outfits. Unlike her daughter, she was undecided.

'You'd look good in this.' Fliss picked up a pale green dress with a square neckline and handkerchief hemline. 'Is it new?'

Sandy nodded. The dress was the result of another trip to *Birds of a Feather* in the expectation of a second invitation from Rob which hadn't eventuated. She slipped it on and gazed at herself in the mirror. Fliss was right. It did look good on her.

Downstairs, Ruby was ready to go. Sandy picked up the cake box and a bottle of wine and the three strolled down the boardwalk to Grace's home. It was still light, and the stiff breeze which had blown up in the late afternoon was stirring up the waves, producing what Sandy's grandmother had called white horses on the water. Ruby kept a firm hold of Sandy's arm, clearly still unsure of her feet on the uneven surface of the boardwalk, while Fliss skipped along beside them, excited to be seeing Zack again, even though she had spent the previous evening with him.

When they reached Grace's gate, the first thing Sandy saw was Rob's dog, Bess, along with the dog's owner. He was on the front deck chatting with Ted and a couple Sandy didn't recognise. Sandy felt herself stiffen, her heart beating madly. *Why hadn't she realised he'd be here?* There seemed to be no way of avoiding him, even if she wanted to… and she didn't. But she wished she knew what he was feeling, why he hadn't contacted her. *Was he regretting sharing his story?* Pasting a smile on her face, Sandy pushed open the gate.

'Ruby… and Sandy, welcome!' Grace came out to greet them with a warm hug and kiss on the cheek, while Fliss disappeared around the corner of the house, no doubt in search of Zack. At Grace's words, Ted and Rob turned, and Sandy caught sight of what looked like a glint of pleasure in Rob's eyes.

Bess ran forward to greet the newcomers, Ruby bent down to pet her, Ted joined them and, in the melee, Rob put his hand on Sandy's arm and whispered, 'I'm pleased to see you. We must talk.'

Sandy glowed, but before she had time to respond, Grace drew her attention to the other couple. 'Have you met Martin and Ailsa? Martin is Bev's brother, and Ailsa is her best friend. They were the first couple to be married in *Pandanus Weddings*.'

'Hello, I'm pleased to meet you both. Bev has spoken about you.' From what Sandy could remember, Martin Cooper was a famous photographer who had met Ailsa here in Bellbird Bay when they were both staying with Bev. She didn't know the details. And Ailsa was the mother of Nate, the young barman who she'd met at the weddings.

'I've heard about you, too,' Ailsa said. 'Bev's told me how you stepped in to bake for the café and to cater for *Pandanus Weddings*… and we've all seen your bright pink van around town.' She chuckled.

Sandy blushed. Then the others started speaking to Ruby, and she twisted round to see where Rob was.

He was leaning against the doorway into the house, watching her. She blushed again.

'The others are in the garden,' Grace said, ushering them around the side of the house to a large yard where several groups were standing around chatting. Grace handed the newcomers glasses of sparkling wine and clapped her hands for silence. 'We're all here to celebrate Ruby's recovery,' she said. 'We've enjoyed her cakes for as long as *The Pandanus Café* has been open, and her accident has reinforced the need for us all to be wary of magpies in the nesting season.' She chuckled, and everyone laughed. 'It's good to see you getting back to normal, Ruby, and we hope you'll continue to provide cakes for us for a good many years to come.'

'Hear, hear,' a voice Sandy recognised as Will Rankin's said. 'Three cheers for Ruby.'

Everyone cheered, and Ruby looked embarrassed.

Sandy felt superfluous. She was only here until Ruby could take over again. Now the old woman was recovered, there was no place for her in Bellbird Bay. It had always been her intention to return to Sydney, so why did she suddenly feel empty?

'Are you okay?'

She turned to see Rob at her shoulder.

'Your face... it turned white.'

'I... I'm fine. I guess I just realised I'm no longer needed.'

'I wouldn't say that.' Rob drew her aside. 'I need to apologise... after our dinner... I felt bad. I shouldn't have unloaded to you like that. I...' he pulled on his beard, '... it's not something I normally do. I never have before. I don't know what made me...' He shook his head. 'Can we forget it?'

Forget it? How could she? It had been an insight into the man she was feeling a growing attraction to. 'It's okay,' she said, putting her hand on his arm, feeling the strength in it, a strength that provided comfort. 'But...' she thought of her own position again, '... Ruby and I need to talk, to sort things out. She seems well again, but I'm not entirely convinced she's capable of...'

'Sandy, do you have a minute?' Bev interrupted their conversation before Sandy could complete her sentence.

'Sure.' Sandy allowed herself to be led away to a corner of the yard.

'I wanted a word,' Bev said when they were alone, the chatter of the other guests fading into the background. 'It's about Ruby. I know what Grace said, and I agree Ruby is looking a lot better, but did you see her face when Grace spoke about enjoying her cakes for many years to come?'

'She appeared embarrassed, but that's Ruby. Is that what you mean?' Sandy asked with a frown.

'Not exactly. I thought she looked more terrified than embarrassed.'

'Terrified? Ruby?' Sandy tried to picture the expression on Ruby's face. *Had she been so tied up in her own feelings, she'd ignored Ruby's?* She recalled her own concerns, and hadn't she been about to say as much to Rob when Bev interrupted them? 'I have wondered lately if the accident had destroyed some of her confidence. It was when I suggested Fliss handing back her bike. Do you really think...?' For a moment Sandy considered what it would mean to Ruby if she could no longer fulfil her daily cake order to the café. For the first time, she wondered just how old Ruby was. She'd always seemed old to Sandy, even when she was a child, but that was natural. She was a friend of her grandmother, the grandmother who'd died over ten years ago.

'She can't go on for ever,' Bev said. 'I guess we've all become so used to her being there, to her wonderful cakes. It never occurred to us the day would come when she was no longer able to provide them.'

Sandy felt her eyes moisten. Poor Ruby. Her mind was still as active as ever, but if her confidence was gone, if she could no longer ride her bike to deliver cakes, to get around town... She'd never driven a car, declaring her legs could take her anywhere she wanted to go, which had been fine... till now. 'She can still bake,' she said, almost to herself.

'You couldn't stay?' Bev asked. 'It would solve all our problems, I know it would be a big upheaval for you, but...' she bit her lip, '... your daughter seems to have settled well, and...'

As if to prove Bev's point, Fliss appeared, hand-in-hand with Zack. 'Mum, is it okay if we head off? Zack knows of a party and...' She gazed pleadingly at her mother.

'Okay, but be home by eleven.'

'Thanks, Mum.' The pair dashed off, laughing.

Sandy turned back to Bev. 'I'd need to think about it. Our lives are in Sydney. Fliss's dad... And I'm still waiting to hear about the report from the fire assessors.'

'But you will think about it?'

'I will,' Sandy promised. She couldn't imagine making such a big move, though there would be some advantages. She loved the town, the peaceful atmosphere, the friendly people. It was so different from the city. There was her business, too. *Celebrations* had really taken off here. In Sydney, she would have to start all over again. If they did stay, if Fliss agreed to the move, where would they live? She couldn't expect to continue to live with Ruby on a permanent basis, or could she? As she'd already told Rob, she and Ruby needed to talk.

'Thanks.' Bev gave her a warm hug and left.

Sandy was still standing there in a state of shock, when Rob walked up, Bess padding behind him.

'I wondered where you'd got to. I saw Bev come back. The food's being served now. Hungry?'

Sandy shook her head. The conversation with Bev had taken away her appetite.

'What did Bev want?'

'She's doubtful Ruby's going to make a full recovery. She wanted to know if I'd consider staying.'

'Wow! Heavy! What was your reaction?'

'I promised to think about it.'

'If you don't want to eat, would you like to go for a walk? Ruby's surrounded by admirers. She won't miss you for a bit. Your daughter…?'

'She's gone off with Zack, some party.' Sandy realised a walk was exactly what she would like, a chance to think more clearly, perhaps talk over her concerns with Rob. He'd shared his problems with her. Perhaps it was *her* turn. She was sure he'd be a good listener. 'Thanks, Rob, I would like a walk, if you're sure you don't mind leaving?'

'Happy to. These events aren't really my thing.'

# Twenty-seven

The moon was high in the sky, lighting their way, as Rob and Sandy climbed down the steps to the beach. Bess ran ahead, stopping from time to time to check they were following. When they reached the edge of the ocean, Rob reached out to take Sandy's hand, pleased when she didn't draw away. He sensed her confusion and wanted to do what he could to help, even if it was only to listen. She'd looked so little and alone when he and Bess joined her in the far corner of Grace and Ted's yard, he'd wanted to comfort her. He knew better than anyone, how it felt to be facing an uncertain future.

'If you don't want to talk, it's fine. But if you do, I'm happy to listen.'

'Thanks.' Sandy's upturned face glowed in the moonlight, making Rob want to throw caution to the wind and pick her up in his arms.

They walked in silence for several minutes, only interrupted by Bess's low growl when she came across a small crab on the sand.

'I don't know what to do,' Sandy said at last. 'When we came here, it was to be a temporary thing, till after Christmas. Fliss didn't want to come and only did on the understanding we'd be going back to Sydney, where she'd finish school. Now...' she sighed, '... if Bev's right in thinking Ruby won't fully recover – and I think I told you about my doubts, too – I'm not sure what to do for the best.'

'What do you want to do?'

'I don't know.' Sandy paused.

They stopped, and she gazed out at the ocean.

'I love it here. My business is going well. It would be easy to stay, if...'

'If?' Rob felt his heart thump.

Sandy sighed again. 'If I didn't have a home in Sydney, if Fliss's school wasn't there, if her dad didn't live there, if...' she shook her head, the highlights in her hair glistening in the moonlight. 'It's all too difficult. Then, there's the issue of suggesting to Ruby she can't continue as she's been doing... and where would we live? We can't stay at *Headland House* for ever.'

'No? I bet Ruby would love to have you there.'

'Maybe, but... No, Fliss and I need our own place, and besides, there are Ruby's B&B guests. We're taking up rooms she could let out.'

'She'd be able to continue with the B&B?'

'Maybe. I think she'll be fine as long as she doesn't need to get back on the bike. The accident really shook her up, but she seems as spry as ever at home.'

'And your daughter? How would she feel about staying?'

Sandy thought for a moment. 'I'm not sure,' she said slowly. 'Right now, I'd probably say she'd be delighted, given how well she and Zack are getting on. But he'll be finishing school soon, going off to uni. I'm not sure if Bellbird Bay will still hold its charm for her with him gone.'

'For what it's worth, I have it on good authority Zack intends to study at the local university and continue to live at home. He's hellbent on the surf championship next year and would never risk that by moving away. Not sure if that helps you with your decision.'

'Not really. I need to discuss it with Fliss, too... and with Grant.'

'Your ex?'

'Mmm. He's overseas at the moment but will be back by Christmas. We were intending to spend it together in Sydney until this came up.'

'And now?'

'Who knows?' Sandy released her hand to throw her arms in the air.

Bess chose that moment to come back from her wandering to drop a wet stick at Rob's feet. He threw it off into the darkness for her, making sure it didn't go into the water. He didn't want to lose her in the sea at this time of night.

'Well, I've always found things tend to sort themselves out. Take it from one who knows.' Rob thought back to the long weeks in hospital and in rehab, weeks when he wished he was dead, when he couldn't imagine ever finding a purpose in life. But he had. He was happy in the life he'd made for himself. It surprised him to realise that now. He looked down at his companion, her auburn hair tossed by the wind, her dress clinging to her body. She looked so lovely, so vulnerable, so desirable. Without thinking, he bent down and pressed his lips against hers which parted to receive them.

*

Sandy felt her heart leap at the touch of Rob's lips on hers. It was so unexpected.

'I'm sorry. I don't know what came over me.' Rob's voice broke through the flash of desire which had taken her by surprise.

'Don't be... sorry, I mean. I... it...' Hell, was she making things worse? He obviously regretted the kiss. There was no need to dissect it, to embarrass him. Hadn't he told her he wasn't looking for a relationship? But he had kissed her, and it had been quite a kiss, one she would like to repeat. She glanced at him out of the corner of her eye, but his attention was on Bess who had now brought back the stick and laid it at Rob's feet.

'No more, Bess,' he said to the dog, then turning to Sandy, 'We should be getting back.'

'Sure.' The moment had passed. That was all it was – a moment between two friends, a result of their mood and the moonlight. It was nothing to get all hot and bothered about. But it had brought back memories of what it was like to desire and be desired. Maybe she'd been on her own so long, she was ripe for the attention of the first man who showed her any affection.

They walked back along the beach side-by-side, no longer holding hands, Bess padding along beside them. Only when they came to the steps up to the boardwalk, did Rob offer his hand to help Sandy. At the top, she put her shoes back on and tried to ignore the tremor she felt at his touch.

When they re-joined the party, it seemed no one had noticed their absence.

But Ruby had.

As they walked back up the boardwalk to *Headland House*, the old woman said, 'I noticed you and Rob disappear for a while. Is there something you want to tell me?'

'No,' Sandy said, flustered, 'we only went for a walk along the beach. I needed to think about something, and he offered to be a sounding board for me.'

'And did you resolve what you wanted to think about?'

'Not quite. It's late now. Maybe we can talk about it tomorrow?' Sandy still had a lot of thinking to do.

'Remember the Bartons arrive tomorrow.'

'I do.' Sandy was looking forward to the arrival of Ruby's first guests. It would make life busier, but the work would take her mind off the decision she had to make. She'd sound out Ruby tomorrow. She valued the older woman's opinion and any decision she made would involve her, too.

Ruby must have sensed her inner turmoil. Just as they reached the gate, she patted the hand Sandy had laid on her arm to help her navigate the path. 'It's all going to work out for you, Sandy. Everything may look complicated right now, but the mist will clear, you'll see. There are clear skies ahead and you may be surprised by the outcome.'

Sandy felt a shiver run up her spine. She knew all about the old woman's weird sayings – what some called predictions – but this was entirely unexpected.

# Twenty-eight

Next morning, Sandy rose early as usual, her mind filled with what needed to be done. After the daily batch of cakes were baked and delivered to the café, she wanted to ensure everything was ready for the guests' arrival. She'd never been involved in taking care of paying guests before and was a little nervous at the prospect. There was no sign of Fliss who'd left even earlier for a game of volleyball. These days, there was no difficulty in prising her out of bed on weekends.

To her relief, when she returned from the café, Ruby seemed to be well organised. 'I've been doing this for years,' she said, in response to Sandy's raised eyebrows at the sight of the freshly baked scones on the benchtop. 'I treat them all like old friends, and that's what many have become, returning year after year. This morning, I decided it was time I got back to baking. I can't let you keep doing it for me.'

Sandy took a deep breath. This was her opening. 'That's what I want to talk with you about, Ruby. But I don't want us to be interrupted. When do you expect this couple to arrive?'

'Not till after lunch. Why don't we have a cup of tea and a scone – check I haven't lost my touch – and take them out to the yard. We can talk there. Things always seem clearer in the fresh air and the sunlight.'

Once outside with cups of peppermint tea and scones with jam and cream, Sandy was able to reassure Ruby she hadn't lost her touch. The scones were as light as ever, much lighter than any Sandy had made, she was sure.

'Now, what's been bothering you?' Ruby asked. 'I've noticed you've been worried these past few days, and I suspect it has something to do with me.' She gazed at Sandy expectantly.

Now the time had come, Sandy was loath to begin. How would Ruby feel about what she had to say? She'd never known Ruby to be angry, but there was always a first time.

'It's *Celebrations*,' Sandy began.

'It's going well?'

'Better than I expected. I could never have done it without your help.'

'Poof!' Ruby waved away her praise. 'It's you who's done it all. Nothing to do with me.'

Sandy knew it wasn't true but didn't want to argue with Ruby. 'Anyway, it's been suggested I stay here in Bellbird Bay, that, instead of going back to Sydney, I continue running *Celebrations* here.' She waited with bated breath.

'And I suppose you mean to take over from me, too?'

'No, not if you don't want me to.' Sandy bit her lip. This wasn't going the way she expected, though what had she expected? 'I know you still bake the best cakes on the coast, if not in the whole of Australia. I could never hope to compete,' she caught the glimpse of a smug smile from Ruby, and continued, 'but I was surprised when you baulked at taking your bike back from Fliss. I don't think it was because of any unselfish motivation.'

Ruby sighed and put down her cup. 'You're right. That magpie scared me more than I can say. The very thought of getting back on my bike gives me goosebumps. I must be getting old.' She sighed again.

'Never. You're indestructible, Ruby. But I do understand how it makes you feel.'

'Do you, Sandy? I doubt it. Just wait till you're my age, when you still feel like nineteen inside, but your body lets you down. So,' she said on a brighter note, 'what are we going to do about it?'

'I don't know,' Sandy almost wailed. 'I don't want to let you down, but there's Fliss to consider, and Grant, our life in Sydney...' She felt if she repeated the issues often enough, she might find a solution.

'I don't think you need to worry about Fliss. She seems to have settled into Bellbird Bay. And as for that ex of yours, he can always visit her here. Why don't you invite him up for Christmas? And Sydney, do you really want to go back to the city, start again, when *Celebrations* is doing so well here?'

Sandy stared at Ruby. It was as if, in a couple of sentences, Ruby had seen through Sandy's concerns and dismissed them. If only it was that easy. But inviting Grant for Christmas was a good idea. She could talk with him then, and Fliss would have her dad with her on the big day.

But Ruby hadn't finished. 'I may not be of a mind to go back to cycling around but there's your van. You can continue to deliver the cakes and, if you don't have to do all the baking, it will give you more time to devote to the other side of your business and to focus on your speciality cakes. Young Liam's doing well as your assistant. You might want to consider taking him on permanently and...'

'Steady on, Ruby.' This was going too fast for Sandy. She had still to decide whether or not to stay in Bellbird Bay. Ruby was talking as if it was a done deal.

'There's Rob Andrews, too,' Ruby said, a twinkle in her eye.

Sandy felt the blood rush to her face. 'What does he have to do with anything?'

'I saw the way the two of you disappeared last night. You were flushed when you came back. I wasn't born yesterday.' She tapped the side of her nose. 'He may not be ready for a relationship yet, but mark my words...'

'No, Ruby, you're wrong there. He's said he's not interested in anything more than friendship. Nor am I,' she added.

'Hmm.' Ruby smiled as if she knew something Sandy didn't. 'I think I'd like a lie down before lunch,' she said, picking up her cup and rising. She walked into the kitchen, leaving Sandy staring after her. *What had all that been about? Had anything been resolved?* She shook her head. She'd never understand Ruby, but hoped she'd be as switched on as she was when she reached her age.

They had barely finished their lunch of ham and cheese sandwiches, Fliss darting off to the beach immediately afterwards, when there was the sound of a car stopping outside. Peering out, Sandy saw an elderly couple emerge from the vehicle and make their way to the front door to be greeted by Ruby like old friends.

After she'd been introduced as *the granddaughter of a dear friend who's come to help me out,* Sandy left the three to enjoy the tea and scones Ruby insisted was always part of the welcome to *Headland House.* Going to the office, she decided to check the computer to find out how many other guests were expected before Christmas. Ruby had been reticent about the exact number, and Sandy feared it was more than just a few of her regulars.

But Ruby hadn't misled her. There were only a few weeks till Christmas and when Sandy checked, she could only find three groups – two families of three and one other couple – who were booked in. Christmas week itself was free. She gave a sigh of relief. That shouldn't be too difficult to manage, allowing her to concentrate on her own bookings which were coming in thick and fast. She couldn't have coped without Liam's help.

She was still sitting there when her mobile rang. Seeing the number of the Mosman police station, Sandy felt a ray of hope. *Had they decided on the cause of the fire? Would she be able to claim the insurance for her damaged equipment?*

'Hello?'

'Mrs Elliot?'

'Speaking.' Her voice quavered.

'This is Detective Bruce Anderson. I apologise for disturbing you on a Saturday. I'm ringing to inform you that the fire assessor has submitted his report. It appears the fire to your premises in...' he paused, '... Neutral Bay has been declared as arson.'

Sandy breathed a sigh of relief. It hadn't been her fault. She was sure she'd been careful, but there was always the chance... He was still speaking.

'It's one of a number of arson attacks on small businesses in the area, and I'm pleased to inform you that the offenders – a group of teenagers – have been arrested and charged. It means...'

'I can go ahead and contact my insurance company again?'

'You can. If you have any other questions, you have my number.'

'Yes, thank you. And thank you for letting me know.' Sandy closed the phone with a lightness she hadn't felt for some time. One hurdle was over. She'd call the insurance company tomorrow. Perhaps she'd need to go to complete the required forms in person, but she'd face that if she had to. It might not be a bad thing to take a trip to Sydney if she could work out the logistics of cake delivery while she was gone. It would remind her what she'd be leaving if she did decide to stay in Bellbird Bay… and she could catch up with Grant who should be back from his trip. All in all, things were looking up.

# Twenty-nine

Rob hadn't slept well. This time, it wasn't the usual nightmare that disturbed his rest, but the memory of the kiss that should never have happened. But it had, and he couldn't forget the thrill of Sandy's soft lips under his, of them opening to receive his kiss. He tossed and turned, wakening to feel exhausted, the bedclothes tangled around him.

A cold shower helped him feel better, as did the large mug of coffee he drank while wolfing down three slices of toast and marmalade.

'No walk this morning, Bess,' he said to the dog as he filled her bowl with food, before the pair of them set off for *Bay Bikes*.

It was another glorious morning, the sort of day which made you glad to be alive... but Rob's mind was filled with regret. *Had he managed to ruin what could be a perfectly good friendship by his impulsive behaviour?* Now wasn't the time for worrying about his mistakes. Sunday was the day when the members of the peloton gathered outside *Bay Bikes*, ready for coffee and chat, and he needed to summon up a cheerful manner ready for their arrival.

The shop was redolent with the aroma of freshly brewed coffee, and he was opening the couple of packets of Tim Tams he'd bought at the store when Zack bounced in full of the joys of life. The youngster's enthusiasm was infectious and, by the time the cyclists arrived, Rob found his own mood had lightened. Aaron was one of the first to appear, followed by Finn and Luke. Their conversation today was all about the charity ride which was to take place the following weekend, and the lighting of the Christmas tree which would occur afterwards.

'You're not taking part?' Aaron asked in surprise. 'Why not?'

'Someone needs to be available on the route in case of mishaps with the bikes,' Rob said with a grin. 'I'll leave Zack in charge here and be out there along with the paramedics and the ambulance. Hopefully we won't be needed, but it's a precautionary measure. Our good mayor insisted on it when he planned the event.'

'Good old Will,' Finn said, grinning widely, too. 'Though a few disasters would make a good news item.'

'Always eager for a good story,' Rob said. He knew as editor of the local paper, Finn was always on the lookout for something to appeal to his readers.

'It's a business, just like yours,' Finn said. 'But I don't really want anyone to come to harm. We have a few younger participants this year. Pity young Zack will be tied up here.'

'I prefer surfing,' Zack said, appearing with the plates of Tim Tams which were quickly consumed by the group. 'But I wish you all well.'

Gradually the conversation slowed, the biscuits were all eaten and the coffee drunk, and Rob and Zack were left to clear up the mess.

'Will it be okay if I leave a bit early today, Rob?' Zack asked when the shop was tidy again. 'There's a group going out to Dolphin Beach this arvo, and I said I'd get there if I could. There's going to be a picnic and...'

'I hope you're not intending to start a fire on the beach there. It's one of the few untouched spots around.'

'Wouldn't dare,' Zack said. 'Not after all the effort we put in to save it from the developers. Will Rankin would never forgive us.'

They both laughed, but they remembered the way everyone had joined in to save the beach and its pristine white sand.

'Have you ever seen a dugong?' Zack asked. 'I know it was the presence of the seagrass which saved the beach, and that the creatures feed on it, but I've never actually spotted one.'

'I have, a couple of times. The first was when I was younger than you. Mum used to take my brother and I there to play and one day we spied a couple grazing close to shore. I guess the seagrass was more abundant in those days. They looked as if they were standing on their tails with their heads above the water.' Rob fell silent, the memory of those happy times with his brother intertwined with the ache of his loss, and his guilt.

'I didn't know you had a brother. Where is he?'

'He died.' Rob spoke more sharply than he intended.

'Sorry.' Zack appeared crestfallen.

'It's okay. You weren't to know. It happened a long time ago.' But he'd always miss Brett. There were some things time didn't heal.

'And the second time?' Zack wanted to know.

'It was after I came back to Bellbird Bay. Bess and I were running along the beach at Dolphin Bay.' Rob remembered the day like it was yesterday. He had not long returned to Bellbird Bay and wanted to get away from everyone. Dolphin Bay, isolated from the town, seemed an ideal place to lick his wounds. 'Bess was chasing a stick I'd thrown into the water when she noticed something in the surf which made her lose interest in the stick. I saw a fin coming out of the water, so I called her back. I thought it was a dolphin in trouble.'

'I've seen dolphins there,' Zack said, 'when we went out in Nick's boat. He's a mate of Dad's.'

'Right, well it was around the time I'd heard about dolphins dying of infection, so I wondered if the creature needed help. But it wasn't a dolphin; it wasn't anything dying.' Rob chuckled. 'It was actually two dugongs mating.'

'Wow! How lucky was that?'

'Yeah, it was.' Rob pulled on his beard. It had been an amazing discovery, one he'd kept to himself until now. He knew he could trust Zack with the story. He wasn't the sort of kid to rush off to see if he could find dugongs for himself. 'They're interesting creatures,' he said. 'They have a broad bristled snout with no neck, rounded flippers and a tapered body.'

'You saw all that?' Zack's eyes widened.

'No, I read up on them later. I also discovered they can live for up to seventy-three years, and sightings of dugongs by early seafarers are believed to have given rise to the mythology of mermaids and sirens. I was lucky to see them both times. They prefer to eat the seagrass in much deeper water.'

'Oh! I'll keep a lookout next time we go sailing with Nick.'

'You do that and let me know if you spot some – they tend to travel in pairs or herds.'

The rest of the day passed uneventfully with a few enquiries about the new electric bikes Rob had added to his range, and two parents bringing in their son's bikes for repair. Rob was glad Zack had left early. Although pleasant company and a good worker, Zack did like to chat – he was almost unrecognisable from the withdrawn lad who had arrived to live with his grandfather a few years earlier – and Rob needed time to process what was happening between him and Sandy.

Rob had arranged to meet with Will for a drink at the surf club when he closed the shop. There were details about the proposed bike parade to iron out. As he climbed the stairs to the club restaurant, the memory of the previous evening with Sandy played over in his mind. Although he'd spent the last half hour or so trying to analyse his feelings, he was still unclear how Sandy Elliot had managed to slip under his carefully constructed barriers and arouse emotions he'd thought dead for ever.

'Hey!' Will greeted him when he reached the bar. 'What'll you have?'

'I think it's my shout,' Rob said with a grin, putting aside all thought of Sandy. 'Yours is Four X, isn't it?'

'Good man.' Will clapped him on the shoulder.

Rob ordered the beers from a barman he didn't recognise. 'Nate not working tonight?'

'He and Owen are otherwise engaged.' Will tapped his nose. 'There's a wedding in the offing – Nate and Han.'

Rob raised an eyebrow. 'Aren't they a bit young?'

'Around the same age I was when I married Owen's mum. If they love each other – and they seem to – it's not a problem. Cleo's happy about it, too. She's looking forward to seeing her daughter settled.'

'Hmm.' There had been so many happy events since he returned to Bellbird Bay, it was no wonder his mother wanted to matchmake. His thoughts turned again to Sandy. If only...

Will was speaking.

'Sorry, Will. What did you say?'

'I was suggesting we take our drinks out to the deck. It's a bit noisy in here for conversation.'

'Okay by me.' Rob picked up his drink. While he had been musing about Sandy, a group had started playing music, and between that and the noise from the pokies it was difficult to make themselves heard.

It was peaceful out on the deck, the only sound the roar of the waves and the squawking of the seabirds as they ducked and dived seeking their evening feed.

'Right,' Will said, producing his iPad, 'let's get started. I was thinking of the afternoon of Christmas Eve. We have the Christmas fundraiser in the morning for the adults, and the kids are usually getting a bit antsy by the time it's over. It would keep them occupied and use up their energy; maybe let the parents get a decent sleep before the big day.'

'Doubt anything would do that.' Although he had no children of his own, Rob could remember the excitement of him and his brother on the night before Christmas. He didn't think they slept much at all, determined to stay awake to see Santa deliver their presents – until the year after Brett died, when it was just him. His parents tried hard, but Christmas was never the same again. Rob had lost his faith in Santa and, consumed with guilt at still being alive while Brett wasn't, he hated the whole idea of Christmas.

'So, you're okay with Christmas Eve?'

'Sure. You're right about the kids needing to burn off energy. I can arrange for all the bikes I'll have put aside to be picked up by the relevant Santa's helpers by lunchtime, leaving me free to officiate in any way you want. Young Zack may be willing to help, too, if he hasn't tired himself out in the fundraiser.'

'That young man has a boundless supply of energy,' Will said. 'He's following in his grandfather's footsteps. Reminds me of Owen at his age; another champion in the making.' He took a sip of his beer. 'Have you had any thoughts about the route?'

'Well, given everyone will have been on the beach all morning, and many will have gone to the surf club for lunch, how about we block off the esplanade and the route from the surf club along to the far end, where the other part of the boardwalk begins. You mentioned something about a party. We could arrange for food and drinks to be set up near the harbour. Maybe you could use your influence with the council re the road?'

'I think I could manage that,' Will chuckled. 'About the food. Do you think we could prevail on the lady who runs the catering business – *Celebrations* – to provide it, or would it be too much for her? You know her, don't you?'

Rob felt his stomach clench. 'I could ask her.'

# Thirty

Sandy began to make arrangements to travel to Sydney. Her apartment was still rented out, so she booked herself into a hotel in the city, reasoning that, with her insurance money coming through soon, she could afford the luxury.

'Will you see Dad?' Fliss asked over dinner one evening in the week before she planned to leave.

'Probably. What would you think about me asking him to come to Bellbird Bay for Christmas?'

'Ooh, it'd be great. By himself?'

It hadn't occurred to Sandy to consider he might want to bring his current lady friend. 'We'll see.' Maybe he wasn't seeing anyone at the moment. She could only hope. She didn't want Fliss to have to cope with spending the holiday with one of Grant's women.

They were discussing her trip, Fliss itemising all the things she wanted brought back from the storage they'd rented before leaving, when Sandy's phone rang. Seeing Rob's number, she felt a jolt of excitement. 'I need to take this,' she said, stepping outside to answer it.

'Hello, Rob.'

'Sandy.'

The sound of his voice sent shivers down her spine. She pictured him, standing somewhere, gazing out at the ocean, his dark eyes shining in the moonlight.

'I have a catering request.'

'Oh!' The pleasure of hearing his voice suddenly diminished.

'It's about the bike parade Will Rankin is organising. I've promised to help. I wondered if we could meet to discuss it.'

'Of course.' Sandy was aware she sounded very businesslike. It was her professional voice. 'When did you have in mind? I'm flying down to Sydney in a couple of days.'

'Oh! Can we meet before you leave? Tomorrow? How about I treat you to lunch at *The Greedy Gecko*? Around one?'

Sandy hesitated. There was no reason to refuse. The poor man couldn't read her mind, know she'd hoped for something more intimate for their next meeting. 'That would be fine,' she said.

'Who was that?' Fliss asked, when Sandy returned. 'Why did you go outside to take the call?'

'Rob Andrews.'

Ruby smiled. 'I knew it,' she said. 'I saw two magpies on the lawn today. You know the old nursery rhyme – one for sorrow, two for joy. When I was attacked there was just one. Two is a sign of joy for your future.'

Sandy chuckled. 'I doubt it, Ruby. He called to talk about some catering he wants me to do... a bike parade.'

'Oh, I've heard Zack talk about it. It's something they want to arrange for the young kids around Christmas. I think Will Rankin's involved,' Fliss said.

'So he said.'

'Don't be too sure,' Ruby said with a gleam in her eye. 'I know what I saw, and I know what it means.' She nodded.

Sandy shrugged. She should be used to Ruby's weird ways, but magpies? 'I'm off to check my emails,' she said. 'I need to make sure I don't leave any loose ends while I'm gone. Liam has promised to deliver the cakes, Ruby, if you're sure you can manage the baking. He's going to drive me to the airport, and I'll leave the van with him while I'm gone. You're sure you'll be okay, both of you? It's only for a few days.'

'We'll be fine, won't we, Fliss?' Ruby grinned at the young girl. 'Remember to tell that ex-husband of yours he's welcome to stay here for Christmas, but to leave his floozie at home.'

Sandy and Fliss laughed. As if Grant would accept instructions from either Sandy or Ruby.

Once in the room she was using as an office, Sandy checked out the local paper online to see if she could find any mention of this bike parade, finally discovering it in the council news. It sounded like fun, like a huge children's party, but it didn't give a date. She supposed Rob would tell her when they met. For several moments she sat gazing into space, picturing the face of the man she'd come to regard as someone she wanted to get to know better, to spend more time with. Well, at least they were to have lunch together next day. Even if it wasn't what she'd hoped for, it was a start. Although she was aware of his challenges, she couldn't help hoping for more. If only Ruby was right.

*

Next day, Sandy couldn't stifle the wave of anticipation she felt at the prospect of seeing Rob again, even if it was to be a business lunch. She dressed carefully in a pair of white pants and a bright pink tee-shirt. It was a favourite and one which matched the pink of her van. She always felt good wearing it and she knew she needed all the help she could get to make it through lunch.

Determined to remain professional and keep her personal feelings in check, Sandy pulled her hair into a tidy bun at the back of her neck. Gazing at herself in the mirror, she was satisfied there was no sign of the vulnerable woman who'd walked along the beach with Rob, who had responded to his kiss... for which he had apologised, she reminded herself.

When she walked into the café, Sandy was pleased to see she was first to arrive. She chose a table in the back corner, took out her iPad and looked around, assessing the café as she always did on a first visit. From what she could see, it was a fairly standard seaside town café. The blackboard menu on the wall listed the usual fish, meat, pasta and vegetarian dishes, and the slightly tattered one on the table included a variety of sandwiches, some with more exotic fillings than she might have expected. She was trying to decide which of them to order when she heard the waitress say, 'Hey, Rob. Your usual?' Looking up, she saw Rob Andrews walking towards her. Today, there was no sign of Bess.

'You came,' he said, sitting down opposite.

'I said I would. You mentioned a booking for catering.' As soon as she spoke, Sandy knew it had been a mistake, his slight intake of breath indicating his surprise. 'Sorry, I didn't mean that the way it sounded... but you did say...'

'*I'm* sorry.' Rob drew his hand through his hair, making parts of it stand on end.

Sandy's fingers itched to smooth it down, to touch his lips, to... Stop, she told herself. He only wants to talk business. But it didn't stem the feelings the sight of him aroused.

'I think I owe you an apology for the way I behaved on the beach,' he said. 'I've been meaning to contact you, and when Will suggested I talk to you about catering for the parade...'

So, it *was* all Will's idea. Sandy's heart plummeted. She should have known. And she'd come prepared. So why the wave of disappointment? 'There's no need to apologise. We both got carried away in the moment, the moonlight...' She waved a hand in the air, hoping she didn't sound as upset as she felt.

Rob appeared relieved. 'Good. I'd hate to think I'd ruined our friendship. I haven't, have I?'

'Not at all.'

'Good,' he repeated. He picked up a menu. 'What would you like? I can recommend the avocado with dried tomato and fetta on rye. It's what I usually have. I often eat lunch here.'

'That sounds delicious, thanks.'

'Coffee?'

'Peppermint tea.'

'I'll order. Won't be a moment.'

While Rob was placing their order at the counter, Sandy had time to recover her composure which had slipped during their conversation. Friends was what they had agreed. Why had she imagined there might be more to their relationship? Surely she wasn't being swayed by Ruby's flight of fancy at the sighting of two magpies?

'Tell me more about this bike parade,' Sandy said when Rob returned. 'Is there a date?'

'Christmas Eve.'

Sandy's eyes widened. Surely everyone would be too busy with family to get involved in something like that on Christmas Eve.

'It's a bit of a special day in Bellbird Bay,' Rob began. 'It starts out in the morning with the annual Christmas fundraiser which raises money the local surf lifesavers use for the maintenance and replacement of equipment and the purchase of surf boats. It's a lot of fun. The surfers, all dressed in Santa outfits, take their boards out and surf into the beach, and there's also a group of swimmers who swim out to the headland, then back again. It's a big deal and attracts a lot of media attention, but it's for the adults. Will's idea is to have the kid's turn in the afternoon with a bike parade culminating with a party at the far end of the esplanade, near the harbour. That's where you come in,' he said, clearly seeing Sandy's startled expression.

'How many kids are we talking about?' Sandy was used to small home parties. This sounded like an enormous undertaking.

Rob pulled on his beard.

She'd noticed he did that when he was thinking. It was an endearing quality.

'Hard to tell. It depends how many sign up for the parade. The form will be in *The Bugle* this week.'

For a brief moment, Sandy's heart sank. What was she letting herself in for if she agreed? But she'd be mad not to. It was such a great opportunity to promote *Celebrations*. She was swamped with a wave of excitement, forgetting she might not be here after Christmas to benefit from the flood of bookings which would be sure to result from the event. All she could think of was the boost it would give her business.

'What do you think?' Rob asked as she hesitated.

'It would take a lot of preparation,' she said slowly, 'but there are a few people I can call upon to help.' Her mind went into overdrive as she considered the possibilities. The parade was on Christmas Eve, but the preparation could be done before that. She could organise her usual children's party menu – mini sausage rolls, hot dogs, quiches and pizzas, along with dips, veggie sticks and potato chips, maybe grilled cheese sandwiches, with water and cordial to wash it all down. Then there would be gingerbread men, and maybe she could talk to the gelato place about providing ice cream. Ruby and Liam would help and, with a bit of luck and the promise of payment, maybe she could persuade Fliss and her friends to pitch in. 'How soon will you know the numbers?'

'I'll have to check with Will, but I'm pretty sure there'll be a deadline for entries.'

'And what's your involvement?' Sandy asked, amused at Rob's interest.

'I'll be providing bikes where needed and be on site in the event of any mishaps on the day. Purely for the bikes. The surf lifesavers will be on hand to cater for minor casualties, and a group of paramedics for anything more serious.'

'You seem to have thought of everything.'

'All Will's doing. He's a powerhouse when it comes to organising fundraisers – part of the reason he was elected mayor.'

'I suspect you had a hand in it, too,' she said, amused to see him blush.

'Well, maybe.'

Their meals arrived, and Rob busied himself with eating, leaving Sandy to do the same.

'This is delicious,' she said. 'Everywhere I've eaten here has been of a high standard. I'm surprised none of the cafés provide catering.'

'They probably think it's too much trouble. *The Firenze* does takeaway, and this place provides takeaway and picnic hampers. But nothing like you offer with *Celebrations*. You still considering staying around?'

Sandy stared at him. Despite sharing her concerns with him, she was no further forward in making a decision. Maybe her trip to Sydney would help her decide.

As if reading her mind, Rob said, 'You mentioned going to Sydney. Will you be gone long?'

'Only a few days. I have a few things to sort out.' She glanced across the table then decided to elaborate. 'The police have decided the fire was arson and have arrested a group of youths. They want to interview me again, and I need to see my insurers.'

'That must be a relief.'

'Ye...es.'

'You sound doubtful.'

'I'm not really, but...' Sandy wasn't sure why she had some misgivings about her trip to Sydney.

'It'll give you a chance to see if you want to go back there to live.'

Sandy was taken aback. Had he read her mind? 'That, too,' she said. 'And I can check with Grant. Ruby has suggested I invite him for Christmas.'

'To Bellbird Bay?'

'Of course. We still have a good relationship.' Why did Rob appear gobsmacked? 'It would be good for Fliss to have her dad with us.'

'Sure. You'll be back for the lighting of the Christmas tree?'

'All going well in Sydney. Ruby tells me it's a special event. Fliss is looking forward to it.'

'It's like a big street party. Happens the evening of the charity bike ride and gets everyone into the Christmas mood.'

'Sounds like fun. Will you be taking part in the bike ride, too?'

'Only on the admin side. My role is to be there in the event of accidents – to the bikes.'

'I see.' Sandy couldn't hide her smile.

'I hope…' Rob looked down awkwardly. 'I hope to see you there. Perhaps we can have a drink together afterwards.'

'Perhaps we can.' Sandy wasn't sure why, but her heart lightened at Rob's suggestion. If at all possible, she intended to be back.

# Thirty-one

Sandy had little time to think about Rob in the rush to get ready for her trip and to fit in a couple of last-minute parties. But finally, she was on her way. As the plane took off and the coastline spread out below, she found herself filled with a sense of regret. After only a couple of months in Bellbird Bay, the town had managed to envelop her in its peaceful atmosphere. Maybe Ruby was right when she said it was a magical place.

As soon as she set foot on the tarmac in Sydney, however, the city drew her back in. This was her home, not the small coastal town, no matter how pleasant it seemed. Hailing a cab, she was soon in streets she recognised, though the traffic was a shock. She'd forgotten how busy and noisy Sydney was. It was a relief to arrive at her hotel.

Once checked in, Sandy pulled out her laptop and phone to confirm her meeting at the police station and her appointment with the insurance company, both of which were to take place next day. Then she made a call to Grant.

As she expected, he had returned from his trip and although still officially on leave, was back in his university office. They arranged to meet for lunch next day – Sandy could fit it in between her other appointments – at a pub close to the university. That done, she sent a text to Fliss to let her and Ruby know she'd arrived safely, before lying down for a nap before dinner.

It was dark when she awoke, and it took her a few moments to remember where she was. She got up and gazed out the window at the busy street below, feeling like a stranger. Although she hadn't lived in this part of the city recently, it had been her home when she was a student, so it should feel familiar. But she found herself longing for the ocean view from Ruby's house on the headland, for the scent of the ocean and the wind in her hair.

Checking her phone, she smiled to read Fliss's reply to her text.

*Don't forget my books and guitar, and my pink dress, and make sure you're back for the lighting of the tree. Have you seen Dad yet? xxx*

Suddenly overcome with the urge to hear her daughter's voice, Sandy pressed Fliss's number on speed dial, but it went to voicemail. 'Love you, Fliss. I won't forget, and I'm seeing Dad tomorrow. I'll give him your love. Hope to be back for the tree lighting.' Finishing the call, she was reminded of Rob Andrews, smiling at the prospect of celebrating the tree lighting with him, followed by the promised drink.

Half an hour later, eating the pasta dish she'd ordered from room service, Sandy was struck again by all she'd left behind in Bellbird Bay, by the realisation she'd made more friends there than she had in Sydney in the years since her divorce. She began to seriously wonder what life would be like if she did decide to stay there.

*

Next morning, Sandy dressed smartly in a blue linen pants suit, a white tee-shirt under the jacket, and made her way to the police station where she was to give her statement. It was a strange sensation to sit in a small interview room where a young police officer took down her words before printing them off for her signature. Then, the senior officer she'd spoken to on the phone appeared.

'Thanks for making the trip, Mrs Elliot,' he said. 'You must be glad we've apprehended the culprits, though they're out on bail. They're underage,' he added, apologetically, 'so it's unlikely they'll see the inside of a cell, even detention. There's been a lot of publicity recently – you may have seen it on television. All too often, these teenagers get off with no more than a slap on the wrist. It's not fair to shop owners like yourself who've had your livelihood destroyed.'

Sandy stared at him in surprise. She'd come all this way... for what?

If the miscreants weren't going to be punished, what was the point of her being here?

He must have read her thoughts. 'I know it's difficult to hear, but we need to go through the motions in the hope this time will be different.'

Still reeling from the news the youths who'd set fire to her shop might escape punishment, Sandy made her way across town to where she had arranged to meet Grant. The pub he'd nominated was a new one to Sandy, but she was out of touch with this part of the city. She found Grant sitting in the beer garden, looking tanned and relaxed, a beer and a glass of white wine on the table.

'Still prefer chardonnay?' he asked, gesturing to the glass. 'You look as if you might need it.'

Sandy nodded, pleased he'd anticipated her desire for alcohol after her experience at the police station. 'Thanks,' she said, accepting his peck on the cheek and slipping into the seat opposite him. 'This morning wasn't quite what I expected.' She took a welcome gulp of wine.

'You saw the police?'

'Yes, gave my statement, but it seems they may get off – too young to be locked up.'

'It's a sad fact of life.' Grant shook his head. 'Youth crime is escalating and there doesn't seem to be any solution. You're looking good. Bellbird Bay must be agreeing with you.'

'Thanks. You, too.' She was glad they'd remained friends after the divorce, unlike some couples she knew. 'How was the trip?'

'Good... pretty good, actually. I've been offered a job there.'

'In the US?'

'In California, at UC Berkeley where I spent my sabbatical.'

'Wow!'

'Yeah, it's a bit of a facer. It would mean...'

'What about Fliss?' Sandy's mind started to think of all the obstacles. Surely Grant wouldn't want Fliss to go there with him? How could she? And, if Grant was no longer in Sydney, it took away one of her reasons to return.

'Fliss will be okay. She's never going to want to live with me, is she?' he asked, a bitter note in his voice. 'But...' he said, sounding more upbeat, '... maybe she could visit me there in her holidays.'

'Maybe.' Sandy tried to think how Fliss would react to the news. 'When would you be going there?'

'January, if I can get out of my contract here. I need to talk with Fliss about it, get her used to the idea. How is she? Enjoying Bellbird Bay?'

'Surprisingly. She has a boyfriend.'

'Wow! Growing up. Would I approve?'

'I think so. He's a couple of years older, but a nice kid. I've met his parents… and grandparents. He's a surfer, so our daughter is learning to surf.'

'Plenty of surf in California.'

'Yes.' Sandy's heart sank. What if Fliss chose to attend university there, to move in with Grant? But that was two years away. A lot could happen in two years.

'We should order. You said you have an appointment this afternoon?'

'Yes, with the insurance company. They may finally be able to pay out my claim.' She picked up the menu.

They didn't speak again till they'd ordered – a house salad for Sandy and chicken schnitzel for Grant, along with refills of beer and wine.

Then Grant said, 'So this Bellbird Bay thing, it's working out for you? I thought you only went there to help out your grandmother's friend, but Fliss tells me you've set up your business again.'

'Yes, I have and yes, I did. It's complicated.'

'Want to talk about it? Fliss sent me the link to some newspaper article with photos of you and your pink van.'

Sandy grimaced. Fliss hadn't said she'd shared it with her dad. But Grant had always been easy to talk to, and there was time while they waited for their meals. 'It's like this…' she began, outlining how she'd been encouraged to set up *Celebrations* in Bellbird Bay, how successful it had been and how people were encouraging her to stay. She said nothing about Rob Andrews, not sure why the thought of him made her feel guilty. 'But I'm not sure,' she finished. 'There's Fliss to consider, and our lives here in Sydney.'

'Let me see,' Grant said. 'What you're saying is that you have a viable catering business in this Bellbird Bay place. Fliss enjoys life there, has a boyfriend. You're enjoying the quieter life. And you're concerned about… what?'

'When you put it like that…' Sandy laughed. 'But our lives are here, our home, Fliss's school, her friends… until what you just told me, you were here, too.'

'Sounds like a no-brainer. Fliss is happy. You can sell the apartment. Why go to the trouble of starting again if you're happy there?'

Sandy pursed her lips. Grant always had had a habit of cutting through her objections. He was right, of course, but this was a more important decision than what television to buy. 'Yes, but… It's a big step, Grant. We've always lived here. It's our home.'

'I'm making a big change, too. Maybe it's time… for both of us.'

'Maybe.' Sandy took a sip of wine as she saw the waiter approaching with their food. 'Anyway, I'm seeing my insurer this afternoon. Then I thought I might check out possible premises.'

'To have the same thing happen again if the bastards get off?'

The same thought had occurred to her. At least in Bellbird Bay, no one was going to set fire to *Headland House*, and perhaps she could even find somewhere to rent there and get out of Ruby's hair. 'We'll see,' was all she said. 'Wow, this looks good,' she added as the plates were set before them, and she realised she was hungry. She'd been too wired about the interview with the police to have more than coffee for breakfast.

By the time they finished eating, it was almost time for Sandy to head off. 'Why don't you come to Bellbird Bay for Christmas?' she said. 'Fliss would love you to be there… especially if you're off to California in January. I can break the news to her before then.' Sandy wasn't sure what Fliss's reaction would be. She didn't see Grant often, but he was always there when she wanted to get away from home for a few hours – or a weekend.

'Stay with you?'

'Ruby says you'd be welcome. She runs the place as a B&B. There's lots of room.'

'Thanks. I'd like that. Give Fliss a hug from me.'

'I will. She sent her love.' Sandy felt bad she hadn't passed this on sooner. She'd been so upset with the police.

'She's a good kid.'

'She is. We did well.'

'Can I let you know about Christmas? I have a few things to sort out.'

'Sure, but don't leave it too long. It's only a few weeks away.'

'No worries.'

They stood up and Grant gave her a hug, before he went to pay, and she left. It felt odd, getting a hug from the man who, until five years ago, she'd been married to, the man who now felt more like a favourite cousin.

Sandy exhaled as she walked away. The insurance agency was situated in the city. She had time to walk there, then she planned to take a bus back across to the north side to visit an estate agency specialising in commercial premises. She still hadn't made up her mind what to do.

*

Two hours later, Sandy sat in a café in North Sydney nursing a cappuccino and feeling as if she had been run over by a truck. It was as if the universe was telling her something – or so Ruby would say. The meeting with the insurance company hadn't gone as she expected. While they accepted the police verdict of arson, they had demanded proof of purchase for all her equipment, before they were prepared to release the full sum insured, reasoning there was no way of assessing the condition of the equipment prior to the fire, and were disputing Sandy's claim of loss of income due to the fire. Sandy left with the impression they held her equally responsible for the fire.

Her following visit to the realtor was no more promising. Given the spate of fires, rents had increased exponentially – as had insurance premiums – the agent told her. It seemed as if her decision was being made for her. Her final visit was to another realtor, one dealing with residential properties. This time, the news was more promising. If she did choose to sell her apartment, she could expect to make a good profit.

Now, all she wanted to do was get back to Bellbird Bay, to see Fliss again, hear some of Ruby's homilies, and… yes, see Rob Andrews again, too. There was something about the bike shop owner that piqued her curiosity and made her want to burrow inside the shell he'd erected around himself to discover the core of the man inside.

# Thirty-two

Sandy had only been gone for two days, and Rob was missing her. No matter how often he told himself there was no room for a woman in his life and this one wasn't likely to stay around, he couldn't help thinking of her, remembering her gentle smile, her vulnerable eyes... and those lips. What had possessed him to kiss her, to break the vow he'd made to himself never to become involved in a relationship? He barely knew the woman, but the image of her attractive face was what kept him awake at night. At least it was better than the re-enactment of his last day in Afghanistan, the horror which had plagued him since he returned. But he knew this was only a brief respite, that the horror and guilt would return when he least expected it... and he had to be prepared.

Meantime, a man could dream.

He was having dinner with his parents again – this time to celebrate his birthday. But, for him, his birthday was no call for celebration. It only served to remind him there should be two of them celebrating, and he always got the impression from his mother that she felt the same. It was the day he missed his twin most, the day they had always enjoyed together until Brett was no longer there to celebrate with him. His parents had always tried to make the day special for Rob, but he was aware how they felt their loss, too. He'd been glad to have been absent for all those years but now he was back and he had to suffer through the memories the day evoked.

Rob found himself begin to tense as he drove through the entrance to the complex and parked in one of the visitor parking bays. As he walked across the path, Bess at his heels, the door to his parents' villa opened and his dad walked out to greet him with a warm hug.

'Happy birthday, son,' Bob said, 'Your mother's in the kitchen. It's a difficult day for her.'

'For all of us.' Rob sighed, wishing he could have avoided this. He'd much rather have spent the evening on his own, maybe on the beach with the sound of the waves and only his memories and Bess for company.

Inside, he made his way to the kitchen to find his mother taking a roast out of the oven. 'My boy!' She pulled him into her arms.

*Why did he feel she was giving him the hug she wanted to give Brett? Had he always felt this way?*

'Mum.' Rob extricated himself.

'Brett would have been fifty today, too,' she said, her voice breaking.

'Now, now, Gwen.' Rob's dad walked into the kitchen. 'No tears today. We're celebrating Rob's birthday.'

'You're right. Sorry. Happy birthday, son.' She managed a smile. 'I can't believe it's fifty years since I held the two of you in my arms, my two perfect little boys.'

Rob shifted uncomfortably. Was he always to be reminded that he was the one who'd survived, to be beset with survivor guilt? He knew how the evening would go. They'd have dinner, perhaps even a cake, then his mother would produce the photo albums, the ones which had stopped suddenly when Brett died. There were no records of his childhood after the age of ten.

The meal passed in almost complete silence, Rob's father making attempts at conversation which neither Rob nor his mother responded to. After slices of a birthday cake which Gwen had baked and on which she had placed five candles, they retired to the lounge room where, true to form, she reached for the photo albums.

Rob could bear it no longer. 'I need to go,' he said, rising so quickly he almost overturned his untouched cup of coffee and startled Bess who had been lying at his feet. 'Sorry, Mum, Dad. I'll let myself out. I'll be in touch.'

Once outside, Rob gave a sigh of relief, wishing he didn't find it so difficult to visit his parents. He loved them and knew they loved him, too. But he was aware how the sight of him must remind them of his brother, make them wonder what Brett would have been like if he'd lived, if he would have married and provided them with the grandchildren they longed for.

It was still early, and Rob didn't feel like going home to his empty house where he'd probably drink himself into a stupor making him useless next day. Instead, he headed for the beach where he'd have preferred to spend the evening.

It was deserted at this time of night, the chatter of the patrons on the deck of the surf club growing fainter and fainter as he left it behind and made his way with Bess to the outcrop of rocks where he always went when he was feeling down. It was where he and Brett had often come together, having sneaked away when their parents thought them snugly tucked up in bed. It was the place where he felt closest to his brother.

'Happy birthday, bro,' he said, holding up the bottle of beer he'd extracted from his parents' fridge before leaving. 'Why did it have to be you? Why did I survive? It wasn't fair!' *Life wasn't fair*, Rob drained the bottle, before pulling his knees up to his chest and wrapping his arms around them. He stared out to sea. It would have been better if he had died with Brett, or in Afghanistan, instead of Ned. He could walk out into the ocean right now, keep walking until... Suddenly, he noticed a figure heading towards him, the light from an iPhone piercing the darkness.

*

Sandy was a mess of conflicting emotions when she arrived back in Bellbird Bay. She was glad Fliss was preparing to go out to meet Zack and her response of 'Okay' to Fliss's, 'How was Dad?' was enough to satisfy her daughter. 'See you later, Mum,' she called as she rushed out the door.

'You can talk to her tomorrow,' Ruby said from her usual chair. 'How was your trip? Did you get everything sorted? Did it help you make up your mind?'

'Oh, Ruby. I wish I knew.' Sandy collapsed onto a chair. She was so glad to be back in Bellbird Bay; it was as if she'd come home. 'There's so much to think about.'

'Did you invite Fliss's dad for Christmas?'

'I did. That was the easy part. He's been offered a job in California and is planning to move there. I can't help worrying Fliss might want to go there too one day.'

'Well, there's no sense in worrying about what the future might hold. Fliss will make up her own mind whatever you or her father do or say – and wherever you choose to live.'

'You're right, of course, but...'

'What about the rest of your visit – your meetings with the police and the insurance agency?'

'They were okay. Now they've determined it was arson and found the culprits, things can move forward. I also checked out premises for *Celebrations*.'

'And?' Ruby's eyes glinted.

*Why did Sandy get the impression Ruby already knew the result?*

'It won't be easy to find one which won't end up the same as before. It seems gangs of youths are taking delight in targeting small businesses. I'd be in their sights again.'

'Sounds like you have a bit of thinking to do, and a decision to make.'

'Mmm.'

'Have you eaten? Fliss and I had some quiche and salad, and there's enough left for you.'

'Thanks. That sounds good.' Sandy realised she was hungry. She'd been so caught up in worrying about what to do, she hadn't eaten since lunch with Grant.

'I'll join you in a glass of wine, then I'm for an early night. You look as if you need one, too.'

'Maybe.' But Sandy knew she was too wired up to sleep.

Once she had eaten, and Ruby had gone to bed, but not before making an oblique statement to the effect that the universe had a plan, Sandy felt restless and, pulling on a light jacket, made her way outside and down the steps to the beach. There, with the breeze in her hair and the scent of the sea, she hoped to be able to see things more clearly and come to a decision. It would be a big step to pull up their roots in

Sydney to start again in this small coastal town. Even if it already felt like home to her, she had no idea how Fliss might react.

She walked along slowly in the darkness, her way lit by the torch of her iPhone, considering the pros and cons of making the move to Bellbird Bay. She had almost made up her mind to broach the subject with Fliss when she became aware of two figures huddled on the sand. She stopped and stared as the man's features became clear, and the dog began to rise.

'Rob?' At the sound of her voice the dog settled down again.

'Oh, it's you, Sandy. What are you doing out here at this time of night?'

'I might ask you the same question.' She sat down beside him and stared out at the ocean. It looked dark and treacherous in this light. She shivered.

'I came here to think.'

'You, too?' For some reason, Sandy felt she'd found a kindred spirit. 'What did you have to think about?'

'Whether or not to move here.'

'Your Sydney trip didn't go well, then?'

'Quite the opposite, but it didn't feel like home anymore.' Until she actually said the words, Sandy hadn't realised how alien she'd felt in the city. 'I need to talk to Fliss first, but if she's agreeable, we might decide to make Bellbird Bay our home. You?'

Rob didn't immediately reply then said, 'I was contemplating how easy it would be to walk out into the ocean and end it all.'

Sandy couldn't believe her ears. 'You're not serious?'

'Probably not.' He sighed. 'I don't have the guts to do that either. Today's my birthday. Fifty. It should have been Brett's birthday, too.'

'Your brother?'

'Mmm. When he died from meningococcal, I kept waiting to catch it, too, but I didn't. I survived. I never forgave myself.'

'But it wasn't your fault.'

'I always felt my parents… my mother… blamed me. Ever since, birthdays have been difficult. Tonight… I couldn't take it anymore… the traditional roast, the cake, the photo album, the guilt. I left and came here. If you hadn't appeared when you did…'

'No!' Sandy's stomach clenched. *He hadn't really been contemplating suicide, had he? Had she been too quick to dismiss her earlier concerns?*

181

'No, you're right.' He grimaced, his expression barely visible in the moonlight now she had switched off her torch.

'What do you mean about the photo album?'

'It's what my mother does, brings out the album of when Brett and me were together. There were never any photos after... It's almost as if she wants to rub my nose in the fact I lived, and he didn't.'

'Have you spoken to your parents about how you feel?'

'What good would that do?'

'I can only speak as a mother and I can't imagine anything worse than losing a child, but I know it would make me treasure the living one even more.'

'You don't know my mother.'

'That's true, but I can't believe... What about your dad?'

'Oh, Dad's all right... most of the time. But Mum...' He shook his head.

'It possibly hurt her more to lose your brother, but she still has you.'

'Are you always so conciliatory?'

'Not always.' Sandy thought of times when she was younger, when her temper had led her into awkward situations, until she'd learned to curb it. It had been her grandmother who had helped her then.

They sat in silence for several minutes then Rob said, 'I'm glad you came along when you did.'

'Because I stopped you from doing something stupid?'

'That, too. I was feeling sorry for myself. I've always thought Brett was the favourite and I...'

'Parents don't have favourites, believe me.'

'Maybe. But I've always felt guilty.'

Sandy could see it took a lot for Rob to admit this. Perhaps he'd never spoken to anyone about it before now. If not, why now, why her?

'You're easy to talk to... or maybe it's the evening air, the darkness... I'm sorry to unload all this on you.'

'Don't be. I'm only glad if it helped to talk about it.'

'Surprisingly, it has.'

Rob rose and held out a hand to help Sandy up picking up the empty beer bottle in the other. 'I'll walk you back.'

'Thanks.' The sensation of his hand clasping hers was comforting, reminding Sandy of the kiss they'd shared on this same beach and making her wonder if maybe there was some truth in Ruby's wild predictions. She had the strong sense Rob Andrews was damaged in ways she didn't understand. Tonight, he'd shared his youthful guilt, but she felt certain there was more to it than what he'd revealed to her.

When they reached the foot of the steps up to the headland, they stopped. 'I'll be right now,' she said.

Rob released her hand but didn't move away. 'We're still on for the Christmas lights?' he asked.

'Of course.' She couldn't believe he'd really intended ending his life when he had so much to live for; he was heavily invested in the charity bike ride and the bike parade on Christmas Eve. Surely tonight had been a momentary aberration. 'I'm looking forward to it.'

She suddenly remembered his initial words. It was his birthday, his fiftieth, a milestone birthday. 'Happy birthday,' she said. Then greatly daring, she threw her arms around his neck and kissed him on the lips. As he met her kiss and pulled her into him, Sandy felt his arousal against her, sending a shudder of desire through her whole being. It had been so long since she'd felt this way, she'd almost forgotten the rush of adrenaline and the ache of longing, the need to be close to a man.

# Thirty-three

*Had he really contemplated suicide?*

Rob made his way back along the beach, his senses reeling from the kiss which had been so unexpected and had broken through his self-imposed barriers, making him realise what he had denied himself for so long. But nothing had changed. The guilt was still there, though perhaps he *would* speak with his parents, if he could find the words to convey the emotions he'd tried so hard to hide behind a brusque exterior.

But he reminded himself, even if Sandy was right about his mother and Brett, it didn't change things about the way Ned died... or put an end to his nightmares. Despite the flash of desire he'd experienced when their lips met – and his unexpected physical reaction – nothing had really changed. He couldn't allow himself to let down his guard, especially with Sandy Elliot.

But suicide? No. He looked down at Bess, padding along beside him, and knew he could never have left her. He didn't have the guts to end his life, not when he'd seen what it could do to those left behind. Still, he was glad Sandy had come along when she did. She was someone whose opinion he could trust, someone who could be a good friend. Nothing more, he reminded himself, as he remembered again his body's automatic response to the touch of her lips, her body against his.

By the time he reached his van, he'd convinced himself his reaction had been purely physical, a normal male reaction to the proximity of a desirable woman. At least, this time, there had been no need for him to apologise.

*

Next morning, everything looked brighter. There was a lot to do in *Bay Bikes* ready for the charity bike ride in two days' time, and Zack wouldn't be in till after school. Rob set to checking out the bikes which were to be hired out on the day, making sure they were all ready to go. Some of the participants weren't local and preferred hiring a bike to bringing their own. Then he checked his inventory, noting the orders he'd received for Christmas delivery and making a list of replacements needed to his stock. It was a never-ending task, but one which he enjoyed. How could he even have imagined giving all this up?

The bell on the shop door tinkled.

'Hey, Rob!'

Rob looked up from the computer to see Will Rankin enter the shop.

'All set for Friday?'

'Getting there. No problems?'

'None I'm aware of. I'm just making some last-minute checks to ensure everything is going to plan.'

'All good here. Can I get you a coffee?'

'Thanks.'

In the back shop, Rob fixed them both coffees and found a half packet of biscuits. 'Should be a good day,' he said when they were both seated.

'Yeah, numbers are up on last year. I'm hoping we'll raise $100,000 for the Women's Centre. It's going well since Ali Wells took over. We were all sorry when Madeline passed away, but Ali has proved herself equal to the task. And she's well-liked.'

Rob shook his head. 'I can't believe how many women suffer from domestic violence, even in a place as idyllic as this.'

'At least we can do something to help.' Will stared into his coffee. 'But enough about that. What about you?'

'What about me?'

'Sandy Elliot.'

Rob gazed at him in surprise. What did Will know about his friendship with Sandy?

'Come on, Rob. You can't keep a secret in Bellbird Bay. You should know that. She's a lovely woman, just right for you, I'd imagine.' He winked.

'No, it's not...' But Rob could see Will wasn't going to give up easily. 'Hell, Will, you don't understand.'

'Try me. I have all day. I'm not going anywhere and I've been married twice. I'm unshockable.'

'We're friends, Will, nothing more. It's all I can ever be with a woman.'

Will raised his eyebrows.

'No, it's not... I'm not... It might be easier if I *were* impotent.' He sighed. 'After my time in the army... I saw things... lost mates... watched my best mate die in agony in front of me. It should have been me,' he choked. 'I still have nightmares about it... and guilt,' he muttered, almost inaudibly.

'But surely the right woman would understand?'

'I can't take the risk.' As he spoke, Rob realised Sandy Elliot might well be the right woman, the one he'd been waiting for, but it was too late. The talk about domestic violence had shaken him; he'd always been afraid of what he might do in the throes of one of his nightmares. It wasn't worth the risk. He'd never be able to forgive himself.

'Life's a risk. Every relationship's a risk. If I hadn't taken a risk, Cleo and I might never have got together. We started out pretending to be a couple, then...' Will chuckled. 'It's amazing how things can happen when you least expect it.'

'You were lucky.' Rob envied his friend. Will had found love twice. He had a son who thought the world of him, and a new wife who loved him. What did Rob have to show for his fifty years?

Rob was glad when Will left. The conversation had made him feel uncomfortable. It had reminded him of what he was missing, of how he'd love to be in a relationship like Will, Martin and his other friends. But he knew it wasn't possible. He'd accepted that when he'd lain in his hospital bed, unable to forget the trauma of Ned's death. So why had meeting Sandy Elliot brought back yearnings for a life he used to dream about?

*

Saturday arrived, the day of the charity bike ride and the lighting of the Christmas tree, and Rob still hadn't found the right time to talk about Brett's death with his parents. It had seemed the obvious thing to do when Sandy suggested it but approaching them took more courage than he could summon up right now. Maybe after today, he'd make time.

Today, he'd left Bess at home and was focussed on the bike ride as participants streamed into town, and crowds of onlookers filled the streets and cafés. Rob hoped Will was right, and they'd make a record sum for the charity.

Zack had arrived at *Bay Bikes* early, eager to be in charge for the day, even if the shop was unlikely to have any customers. Most would either be taking part in the event or watching somewhere along the route. 'All set?' he asked, when he saw Rob packing the van with everything he might need.

'I think so.' Rob scratched his head and pulled on his beard. He mentally checked the list he'd made earlier then, adding the flask of coffee he'd thought to fill, along with several bottles of water and a packet of sandwiches. He grinned. 'Yeah, I'm good to go, and I know I'm leaving *Bay Bikes* in good hands.'

'Thanks, Rob. I promise to do my best.'

'Cheers. See you later.'

Rob set off. He planned to meet Will at the start of the race and make his way along the route slowly, ready to be on hand if required. He was only there in case of emergencies; there were plenty of other volunteers providing water along the way.

Rob parked the van and headed to where Will was standing ready to set off the starter's pistol. There were more competitors than he had expected. It looked as if Will was right, and this year would be the largest yet. He just hoped they'd all keep to the rules and there would be no daredevils trying to outsmart the others.

Suddenly, as if hearing some unspoken command, they all fell silent. Will fired the pistol and they were off. The street which had been crowded with cyclists and spectators quickly emptied, and Rob went back to the van to follow them.

Luckily for everyone, there were no serious mishaps. Only two cyclists managed to collide, and neither they nor their bikes were seriously harmed. By the time they all reached the finishing line, back in Bellbird Bay, everyone was exhausted but grinning with pleasure at their achievement.

'A beer?' Will asked Rob, when the last rider had arrived and been greeted with applause. 'A few of us are heading to the club.'

'Thanks, but no. I've left Zack on his own for long enough. I need to get back to give him a break.'

'Okay, but we'll see you at the lighting of the tree tonight?'

'Wouldn't miss it.' Rob grinned. Despite his determination to avoid any romantic relationship, he was looking forward to seeing Sandy again, and to the promised drink afterwards.

# Thirty-four

Everyone seemed to be either taking part in the charity bike ride or had gone to watch it. Sandy hadn't realised it was such a big deal. But, at least, she had no parties booked today so was able to relax and prepare herself for the evening when she was meeting Rob again. She wasn't sure what to think after their meeting on the beach. The poor man, being so weighed down with guilt for a death which hadn't been his fault. To think he had carried that guilt for most of his life. She could only hope that, by now, he'd managed to speak to his parents and resolved the issue. And there had been that kiss! She hadn't intended to kiss him. It was as if she had no power to control the impulse that had forced her to throw her arms around him... and his response had sent her emotions swinging out of control.

Next morning, Ruby had known something had happened – not much got past her. But she hadn't said anything, merely given one of her enigmatic smiles when she asked how Sandy had slept.

Sandy still hadn't had an opportunity to discuss her future plans with her daughter, so when they had finished breakfast, she said, 'I need to talk with you, Fliss.' She had made her delivery to *The Pandanus Café* earlier.

'Can't it wait, Mum? I promised to meet Jenny and Megan to watch the start of the bike ride.'

'No darling, this is important.'

'Huh!' But Fliss followed her out into the courtyard, taking a seat at the table and folding her arms.

'What is it?' she asked impatiently.

'You like it here, don't you?'

'Duh! Of course I do. Ruby's great, the town's great. I love the beach and I've made friends.'

'So, not as boring as you expected?'

'Definitely not. Is that what you wanted to ask me? Can I go now?'

'Not exactly.' Sandy paused. 'As you know, I've started up *Celebrations* here, and it's been successful. When I was down in Sydney...'

'What?'

'How would you feel if we stayed here, if we didn't go back to the city?' Sandy held her breath.

Fliss didn't answer immediately, then said, 'What about Dad?'

Sandy flinched. She should have known he would be Fliss's first concern.

'Your dad's moving from Sydney. He's been offered a job in California. He plans to move in the new year.'

Fliss's eyes widened, and Sandy thought she saw the beginning of a tear. 'Dad's going to the US? He's leaving me?'

'You'll be able to visit.' Sandy knew it was faint comfort. Instead of being in the next suburb, Grant would be thousands of miles away. 'And he'll be here for Christmas.'

'Good. Is that all?'

'About moving here, how do you feel about it? It would mean selling the apartment, you leaving *Geraldine Spence College*, Eva, your other friends in Sydney...' She bit her lip, trying to gauge her daughter's reaction.

'You mean it? We could stay here? I could keep seeing Zack and maybe make the volleyball team next year. Wait till I tell Jenny and Megan.'

'Won't you miss Sydney... your friends... Eva?'

'Eva's become a pain. She's jealous of me having Zack, doesn't understand how I love surfing and volleyball. All she can think of is the boys at Grammar. As if...' Fliss grimaced.

'So you're happy if we stay? We'll need to find a place of our own. We can't live here with Ruby for ever.'

'Why not? I love it here. Ruby's great. She's like the grandma I never had. Can I go now?'

'Sure.'

Fliss walked away, leaving Sandy somewhat dumbfounded.

'Well?' Ruby asked when Sandy walked back inside.

'She seems... well, she seems remarkably okay with it, but not so much with Grant going overseas.'

'Not your problem, Sandy. She'll survive.'

'No. I mean, yes. It's just, I thought she'd be more upset about leaving Sydney, but...' She shook her head.

'Fliss is young and resilient. I can see how happy she is here. As I may have said before, Sandy, everything happens for a reason, and those two magpies on the lawn...'

'Two for joy. Yeah, yeah.' Sandy laughed.

Ruby raised an eyebrow but said no more.

Joy, Sandy thought. That was certainly a word to describe how she was feeling right now. Joy, at this magical place that was Bellbird Bay. Joy, that Fliss seemed to be so happy here and so accepting of a proposed move.

And then there was... her own joy, at how *Celebrations* and taken off here with such... *gusto* was the word.

And something else... the legend that was Rob Andrews. A familiar warmth prickled through her at the memory of their kiss – his closeness – his...

'Penny for them?' Ruby asked, the same words Rob had used not so long ago.

Sandy realised she was grinning.

'Thanks, Ruby,' she said.

'For what?'

'For bringing joy.'

The old woman chuckled. 'I'll tell the magpies when I see them next.'

Sandy spent the rest of the day planning for two events she had scheduled the following week, one a party for five-year-olds, the other a twenty-fifth wedding anniversary, and she had several orders for birthday cakes, too. She was still delivering cakes to the café each morning, but Ruby had taken over much of the baking and was enjoying being what she called, back to normal. While still undecided about staying in Bellbird Bay, Sandy had been cautious about taking on more than she could handle, but now she had Fliss's approval, the way was open for her to ramp up her business, and she was looking forward to it.

'Did you say you were meeting Rob Andrews at the tree lighting?' Ruby asked, when they were preparing an early dinner.

'Yes,' Sandy felt herself blushing, 'but I can drive you down and back, too.'

'Poof! I've seen it often enough. A quiet night in will suit me fine. Maybe the Smiths will join me,' she said, referring to the elderly couple who had arrived the day before and planned to stay over the weekend.

'If you're sure...' Sandy hoped Ruby wasn't only saying this to enable her to spend time with Rob, even though it was what she wanted.

'I am. You go and enjoy yourself and see if you can break through the barriers he's erected around his emotions. There's a warm, loving man inside, if he could just bring himself to... Well, I'm sure you'll find out.'

Not for the first time, Sandy felt Ruby knew more than she was saying, but how could she know more about Rob? As she said, he had these barriers which kept his emotions well hidden. He'd broken down and shared the guilt about his brother dying, but there was more he was keeping hidden. Perhaps she'd never know, never discover what made him shy away from becoming closer. But if she stayed in Bellbird Bay, there was the possibility of it happening. At the thought, she was bathed in a warm glow.

*

The esplanade and beachfront were crowded when Sandy arrived, making it difficult to distinguish Rob in the throng of people jostling for position by the huge Norfolk pine festooned with decorations and lights which were still unlit. A group of musicians were playing carols, and many of the crowd were singing along. It was a happy, festive atmosphere. Sandy was glad she'd decided to wear the red and green patterned dress she'd purchased in *Birds of a Feather*, the owner having assured her it was perfect for Christmas.

'Mum!'

Sandy turned to see Fliss, arm-in-arm with Zack and accompanied by Rob. Tonight, he was looking especially attractive. He had trimmed his beard and was wearing a white tee-shirt with the outline of a Christmas tree, over a pair of jeans. Surprisingly, his tattoos no longer bothered her.

'Glad we found you,' Rob said, taking her arm and leading her over to a spot from which they had a good view of the platform where Will Rankin as mayor would stand to turn on the lights.

When she turned to greet Fliss, Sandy discovered her daughter had disappeared, swallowed up by the growing crowd.

'She'll be fine with Zack,' Rob said, clearly seeing her expression. 'I've never seen so many people here. I suspect many of those who came for the ride have stayed around.'

'Oh, the ride. Was it a success?'

'Amazingly so. The money raised exceeded Will's expectations. Ali and the Women's Centre will be delighted.'

'I'm glad.' Sandy had been meaning to visit the centre, to offer to volunteer. Maybe now she planned to stay, she would. She had always felt grateful she wasn't one of those women who had suffered violence in a relationship. She couldn't imagine what it must be like.

'Look, there's Will. It's almost time.'

Sandy was very conscious of Rob's arm snaking around her shoulders as Will Rankin took to the stage. The music stopped. The microphone crackled. Then Will was speaking, welcoming everyone, wishing them a Merry Christmas, then without any fuss, he pressed a switch and the tree burst into light, causing a chorused 'Ooh!' from the crowd.

Rob had just said, 'Let's get out of here,' and removed his arm to take her hand, when the first volley of fireworks exploded in a burst of colour and noise. Everyone gasped and cheered. It was a few moments before Sandy noticed Rob's reaction. He had let go of her hand, had dropped to his knees and was huddled on the ground, his eyes tightly shut, his hands covering his head.

'Rob!' She dropped down beside him, heedless of the crowds surrounding them. 'What's the matter? Are you all right?' she asked, even though it was clear he was far from all right.

# Thirty-five

One minute Rob was holding Sandy's hand intent on taking her across to the surf club for a drink, the next he was back in the war zone, with missiles exploding and shrapnel flying everywhere. He covered his head and tried to hide, but there was no escaping the sounds of battle. 'Ned!' he yelled. 'Ned!'

'Shh. It's all right. I'm here.' It was a woman's voice, breaking through the clamour. *Where was Ned? He had to get to him before…* Gradually, he became aware of his surroundings. The noise abated somewhat. He opened his eyes to see a familiar face wearing a concerned expression. 'Sandy?'

'It's all right,' she said.

Rob became aware they were surrounded by people. The bangs continued, accompanied by flashes. Fireworks! He tried to rise, but his head was spinning. 'I… I…'

'I think we need to get you home. Can you stand?'

'Give me a minute.' Rob closed his eyes again, took a deep breath then opened them again and, with a mammoth effort, managed to rise to his feet with the help of Sandy's hand on his arm. Feeling like a fool, but too weak to object, he allowed her to lead him away from the noise and crush of people to where her van was parked.

'I'm feeling better now,' he said, only to have his legs crumble. 'Sorry.'

'I'll drive you home, then we'll see.' Sandy helped him into the passenger seat of the van.

Rob closed his eyes and leant his head back on the headrest. He was vaguely aware of the vehicle starting up and moving, then it stopped.

'We're here.'

He opened his eyes, relieved the noises and flashing lights had stopped. He tried to dismiss the dizziness, but it was still there. *Could he make it into the house without making a fool of himself?*

'Don't try to move.'

It seemed much simpler to do as he was told. The van door opened, and Sandy helped him out and along the path. They paused for a few moments while she edged his keys out of his pocket and opened the door. Then they were inside.

'Which way is your bedroom?'

Too confused to argue, Rob pointed, to have Sandy steer him into the room where he collapsed onto the bed, the room swirling around him as his eyes closed again.

*

Sandy didn't know what to do. When Rob had collapsed on the beachfront as soon as the fireworks started, she worked out he was having some sort of flashback to his army experiences. But she felt helpless. All she could think of was the need to get him away from whatever was upsetting him.

Now he was back home, but still seemed disorientated. She couldn't leave him like this. What if something happened during the night? Deciding to stay for a little while at least, she made her way to the kitchen. Surely Rob wouldn't mind if she made herself a cup of tea?

In the kitchen, Bess came lumbering out of her basket to sniff at Sandy's ankles. She'd forgotten about the dog. Did she need feeding? Sandy checked the animal's bowls, but they were both partially full. The dog wandered around the kitchen, which was surprisingly neat and tidy for a bachelor, she thought, then settled back in her basket. Sandy easily managed to find some camomile tea, then took it into the living room and sat down on the sofa. This room was more lived in, with a laptop open on the coffee table along with various books about bikes and cycling and the latest Adam Holland thriller.

Finishing the calming tea, Sandy's eyes began to close. She forced them open and went to check on Rob. Opening the bedroom door, she peered in to see he was sound asleep. She tiptoed in and gently placed a blanket over him, then crept out again.

Back in the living room, she debated what to do, finally deciding she couldn't leave him. She sent a text to Ruby, then curled up on the sofa with another blanket and closed her eyes.

A loud yell awakened her. Startled, Sandy sat up, taking a moment to remember where she was. Then she rushed to Rob's room. He was thrashing around on the bed, his legs tangled in the blanket, strange yells and grunts coming from him. She thought she recognised the name Ned. Wasn't that what he'd been shouting on the beachfront?

Without thinking, she climbed onto the bed and took him in her arms, holding him tightly and hushing and rocking him as if he were a baby. Gradually he began to calm down and finally went back to sleep, clutching her hand. Unwilling to disturb him, Sandy remained beside him, pulling the blanket over them both.

*

Sandy wakened to the sun shining through the window, and Rob's face close to hers. From where she was lying, she could see every line and wrinkle and the grey streaks in his beard which looked so soft she wanted to touch it.

He opened his eyes. 'What...?' He sat up suddenly and looked around. 'What are you doing here? What happened?' Then, realising they were both fully dressed, he slid down onto the bed again. 'Hell, it was those damned fireworks, wasn't it? I didn't know... They've never had them at the tree lighting before. I've always managed to keep away when I knew there was to be a display, in case... What did I do? Did I make a fool of myself?'

'No. You were upset, disoriented. I brought you home and... I didn't think you should be alone, so I stayed... on the sofa.'

'But you're not on the sofa.' The hint of a smile appeared on the corner of his mouth.

'You were having a nightmare. I came in to help and... you were holding onto my hand so tightly, I stayed.'

Rob's face paled. 'You shouldn't have seen that. No one should.' Then he seemed to remember. 'Bess?'

'She's fine. I checked on her when we got back.' As she spoke, the dog nosed the door open and padded to the side of the bed. Suddenly embarrassed by their closeness, Sandy rolled away from Rob. 'I should move. You'll want to…'

Rob ran a hand through his hair. 'Don't go yet. At least stay for breakfast. I just need to… Hell!' His eyes glazed over. 'Was I really bad? Did I…?'

'You were upset. I tried to comfort you. It seemed to work. You went back to sleep.'

'I did?' Rob shook his head. 'I normally have to get up and walk around, make myself a drink. It's usually Bess who helps calm me. She's a therapy dog, at least she started out that way. Sorry, I'm babbling. Let me have a shower and make you some breakfast. It's the least I can do.'

Sandy smiled. 'Why don't I make breakfast while you shower? If you trust me in your kitchen.'

Rob gave her a wide grin. 'You're the cook.'

Pleased to see him looking so well, so different from the wreck he'd been the night before, Sandy made her way to the kitchen, followed by Bess. First, she managed to find the dog food to fill the animal's bowl, then she foraged in the fridge and pantry to find eggs, bacon and mushrooms which she decided to turn into an omelette. The omelette was almost ready, the coffee brewing and two slices of bread toasting, when Rob appeared in the kitchen wearing a pair of khaki shorts and a white tee-shirt, his hair damp from the shower. She swallowed. *How could she ever have thought this man unattractive?*

'Wow, something smells good,' he said, patting Bess who padded over to greet him. 'I'm really sorry about last night. If I'd known there was to be fireworks, I'd have made sure to leave before they began. I'm sorry you had to see me like that… and in the night, too.' He reddened.

'It's okay. I guessed it was a hangover from your time in a war zone.'

'Yeah.'

'Who's Ned?' she asked, when they had begun to eat. 'You mentioned him during the fireworks and again in your nightmare.'

When Rob didn't answer, Sandy gazed at him, seeing his eyes glaze over again. It was as if he'd gone somewhere she couldn't follow.

'Sorry,' he said again just when she thought the silence was going to go on for ever. 'Ned was my mate. He was killed. The poor sod didn't stand a chance. I was right there… It should have been me.'

Sandy inhaled sharply. No wonder Rob was so plagued with guilt. Not only had he harboured guilt for his brother's death, but he felt responsible for the death of his mate in Afghanistan, too. She wanted to reassure him, but what did she know of the situation? 'I'm sorry, Rob.' There was nothing more she could say. Instead, she patted Bess's head, the dog having chosen to lie at her feet.

No more was said about Rob's collapse or his heart-rendering confession.

When they finished eating, he said, 'No need to clear up. I can do it. I'm going to need to go into the shop today. I have a lot to organise after yesterday. I'm sure you have things to do, too.'

'Of course,' Sandy said stiffly, accepting what she saw as a brush off. 'I'll leave you to it. Your van is still in town. Do you need a lift?'

'No thanks. The walk will do me good, and Bess will enjoy the exercise.'

'Okay.' It didn't seem right to leave him after such an intimate experience, but she recognised his embarrassment at waking up to find her in his bed, and later to share his confidence with her. It wasn't the best way to establish a relationship. Shocked at her thoughts, Sandy quickly grabbed her bag, ready to leave. She had just reached the door, when Rob caught her by the arm, sending shivers down her spine.

'Sorry if I seem rude. I owe you for what you did for me last night, for putting up with me when…' He pulled on his beard. 'We never did have that drink. Can I make it up to you? Dinner tonight? Pick you up at seven?'

Stunned, a thrill of excitement shooting through her, Sandy agreed.

# Thirty-six

What started out to be the one of the most horrible nights of his life, resulted in one of the best. After his initial embarrassment at Sandy having seen him at his worst, Rob discovered she was a pleasant companion, someone who wasn't repelled by the sight of him in the throes of a nightmare. And although he had no intention of allowing her to see him like that again, he did wonder if perhaps one day...

That evening was the beginning of many, and the kiss she'd stolen from him on his birthday was repaid many times over. But that was all. Despite Sandy having seen him in a nightmare, it wasn't something he was anxious to repeat. So, in spite of the ache of desire he experienced each time they were close, he steadfastly refused to give in to his longing for anything more intimate.

Suddenly, it seemed, Christmas Eve arrived and with it both the Christmas fundraiser and the children's bike parade. Rob had liaised closely with Sandy regarding the latter and, although he was aware her ex had arrived to spend Christmas in Bellbird Bay, he was hoping they might be able to fit in a celebration of their own.

Everyone in Bellbird Bay seemed filled with the Christmas spirit as customers arrived to pick up their Christmas orders, ready to be hidden away until the next morning. He had prevailed upon Sandy and Ruby – with whom he'd developed an understanding – to provide him with a selection of fancy shortbread and gingerbread cookies which he and Zack served with coffee to those who were waiting to be served.

It was late morning before the rush died down, and Zack dashed off to take part in the fundraiser, leaving Rob to tidy up before heading to the beachfront himself, just in time to see the end of the race and join in the laughter as, one after the other, the surfers emerged from the water, their Santa outfits sodden and falling apart. He accepted a glass of champagne from a weary Will Rankin whose responsibility it had been to organise the event, then looked around for Sandy. She was nowhere to be seen, but Fliss was there, hanging onto Zack's arm, a tall stranger on her other side.

'Your mum here?' Rob asked.

Fliss shook her head. 'She's busy getting ready for this afternoon. Have you met my dad?' She nodded to the man now gazing at Rob with an amused expression.

'Hi, you must be...'

'Grant Elliot.' He held out a hand.

Rob shook his hand. 'Rob Andrews I'm...'

'Sandy's friend. I knew there was someone... when we met in Sydney. Pleased to meet you. Fliss tells me you're a good man. Sandy deserves to have found someone... after the way I treated her. Despite everything, I've always tried to be there for her and Fliss, but I won't be in the future. I'm off to the US next month, so I hope...' he nodded, before Fliss and Zack dragged him off.

Rob stared after them, unsure exactly what Grant had meant, but suspecting he was reading more into Rob's relationship with Sandy than was warranted. He suddenly felt very small. Was he being unfair to Sandy, taking up her time when she could... should... be finding someone else, someone more deserving, someone who could make her happy, be a good stepdad for Fliss and...?

'All set for this arvo?' Will's voice brought Rob back to the present.

'Sure. All my orders have been collected and I've closed up shop till after New Year. Can't believe I'll have a whole week off.'

'Good man.' Will clapped him on the shoulder. 'You deserve a break, time to spend with that woman of yours.'

'We're not...' But Will had already gone off to check with someone else.

\*

'Met your fellow.'

Sandy looked up from the kitchen bench where she'd been working all morning along with Ruby and Liam, preparing for the after-parade party. Grant was leaning against the doorway. He was grinning. 'Seems like a decent sort.'

'He is.' Sandy was too busy to have this conversation right now. Things were going well with Rob. They were spending time together. They enjoyed each other's company. But… their relationship seemed to have stalled, when it should have been moving forward. After the night she'd spent with him, having seen him at his most vulnerable, she'd thought things would progress more quickly. It was what she wanted, and she could tell he wanted it, too, but something seemed to be holding him back. It wasn't the sort of thing she could discuss with Grant, or even Ruby, though she had seen an odd expression in Ruby's eyes from time to time, as if the old woman wanted to say something to her but had decided not to.

Grant didn't move.

'Look, Grant, if you're going to stand there, you could at least make yourself useful. I have five more batches of sausage rolls to make, and Liam could do with help chopping carrot and celery sticks for the dips. There's another apron over there.' She nodded towards a hook on the back of the door.

Ruby, who was busy mixing up the ingredients for a batch of brownies, chuckled. 'There's no room for slackers here today, Grant. Even Fliss did her bit before she went out.'

'Okay, okay.' With good humour, Grant donned an apron and, picking up a knife, began to help Liam.

They all worked together happily until Sandy called a halt. Pushing back a stray strand of hair from her forehead, she said, 'Okay, folks. I think we've done it. We should have a bite to eat before we start packing the van. Then you can both take a rest while Liam and I deliver the food,' she said to Ruby and Grant.

'I'll come with you,' Grant said, surprising Sandy. 'Fliss said she and Zack plan to help out serving the kids, and I want to see as much of her as I can while I'm here.'

'Okay, but I'm sure you want to rest, Ruby.'

Ruby nodded. 'I'm too old for partying,' she said, her cheeky grin belying her words. Sandy took a bag of rolls, a dish of butter, a packet of ham, and a slab of cheese from the fridge. 'It's help yourself for lunch, I'm afraid.'

After lunch, Ruby went to have a nap, while the others packed the van with what seemed to be enough food to feed an army. But Sandy knew it would all disappear in a flash. She always found it rewarding to see her carefully prepared food being enjoyed, and children were great judges of the quality of what they were served.

'I think that's it.' She mentally ticked off her list, before getting into the van with Liam – Grant was to follow in his rental car – and they set off.

When they reached the harbourside, Sandy could see Will and his helpers – which included Fliss and Zack, plus several of their friends – had already set up tables ready for the food. Grant joined in, and they had just finished setting everything out when there was a shout, and the first cyclists appeared, their bikes festooned with tinsel and streamers. When the final group rode in, Rob bringing up in the rear with his *Bay Bikes* van, there was a huge cheer, and parents rushed to their children, who were more interested in the food than in their parents' congratulations.

As Sandy had expected, the food went quickly. Then there was the sound of jingle bells and an open-topped car drove in with a tall figure dressed as Santa, who began to hand out gifts. It was all a great success.

'You did well,' Rob said to Sandy as they stood together watching the spectacle.

'Thanks.' Sandy was grateful for his arm around his shoulders, but she sensed a reticence in him that hadn't been there before. *Had something happened?*

'I have to spend tomorrow with my parents, but can we meet tonight?' he asked. 'I've booked a table at *The Beach House*,' he said, mentioning the restaurant on the beachfront. 'Or do you need to be with your family?' He gestured to where Fliss and Grant were standing together chatting.

'No, I can be with Fliss any time. It's good for her to spend time with her dad, though I suspect Zack may prove more attractive company,' she added, as Zack joined the pair, and Fliss immediately turned her attention to him. 'But it's not my problem.' She'd never been inside

*The Beach House*, but had heard Cleo mention it, and was keen to see it for herself. 'I thought *The Beach House* would be fully booked tonight.'

Rob tapped his nose. 'I have a few contacts. There are some advantages to growing up here, even if I was away for years.'

Sandy smiled. It was one of the things she'd discovered – and liked – about the town, the sense of community, the way it looked after its own. And she was about to become part of it.

*

While she was getting ready for her date, pulling on the candy-striped dress with shoestring straps and stepping into the pair of high-heeled sandals she could barely walk in, Sandy felt the flutter of butterflies in her stomach. Tonight could be the night their relationship moved to the next level, she thought, as she tried to stifle the strange feeling she'd had on the esplanade, sure she had been imagining it.

*The Beach House* lived up to its reputation. Located on a rocky outcrop, it sat right on the edge of the ocean and tonight the sky was lit by a myriad of stars, giving everything a festive and magical appearance. They ordered the shared seafood platter with a bottle of champagne, and Sandy put her worries aside, determined to enjoy the evening.

They had finished the meal, and had ordered coffee, when Rob took Sandy's hand. Her heart thumped. What was he going to say? But what she heard next wasn't what she expected.

'Sandy, I don't think I've been fair to you. You're a lovely woman, wonderful company… You know how much I enjoy our time together, but…'

Sandy's eyes widened. Her mouth went dry.

'I can never offer you any more than what we have right now. It was hearing Grant say…'

'Grant? What does he have to do with it?' If Grant had put a spanner in the works, had somehow turned Rob off her, she'd wring his neck.

'Nothing really. He told me he was happy you'd found me. It was what made me realise… Oh, I'm not handling this very well. You deserve better than I can give you. I'll never… I can never form a proper relationship.'

Sandy's eyes widened further. What was he trying to tell her?

'Oh, it's not... I'm not... But, after everything I've been through... I can't inflict myself on a lovely woman like you.'

'What if I don't mind? I've seen you when...'

'No.' Rob shook his head. 'I don't deserve you. I'm sorry. I should never have...'

Sandy's evening was ruined. They drank their coffee and left. Rob drove her home in silence, as she tried to come to terms with what he had told her. It didn't make sense. They got on so well. She knew he desired her as much as she did him. Why was he so determined to ignore the special connection, the chemistry between them?

She was glad Ruby was in bed when she returned to *Headland House*, and there was no sign of either Grant or Fliss. She couldn't have coped with their company. Taking off the sandals she'd put on with such pleasure and which now seemed to mock her, Sandy ran upstairs, closed the door of her bedroom behind her, threw herself on the bed, and burst into tears.

# Thirty-seven

Christmas Day morning broke, another glorious day, but Sandy's mood was anything but. She had barely slept, her mind going round in circles as she tried to make sense of the way Rob had put an end to their relationship, just as she thought they were going to...

There was a knock at her bedroom door. It opened and Fliss bounced in and gave her a hug. 'Merry Christmas, Mum. Look what Dad gave me!' She held up a brand-new iPhone. 'Isn't it amazing? Are you going to get up? Ruby's making croissants for breakfast, and Dad's made coffee. I'm meeting Zack on the beach for a swim before he has lunch with his folks and...'

Sandy put her hands over her ears and smiled. 'Merry Christmas, darling. That was very generous of your dad.' Sandy had the fleeting thought Grant was attempting to assuage his guilt about going to California. 'And, yes, I'm getting up for breakfast. I couldn't miss Ruby's croissants. You'll be back for lunch, won't you?'

'Course. Ruby says we're having prawns and lobster with salad, and a pavlova.'

'We are,' Sandy said, trying to summon up an energy she didn't feel, and to forget Rob's rejection. 'And I have a gift for you, too,' she added, wondering how the stack of books carefully chosen from *Bay Books* could compete with the latest iPhone. Trust Grant to outdo her again. He'd always been competitive.

Breakfast passed without incident. Fliss was delighted with her choice of books, while Sandy was pleased and surprised by the beach bag Fliss had bought her from *Sassy's*, less so with the cookery book Grant had given her, which she and Ruby would have a laugh about later.

Breakfast over, Fliss set off for the beach, and Grant decided to join her, leaving Sandy with Ruby.

'Something happen last night?' Ruby didn't beat about the bush. 'You're trying to hide it, but I can tell.'

'Oh, Ruby!' The tears which Sandy had been managing to stifle began to stream down her cheeks. 'It's Rob... he...'

'What has the silly boy said?'

Sandy blinked her eyes and repeated Rob's words, as clearly as she could remember. 'I can't believe it,' she finished.

'Then don't. I know it's difficult to believe right now, but it'll all come good. I know what I saw.'

'Not the magpies again?' Sandy managed to raise a smile. Ruby and her damned birds.

Ruby smiled enigmatically. 'Now,' she said, handing Sandy a tissue, 'dry your eyes. We have a Christmas lunch to prepare.'

Sandy was glad they'd decided on a cold meal. Originally, it had been because of all the work they'd had for the children's party on Christmas Eve, but now there was no way she could have contemplated cooking roast turkey with all the trimmings. She always felt it was too hot in Australia for what was a traditional British Christmas meal.

Once the meal was ready and the table set with branches of Christmas bush, Christmas crackers at each place, Sandy was in a better frame of mind. She didn't need Rob Andrews, she told herself. She had all she needed with Fliss and Ruby. Even Grant's company proved pleasant as he and Fliss competed to see who could tell the best joke.

After lunch, the adults retired for a rest while Fliss set up her new iPhone and spread the word with her Sydney friends that she was going to be staying in Bellbird Bay. Then, in the late afternoon, they all went for a walk along the beach before heading back for a snack in front of the television.

It wasn't till she was in bed, that Sandy allowed her tears to fall again, wondering for the hundredth time if there was anything she could do or say to change Rob's mind.

*

Rob spent the day with his parents, eating a traditional Christmas meal of turkey and roast vegetables followed by plum pudding and hard sauce. Not for the first time, Rob wished his mother would follow the local custom and serve a cold meal, maybe prawns and salmon. Over lunch, his mother made several references to his "lady friend", all of which he managed to dodge. He felt bad about the way he'd ended things with Sandy. But it was better it ended now, rather than carry on till her emotions were more invested in the relationship. He ignored his own feelings, reminding himself he didn't deserve happiness.

It was late afternoon before Rob plucked up the courage to mention Brett's death. He knew it would probably make his mother cry, but he hoped his dad would be prepared to listen and perhaps put his worries to rest – if Sandy was to be believed. He took a deep breath. 'Mum, Dad, there's something I need to talk to you about.'

'I knew it,' Gwen said. 'You and this woman... Sandy Elliot, isn't it?' She smiled smugly.

'No, Mum. There's nothing between me and Sandy.'

'But I thought... Dot saw you...'

'Hear the boy out.' Bob put a hand on his wife's arm.

'It's about me... and Brett.'

'Your brother?' His mother's voice rose, breaking as he knew it would.

*Why had he brought this up? But he'd started now.* He continued, 'When he got ill and died, I could never understand why it was him and not me, or why I didn't get sick, too.' He stopped and took another breath. 'I've always felt it was my fault Brett died, that you blamed me for his death, for living when he didn't.' *There, he'd said it.* He looked at his parents who were staring at him, their eyes wide.

His mother was first to speak. 'Oh, my darling boy,' she said. 'Of course we didn't blame you. We were so grateful you'd been spared. You were all we had left of our two beautiful boys. It was a difficult time...'

'Your mother took it hard. To lose a son...' Bob shook his head. 'You were probably too young to understand, but she went into a depression. They were dark days... But how could you imagine we blamed you?'

'It was how it seemed. I'd lost my brother, my twin, my other half, and... there was no one to tell me why. Is it any wonder I blamed myself?'

'Then you left, too,' his mother continued as if he hadn't spoken. 'I felt as if I'd lost both of you... then when you were almost killed in Afghanistan... We were so relieved when you came home to us.' She began to weep, the tears trickling down her cheeks unchecked.

'Look what you've done now. You've made your mother cry,' his father said. 'We never stopped loving you, Rob. I'm sorry if it seemed that way. I wish you'd said something back then.'

'I was too young to know any better. All I could see was both of you grieving. It seemed you didn't have time for me, so I felt guilty for being alive when Brett wasn't.'

'Come here, you fool.' Rob's mother pulled him into a warm hug. 'I'm so sorry, sweetheart. You were what kept me going in the dark days after Brett's death, the knowledge I still had one son who was alive. When they brought you back from Afghanistan, I thought it was all going to happen again... and now, look at you.' She smiled through her tears.

'Your mum's right,' Bob said. 'When we saw you lying there, it was like Brett all over again. But you survived, and we give thanks for that every day.' Rob's mum had released him from her hug and his father threw an arm around his shoulders.

For the first time since before Brett died, Rob felt the warmth of his parents' love. It was a good feeling, and he was grateful to Sandy for her suggestion, unsure why he'd kept his emotions bottled up for so long. It would have saved him so much angst if he had spoken of it before now, but he had been so young when he lost his brother, the blanket of mourning and grief which filled the household had overwhelmed him and sent him into his shell.

'I wish I'd known,' he said. 'I thought it was all my fault.'

'We were all caught up in the grief of Brett's death, son. We should have realised... Was that why you left... joined the army?' his dad asked.

'Partly. We... Brett and I... always intended to. We promised ourselves we would and when he died, it was something I could do for him... keep my promise. It was a good life. I enjoyed it until...'

'But you're home now, back with us again. Now, my only wish is to see you settled and happy.' His mother looked hopeful.

Rob didn't want to disappoint her, so said nothing. There was no point in sharing his belief that he carried bad luck wherever he went.

'Now, I think we deserve a glass of something,' his father said, going to the cupboard where he kept his secret stash of spirits and liquors which were only taken out on special occasions. He took out a bottle of Chivas Regal and, polishing the bottle with his sleeve, poured three small measures. 'Here's to better days,' he said, raising his glass.

'To better days,' Rob said, dutifully swallowing his portion. 'Now, I need to leave you. Bess will need a walk.' He had chosen to leave her at home for once, as it gave him an excuse to leave. 'Thanks for the lovely lunch, Mum, and the voucher.' His parents had given him a voucher to the local menswear store for Christmas.

'We didn't know what to get you. I hope...'

'It's perfect,' he said, giving both her and his dad a hug. 'I'll see you soon.'

It was a relief to get out into the fresh air, away from the atmosphere of his parents' home which had become claustrophobic. Rob had a lot to think about and he could best do that on the beach. But first, he had to go home to pick up Bess.

# Thirty-eight

There had only been a trickle of guests since Christmas, and Sandy was glad Ruby seemed to be winding down the B&B business. From what she could make out, the old woman didn't need the money. It was the company she enjoyed, and now she had Sandy and Fliss, she had plenty of that. But it was difficult for her to refuse guests who had come there year after year.

The call Sandy answered didn't fall into that category. Judith Forsyth was a single lady from Canberra who said she'd heard wonderful reports about Bellbird Bay and *Headland House* and wanted to make a booking for a weekend stay. Unsure what to reply and aware this was Ruby's territory, she called the old woman.

'Book her in,' Ruby said, when Sandy gave her the dates. 'I have no one else staying that weekend. It'll be no trouble.'

Rolling her eyes, Sandy did as she requested and booked her in for the last weekend in January. It coincided with Australia Day, and Sandy had several bookings of her own for the weekend, but she and Liam could easily take care of them.

She was now settled in Bellbird Bay. She and Fliss had taken a trip back to Sydney after the New Year to pack up the apartment, and for Fliss to say goodbye to her friends – the friends she didn't appear too sorry to leave. It had also given them the opportunity to wave Grant off to the US with Fliss promising to visit him there in her school holidays – though not at Easter when Zack would be competing in the surfing championships. The apartment was now on the market and attracting buyers, and Sandy was looking for premises in Bellbird Bay to be a shopfront for *Celebrations*. Life was good. The only downside was her failure to sustain the relationship with Rob Andrews. She still saw him around town from time to time and heard about him from Fliss via Zack. She had even bumped into him at the surf club on New Year's Eve when she was part of a party with Cleo and Will. But there had been no renewal of the close friendship they'd enjoyed... and Sandy missed it.

*

When Judith Forsyth arrived, she proved to be a pleasant woman a few years older than Sandy, who immediately felt comfortable with her. Ruby produced her usual welcoming afternoon tea with scones and, from the kitchen where she was busy making a birthday cake for twin six-year-olds, Sandy could hear the old woman conduct her standard interrogation, disguised as a friendly chat.

Listening with one ear while she iced the pink cake with two white unicorns, she was startled to hear Judith ask, 'Do you know where I can find Rob Andrews? I understand he owns a bike shop here in Bellbird Bay.'

Sandy felt numb. She didn't hear Ruby's reply. Suddenly it made sense. *Canberra... the army. Judith Forsyth must be part of Rob's past, a link to his mate, Ned, the one who died... his widow? But why was she here? Why now? Was she the reason Rob couldn't make a commitment to a relationship with her? Had Sandy been a fool to imagine there could ever be more between her and Rob?*

She wiped away a tear then, realising she had messed the head of one of the unicorns and set about fixing it. Her business was more important than Rob Andrews.

'Did you hear?' Ruby came into the kitchen, just as Sandy finished the cake.

'Has she gone?' Sandy whispered.

'To *Bay Bikes*. I told her where to find him.'

'Well, now we know.'

'What do you mean? There could be all sorts of reasons why she wants to find Rob.'

'A woman like her? Well-dressed, elegant? I doubt it.'

'We'll see.' Ruby tapped her nose in the infuriating way she had – as if she knew something no one else did.

*

Rob was finishing up for the day, when he heard the shop doorbell. He looked up to see a familiar figure but not one he expected to see here. Judith belonged in Canberra. What was she doing in Bellbird Bay?

'Judith!' Rob wiped his hands on a dirty rag. They were oily from the repair he had been busy with for the past thirty minutes.

'Sorry if I gave you a shock.'

'You didn't say you were coming.'

'It was a spur of the moment decision. Can we talk?' She glanced around at the array of bikes.

'Give me a minute.' Rob disappeared into the back of the shop. He washed his hands, drew his fingers through his hair and grimaced at himself in the mirror, before returning to the shop.

'I didn't realise *Bay Bikes* was such a big establishment,' Judith said.

'It is what it is. It's grown over the years.' Rob was proud of what he'd established, how the small shop he'd set up had grown to include the neighbouring one, allowing him to have the display area along with a workroom and a fairly spacious back shop. 'Come through.' He led her through to the back room which housed a table and a couple of chairs. It was where he ate lunch when he didn't go to the café. 'Coffee?' he asked, turning on the coffee maker.

'Thanks.' Judith took a seat, and Rob was conscious of her eyes on him as he brewed the coffee.

'So, to what do I owe the honour of this visit?' he asked, when they both had their drinks. 'I don't imagine you've come all the way to Bellbird Bay to see me.'

'Actually, I have.'

Rob stared at her in surprise.

'I… after your last visit… you said something that stuck in my mind. I'm sorry it's taken me all this time to act on it.'

Rob stared at her again. They'd last met on his trip to Canberra when he'd done the right thing by Ned and visited his widow. But that had been nine months ago, Anzac Day. When he could, he liked to make the effort to attend the dawn service at the Australian War Memorial. There was a war memorial right here in Bellbird Bay, but somehow it meant more to him in the capital. It was the one day of the year when he revisited his army days, when he got together with those of his mates who'd survived, who were in the country not overseas fighting other people's wars. That's how he thought of them now, though it hadn't seemed so at the time. These days he was aware of the futility of war, of all wars. But a part of him still enjoyed the camaraderie of getting together with old mates.

'I know it's been a long time... months. I'm sorry it's taken me so long.'

Rob dragged a hand through his hair. What had he said that Judith had mulled over for months, that had brought her up here so close to the anniversary of Ned's death, a time when most people wanted to be with their families. He tried to remember if Judith had family in Canberra.

As if reading his mind, she said, 'I'll be going back home for the anniversary. I always spend it with my parents and Ned's.'

At the reference to Ned, Rob was flooded by the guilt he always experienced when he thought of his mate, of the conviction the wrong man had died.

Judith continued, 'That day, you came straight from the service. You were distressed.' She glanced at him. 'I understand how moving the ceremony is, how it brings it all back. I avoid it for that very reason. I don't need the dawn day service to remember Ned, I remember him every single day.'

Rob winced. As if he needed reminding. He relived Ned's last moments too often. Even now, he could feel himself break out in a cold sweat, his hands slippery on the mug of coffee. 'So do I,' he said gruffly, afraid to say more lest he break down.

'To get to the point, you said something about guilt, about feeling guilty it was Ned who died, not you. At the time, I thought it was the drink talking. I think you'd had a few before you dropped round.'

Rob remembered. He'd gone to the pub with a few of the guys; he'd needed some Dutch courage to face Judith, his mate's widow. He always felt she'd blamed him for Ned's death, for her losing the baby. It had all been his fault, something he had to live with for the rest of his life.

'But why now?'

'It was at Jacko's funeral…'

Rob winced. Jacko had been a mate, another who'd survived, only to be overcome with survivor guilt. Unable to handle it, he'd committed suicide a month earlier, just before Christmas. He should have been there for him, gone to the funeral, but couldn't face it… the grief, the recriminations, the feeling that there but for the grace of God and his pigheaded determination, the knowledge of what it would have done to his parents to lose another son, it could have been him.

'I spoke with Tom Hardie.'

*The brigadier. He had been Rob's command chief during the conflict.*

'We were talking about Ned and your name came up…'

Rob flinched. He didn't need to hear this, but there seemed to be no way of stopping her. Bess, sensing his distress, moved closer. Rob put a hand on the dog's head, the feel of her soft coat providing some comfort.

'He was unflinching in his praise, said you did everything humanly possible to save Ned, but he was too badly injured. He said you should have got the Victoria Cross but doubted you'd have accepted it. So, you see, Rob,' Judith's voice was gentle, 'you have nothing to blame yourself for. You were a hero.'

Rob swallowed. It was all very well for her to say that, for the brigadier to act as if he had nothing to reproach himself for, but he'd been there, been the one who… He replayed the scene in his mind, but this time, it looked different. This time, he saw himself run towards Ned yelling to him, then… nothing. He'd woken up in a field hospital. *Had he been beating himself up all these years for something that didn't happen?*

'Are you okay, Rob?' Judith put her hand on his arm, causing Bess to emit a low growl.

'I think so. It's a shock. I've always thought… if I had acted sooner… if I had…' He shook his head. 'Sorry, Judith, I can't get my head around this.'

'I wish I'd known sooner. I could have saved you a lot of angst.'

'No, not your fault.'

'I'm sorry.'

Neither spoke for several moments then Judith said, 'Will you be all right if I go now? I plan to be here till Monday. Maybe we can...'

'Can I call you? Where are you staying?'

'*Headland House.*'

Rob flinched again. What a bizarre stroke of fate that Judith was staying with Ruby and Sandy, with the one woman who, if things had been different, he could have... But things *were* different... if he could believe Judith. But he couldn't suddenly wipe out years of nightmares and guilt – and coming so soon after the discussion with his parents about Brett's death... it was almost too much. He needed time to come to terms with it, to decide what, if anything, had really changed. 'You'll have met Sandy Elliot,' he said, unable to stop himself, taking pleasure in speaking her name.

'The young woman who helps out at the B&B? I have. She seems lovely.' Judith peered at Rob. 'Is she... are you and she...?'

Rob shook his head. 'At one point it seemed as if we could be, but it wasn't fair to inflict my guilt on her. She deserves better.'

'But there's no need for you to feel guilty, Rob. That's what I came to tell you. So, surely you can...' Her voice trailed off at his pained expression. 'Sorry. I seem to keep apologising. I'll leave now. You will call me?'

'I promise. We can have dinner. It's the least I can do for Ned, and to thank you for coming all the way here. I just need time to think it all through.'

'Sure.' Judith gave him a brief hug and she was gone.

Rob sat without moving for what seemed an age then, getting up, he placed the *Closed* sign on the door and locked it, then called to Bess to come, before heading to his van to drive home.

# Thirty-nine

Sandy tried her best to keep a smile on her face for the rest of the weekend, but every time she caught sight of their guest, she found it difficult to disguise the flash of jealousy that flared up. Regardless how often she told herself there was no reason for it, that Rob Andrews had never promised her anything, that she didn't need a man in her life, that she didn't care for him, anyway, the thought of him with Judith made her feel sick.

It was a relief when Monday arrived, and she could distract herself with the Australia Day celebrations.

'Would you like a ride down to the esplanade, Ruby?' Sandy asked after breakfast, when Judith had disappeared. She was leaving town later today and had already checked out, after giving Sandy a strange look. Sandy wondered if Rob planned to follow her back to Canberra or if Judith would move here. *It was none of her business.*

'That would be lovely thanks, Sandy. I'm not up to the walk, and I'm still not inclined to attempt the bike again yet. Maybe I need to get one of those motorised scooter things,' she chuckled.

'You mean a mobility scooter? It might not be a bad idea.' Sandy knew how Ruby hated being reliant on her for transport. She'd always been so independent till her accident. It had really taken the stuffing out of her. She made a mental note to speak to Will Rankin about it. Ruby was a well-loved member of the community. Surely they could help support her with the purchase of a means of transport?

'There's so much more happening here than in Sydney,' Fliss said, appearing in a pair of brief shorts and a tee-shirt proclaiming *Happy Australia Day* with a picture of a koala and the Australian flag.

'It just seems that way, Fliss,' Sandy said.

'It's because Bellbird Bay is smaller. It's easier to become involved,' Ruby said. 'I'm sure there were Australia Day celebrations in lots of parts of Sydney, too. Maybe your friends didn't take part in them.'

'I guess not,' Fliss said. 'Anyway, I'm glad we're living here, now, Mum.' She gave Sandy a warm hug, making her glow with pleasure. She was glad she'd made the move here. Ruby had been right. The fire – and Ruby's accident – had changed their lives for the better.

\*

It was busy on the esplanade and beachfront, the glorious weather seeming to have encouraged everyone to join in the celebrations. A group consisting of three young men and a girl were playing Australian ballads. Sandy was singing along to the chorus of *I Still Call Australia Home*, and about to bite into a roll filled with sausage and fried onions when she caught sight of Rob with Judith. Something shrivelled in her gut as she watched them walking along with Bess.

'Everything is all right,' Ruby said.

Sandy stared at her in surprise. Surely she meant, "Is everything all right?" She tried not to look towards where Rob and Judith were now standing, but it was as if her eyes were drawn towards the pair.

'Hey, Mum!' Fliss appeared with a large stick of fairy floss in one hand, the other grasping Zack's. 'Did you see the indigenous dancers? They were amazing.'

'Yes, honey.' Sandy was too distracted to say more. What was going on between Rob and Judith? As she watched, Rob gave the woman a kiss on the cheek, then hugged her, before they went off in different directions. She went towards the car park, while he headed up the boardwalk with Bess.

'It'll be fine.' Ruby placed a hand on Sandy's arm.

Sandy shook it off. Ruby wasn't always right. Look at that ridiculous thing about magpies. Sometimes she wondered if the old woman was losing it. She took a bite of the sausage-filled roll, but it tasted like sawdust. She looked at it in disgust and threw it into the bin. What had possessed her to buy it? 'Why don't we head to the surf club for lunch? My treat,' she said.

The club was busy, too, making Sandy regret her offer of lunch, but Ruby was in her element, greeting everyone she knew and nodding to those she didn't. It made Sandy wish she'd suggested this more often. Poor Ruby must be feeling trapped in the house at the top of the boardwalk.

After ordering their meals – fish and chips for Ruby and a salad Sandy didn't expect to eat, for herself, Sandy ushered the older woman out onto the deck where there was fresh air. 'Wow, I didn't expect it to be so busy,' she said when they were settled.

'Always is on Australia Day,' Ruby said with a grin. 'Brings everyone out to celebrate. You feeling better now?'

'What do you mean?'

'I saw your face out there when you noticed Rob with Judith Forsyth.'

Sandy felt herself redden. 'It's none of my business who he talks to.'

'Maybe not.' Ruby looked as if she was about to say more, but the arrival of their meals prevented her speaking.

Sandy was pushing the food around her plate, when her phone pinged with a text. Seeing Rob's number, her stomach churned. *What did he want?* They hadn't spoken or communicated since Christmas Eve.

'Who's that?' Ruby pointed to Sandy's phone.

'No one.' She wasn't going to tell Ruby it was Rob and have her making all sorts of insinuations. She'd read the text later – or maybe just delete it.

*

Sandy waited till they were back home, and Ruby had lain down for a nap, before she opened the text. It was brief and to the point.

*I owe you an apology. We need to talk. Can we meet? Please?*

Sandy stared at the message trying to read more into it. But, no matter how long she looked at the words, she couldn't detect any hidden meaning. She wavered between agreeing to meet and ignoring it, but finally her curiosity won the day and she replied, *Okay, when and where?*

To her surprise, the reply came immediately.

*Can we meet below the headland in an hour?*

Now, consumed with curiosity as to why he seemed to be in such a rush, she answered, *I'll be there.*

Butterflies doing cartwheels in her stomach, Sandy changed three times before deciding on a blue and white striped sundress with wide straps and a white belt. Slipping her feet into a pair of white sandals, she tidied her hair, renewed her lipstick, grimaced at her reflection in the mirror and, leaving a note for Ruby, set off to climb down the steps to the beach. In her haste, she'd forgotten a hat, and the late afternoon sun beat down on her head as she made her way to the edge of the ocean where she could see Rob standing, looking out to sea. There was no sign of Bess. He was alone.

As if sensing her presence, he turned.

Sandy was shocked to see the pain in his eyes. *What had happened to him since they last spoke?*

'You came.'

Sandy nodded, a light breeze blowing up and whipping her hair around her face. She pushed it back and gazed at him, trying to figure out what he was thinking. *Why was she here?*

'Sandy, I'm sorry. I... When we last spoke, I was a mess. I didn't think it fair to inflict myself on you, on any woman, but especially you.'

Sandy waited, her stomach churning.

'I didn't think I deserved to be happy, to deserve the affection and friendship of someone as lovely as you. I told you about my brother, but it wasn't the whole story. Oh,' he said, clearly seeing the question in her eyes, 'I took your advice and talked to my parents – on Christmas Day. You were right. They never blamed me. All those years...' He shook his head. 'But the rest... It took Judith to make me see reason.'

Sandy felt her heart lurch. He was going to tell her he was leaving, moving to Canberra to be with Judith. She steeled herself for his next words.

'Judith is my mate's widow. Ned was with me in Afghanistan. He died... was killed right in front of me. I think I told you, after the night of the fireworks, when I called out his name. Ever since, I blamed myself, thought it was me who should have died that day. He had a wife, a child on the way. He didn't deserve to die.' His voice broke.

Sandy wanted to comfort him, to throw her arms around his neck, but she restrained herself. He needed to tell this in his own way, in his own time.

'For years, I blamed myself. The nightmare you saw... I was reliving Ned's death, like I did, night after night... knowing it should have been me, wishing it had been me.'

Sandy waited.

'What Judith came to tell me was something our brigadier told her. It was at the funeral of another of the guys – he committed suicide, something I never had the guts to do.'

Sandy recoiled, shocked. *Had he really been suicidal that night on the beach?*

'The point is... I was wrong, terribly wrong. When I met you, there was something about you that spoke to me, a connection I'd never felt before. But, because of my past, I stifled it, pretended it didn't exist. Then I forced myself to distance myself from you, to let you find someone more deserving. Can you forgive me? Is there a chance you can feel something for me? Can we start again?' He reached out to take Sandy's hand.

For Sandy, it was as if the sun had come out from behind a cloud. Rob wanted to... what exactly?

'As friends?' she asked, trembling.

'As friends... and perhaps more?' He smiled.

'I'd like that,' Sandy whispered, feeling a warm glow start at her toes and spread through her whole body.

'Can we start with a drink?'

'No, I should get back to Ruby.' Sandy needed time to digest this new version of Rob. While she didn't doubt his sincerity, it was a lot to absorb.

'Okay.'

Still holding hands, they strolled back to the steps leading up to the headland. They didn't speak much, but from time to time, Rob squeezed Sandy's hand as if to remind her of his words and his intention. Each time he did, she felt another warm glow enfold her.

They climbed up the steps, stopping at the gate to *Headland House*. Rob put one finger under Sandy's chin to tip it up and kissed her. As their lips met, Sandy felt her world stand still.

# Forty

Rob returned home feeling euphoric. It had taken Judith some time to persuade him, but she'd finally done it by telling him he owed it to Ned, that having survived, he owed it to his mate to live the best life he could. Now he'd reconnected with Sandy, he'd text Judith to thank her.

But even though he'd overcome the first hurdle, he knew there was still a way to go before he could fully convince Sandy of his change of heart. Before they'd parted, he'd managed to extract her promise to have dinner with him on Wednesday, and he couldn't wait. It was as if, all of a sudden, the cloud which had been hanging over him for so long had lifted to reveal a glorious future.

In a rare burst of energy, he set about cleaning his already spotless kitchen, causing Bess to whine with annoyance as she was forced to move from her favourite spot. Then, taking pity on the poor creature, he decided to take her for a walk, this time heading in the opposite direction from the boardwalk.

As he walked, his thoughts wandered back to Sandy, reliving how she had felt in his arms, the touch of her lips. It was a heady sensation to imagine how it might feel to lie next to her in his bed again, this time naked, her soft body against his.

He wanted to do something special, something which would prove to Sandy how he felt, prove he was sincere. His mind whirled with one idea after another, till it came to him. He remembered seeing a programme on television. It was one of those reality shows – *A Farmer Wants a Wife*. Not something he normally watched. He must have caught it by accident. From what he could recall, this guy had set up a special date for his lady – a table just for the two of them set up on a private deck. At the time he'd thought it ridiculous, organised by the producers of the show to titillate the television audience, and had quickly switched channels. But now it didn't seem so silly as he pictured a table on the beach, a romantic dinner, just him and Sandy, the ocean and the stars. He began to wonder how it could be organised. Maybe he could rope in Fliss and Zack.

By Wednesday, the idea had taken hold, but Rob knew it would take some time to arrange. For tonight, he'd booked a table at *The Leonard Family Resort*. The hotel was under new management and, despite the name, didn't only cater for families. Rob had heard good reports about the restaurant since Leo Carlson had taken over and thought Sandy might enjoy eating there and checking out the menu.

He was feeling nervous as the time drew near for him to pick Sandy up. Unlike their previous dates, this one felt important, serious. Was he about to fulfil his mother's dearest wish and form a proper relationship? 'What do you think, Bess?' he asked his dog, as he dressed in the pair of cream pants and chambray shirt he'd purchased with his parents' Christmas gift. 'Am I making too much of an effort?' Bess opened her mouth wide and yawned, clearly unconcerned with her master's dilemma.

By the time he reached *Headland House*, Rob had convinced himself Sandy would have changed her mind. He was in such a mess, it was a relief when Ruby opened the door and said, 'She's almost ready. Do you want to come in?'

Stepping over the threshold, Rob was struck by the sense of comfort that immediately surrounded him. This was only the second time he'd actually been inside the house which had provided such a focus of his childhood fun – he and his friends had taken delight in knocking on the door and running away, laughing when Ruby, who they regarded as a witch, came to the door and looked around. Now he knew better and regretted his youthful thoughtlessness.

'So, you've come to your senses at last,' Ruby said.

'Umm.'

'I knew you would when I saw the two magpies. I told Sandy, but I don't think she believed me. Many don't,' she said with a shake of her head.

Magpies? What was she talking about? Rob knew some people still called Ruby a witch, while others swore by her predictions. Before he could reply, Sandy appeared in the doorway. Tonight, she took Rob's breath away. She was wearing something which shimmered in the light shining through the window and had done something different with her hair. He was tempted to pull her into his arms right there and then. Only Ruby's presence stopped him. 'Ready?' he said.

'Ready,' she replied. 'I won't be late, Ruby,' she said to the old woman who was regarding them both with a fond smile.

'No need to hurry home on my account,' Ruby said, winking at Rob, who immediately felt guilty without knowing why. *Had she read his mind?*

\*

Sandy couldn't believe how happy she was. Even Fliss had caught some of her excitement and helped her decide what to wear before heading out herself. When she stepped into the hallway and saw Rob's eyes widen, Sandy knew the white dress, covered in tiny silver halfmoons, was a good choice. Although she had been to dinner with Rob on many previous occasions, this one felt different, and she was reminded of Ruby's words, the ones she'd ridiculed.

She hadn't been inside *The Leonard Family Resort*, but had driven past several times, and Cleo had recounted how she and Will had enjoyed a meal there before they were a couple, when they'd been set up by her friend, Ailsa. Now it had a new owner, a man who had come to live in Bellbird Bay when he renewed an old relationship with the woman who owned *Birds of a Feather*. It still amazed Sandy how much she'd learned about the people she met every day in the short time she'd lived here. It shocked her to think they probably knew just as much about her.

Entering the restaurant, they were greeted by the low sound of music from a grand piano in one corner and were shown to a table near a large window from which they had a view of perfectly landscaped gardens, with a pool and tennis court in the distance.

'Very nice,' she said, looking around to where several tables were occupied by families, others by couples like themselves.

'I've heard it used to be a lot more upmarket,' Rob said. 'The previous owner wanted it to cater to the wealthy Sydneysiders and Melbournians. Leo understands the needs of Bellbird Bay better.'

'You know the owner?'

'Not really, but we've met. Difficult not to. And he's friends with Will and Martin.'

'Small towns.'

Rob grinned.

By the time the wine was served, and they had ordered the fish burritos which were the blackboard special, Sandy was feeling more relaxed and beginning to enjoy Rob's company.

'Tell me more about yourself,' Rob said when they were waiting for their meals to be served. 'When I met your ex, it seemed you were on good terms... and he's off to the US?'

'Yes. He teaches university and was offered a position there. Unlike a lot of couples, we've managed to remain friends, more for Fliss's sake than anything else. But he was very supportive of my business. It'll be strange not having him around; Fliss will miss him. But she wouldn't have been able to see him so often anyway, now we've moved here.'

'You don't regret the move?'

'Oh, no!' Sandy blushed. 'It was good from everyone's point of view – mine, Fliss's, and Ruby's.'

'You and Ruby... you said you're not related?'

'No, as I think I said, she was my grandmother's best friend, and when Gran was dying, she made me promise to keep in touch with Ruby. I would have anyway. Gran brought me up after my parents died and I spent most of my holidays here when I was growing up. It's thanks to Ruby I chose the career I did. I have a lot to thank her for.'

'She's an interesting lady.'

'Mmm.' Sandy smiled.

Their meals arrived and the conversation turned to discussing food and how *Celebrations* was faring.

'You intend to continue working out of *Headland House*?' Rob asked.

'I'm not sure. I think Ruby would like it if I did, but it's not really a commercial kitchen. I've been looking around for premises. It would be good to have a shopfront like I did in Sydney before the fire. I could take on more staff and sell cakes retail.' Sandy felt a surge of excitement as she laid out her plans.

Rob had been quiet for several moments. Suddenly he said, 'The shop next to *Bay Bikes* is becoming vacant.' He cleared his throat, then pulled on his beard. 'I know it may not be what you're looking for, but it is in a good part of town. It might be worth checking out. I can speak to the owner if you're interested.'

Sandy stared at him in surprise. It would be perfect, but to set up right next door to Rob. It would mean she'd see him every day. What if things between them didn't go well? 'I…' She needed time to consider.

'You don't need to decide right now, but I could think of nothing better than to have you next door to me every day.' He reached across the table to take her hand. 'Sandy, I know I've acted like a fool. I hope you can forgive me. When I asked if we could start again, I meant it from the bottom of my heart. I want us to have a future together, and I hope it's what you want, too. It may be too soon for you. If so, I can wait. Just don't keep me waiting for too long.' He smiled and Sandy felt something shift inside her, as she realised just how much Rob had come to mean to her.

She'd been disappointed – devastated – when they'd parted. Now, she was finding it difficult to believe how much he'd changed. 'I…' she repeated, the butterflies in her stomach doing cartwheels. Could she believe him? He seemed sincere.

Rob glanced around, then threw some dollar bills on the table. 'Let's get out of here,' he said.

Giggling like teenagers, they left the restaurant. They piled into the *Bay Bikes* van and Rob started it up.

'Where are we going?' Sandy asked. But she didn't care. She knew she was safe with Rob. She trusted him more than she'd trusted anyone she'd ever known. When they pulled up above the most beautiful bay she'd ever seen, the moon glistening on the water, she gave a sharp intake of breath.

'Dolphin Beach,' Rob said, helping her out of the van and pulling her into his arms. 'I knew there wouldn't be anyone here at this time. I needed to get you alone so I could kiss you properly… and he proceeded to do just that, kissing Sandy until she lost all sense of time and place and just wanted to stay in his arms for ever.

# Forty-one

It was Valentine's Day, and Sandy couldn't believe how much had happened in the past two weeks. After the dinner she now thought of as the one which changed her life, she and Rob had met every day, either for lunch in the backroom of *Bay Bikes*, or for dinner, often in Rob's home, where they'd talked and talked about their pasts and their dreams for the future as they cuddled up together on his sofa, Bess lying contentedly beside them. Also, she had not only viewed the shop next to *Bay Bikes*, she'd signed the lease, was in the process of having the inside remodelled to suit the needs of *Celebrations*, and had ordered replacements for the equipment she'd lost in the fire. Thankfully, her insurance payout had arrived making it all possible.

Now she couldn't imagine life without Rob. Though they still had to consummate their relationship, she knew it wouldn't be long before they did. Meanwhile, she had to suffer Ruby's veiled innuendos and sly glances when she thought Sandy wasn't looking.

Today, she was flat out delivering all the special Valentine's Day cakes her customers had ordered. Thank goodness for Liam's help and that of his friend, Cheryl, who he had introduced to Sandy and who fitted right in. They were studying together, and Sandy suspected they were more than just fellow students.

This morning, she'd been surprised to receive not only a card from Rob, but a large bunch of red roses which must have cost the earth. It was the first time she'd received a card on Valentine's Day for years, and the first time ever for a bunch of roses – Grant had never been one for grand gestures. It made her feel special. Opening the card, Sandy was intrigued to see a smaller one drop out. It was an invitation to dinner that evening at an undisclosed location with instructions to be ready at seven o'clock.

As the day progressed, so Sandy's sense of anticipation grew. *What did Rob have in mind? Would tonight be the one when they took the next step in their relationship?* He'd confided his nightmares had almost ceased, joking that thoughts and images of her filled his dreams instead, and she hoped he was right. Hers were certainly filled with images of him, and she couldn't wait till her dreams became a reality.

By the time seven o'clock came around, Sandy had imagined all sorts of scenarios. As she dressed in a mid-length shift in pale pink and brushed her hair till it shone, she remembered her first impression of Rob, smiling at her foolishness. Now she knew him, the beard and tattoos were so much part of the man she loved that... She stopped, her hand in the air. Loved? Until now, she hadn't admitted, even to herself, that she loved Rob Andrews. But she did. She loved him with all her heart, and she was pretty sure he felt the same way about her. Love was the last thing she'd expected to find in Bellbird Bay, but find it she had, and she'd always be grateful to Ruby – and the magpie – for bringing her here. Maybe she should also be grateful to the youths who burned down her shop, she thought, chuckling.

'He's here, Mum!' Fliss popped her head around the door. 'Oh, you look lovely.' She hugged Sandy, careful not to mess up her dress or her hair. 'You're going to have a wonderful time.'

Giving her daughter a strange look, her stomach churning with excitement, Sandy made her way downstairs to where Rob was waiting. Dressed in a pair of neatly pressed jeans, his white shirt gleaming against his tanned skin, he was oozing sex appeal. She took a deep breath.

Once outside, Rob took her in his arms and gave her a kiss on the lips. 'Happy Valentine's Day,' he said.

'Thanks for the card and the flowers,' she said when she recovered her breath. 'Where are we going?'

Rob didn't reply, but instead of going out the front gate to the roadway he led her through the back fence to the boardwalk and the stairs which led down to the beach.

'How did you...?' Sandy gazed at the table covered with a white cloth, the two chairs similarly decorated, the red flowers – more roses – the champagne goblets, the cake.

'I had some help. Zack and Fliss.'

'Fliss? The little devil. She didn't say.'

'Wouldn't have been a secret if she had. And the cake's Ruby's contribution.' Rob grinned clearly delighted to have made such an impression.

'Wow! You planned all this... for me?'

'I thought you deserved a bit of pampering. You're usually the one to organise special events for others. This one is for you. Our own celebration.'

Sandy was speechless. She'd never imagined Rob as the romantic type. But he'd surprised her before now, this man with his beard and tattoos.

'I'm afraid it's a cold meal,' he said, reaching down to the esky she hadn't noticed, to unpack a platter of smoked salmon, a tub of pâté, cheeses, a loaf of sour dough bread, and a container of chocolate covered strawberries. 'It's the best I could do.'

'It's perfect.' Sandy was blown away by how he had managed to organise all this, how he'd even thought of it.

'To us.' Rob held up his glass of champagne to meet Sandy's.

'To us,' she replied, wondering how life could get any more perfect.

'I need you to know how much you mean to me,' Rob said, placing his glass on the table and taking Sandy's hands in his. 'If we hadn't met, I might still have been stuck in that dark place I'd inhabited since I returned from Afghanistan, filled with guilt and wishing I was dead.'

Sandy tightened her fingers around his hands, shaken to hear how much she had contributed to the change in him, remembering the night on the beach when he'd revealed the depth of his distress.

Rob continued, 'Judith helped too, helped me to see I wasn't responsible for Ned's death. It'll never leave me, but at last, I'm beginning to realise that I'm not to blame for his death – or for Brett's. I still don't believe I deserve you, but... if you're prepared to give me a chance, I'll do my best to make you happy.'

'Oh, Rob!' Sandy felt tears begin to well up. Releasing her hands, she made to brush them away, but Rob's finger was there first, tracing the trail of moisture on her cheek. She caught it and kissed the palm of his hand, revelling in the taste of his skin. 'You're everything I could ever hope for in a man. When I came to Bellbird Bay, I was intent on leaving again when Ruby had recovered. It was why I hesitated, why I didn't want to form a relationship. I didn't expect to meet someone like you, someone who...' Her voice broke. 'I'm glad I did,' she said softly.

Rob took her hands again, gazing into her eyes for what seemed like an eternity. Then, 'We should eat,' he said, pulling his hands away. 'It'd be a shame to waste all this food... and Fliss and Zack would be disappointed, not to mention Ruby.'

At the mention of the old woman's name, Sandy grinned. Maybe Ruby did have special powers. Maybe she had seen Rob and her together. She'd never know.

After they'd eaten the food and consumed most of the champagne, Rob took Sandy's hand, and they wandered along the edge of the ocean in the moonlight. When they stopped, he turned her towards him and put his arms around her. 'You know I love you, don't you?' he murmured between kisses, sending shivers of delight right down to her toes.

'I love you, too,' she said, knowing it was true.

'Will you come home with me?' he asked, his voice husky with desire.

Sandy didn't need to reply. Her kiss did it for her.

Later, as they lay entwined in Rob's king-sized bed, his lips travelling across her forehead, over her eyelids and down to her lips, she knew she'd found the place where she belonged.

## The End

If you've enjoyed Sandy and Rob's story, a way you can say thank you to me is to leave a review on Amazon and/or Goodreads. A few words will suffice, no need for a lengthy review. It will mean a lot to me and help other readers find my books.

The next book in the series, features Cass Marshall, owner of *Sassy's*, the beachwear shop next door to *Birds of a Feather*, and those of you familiar with the series will find all of your old friends there too. It's book nine in this series but, like all my other books, it can be read and enjoyed as a standalone novel.

It's been over twenty years since Cass Marshall's relationship fell apart, and she returned home to Bellbird Bay. Now, although happy with the success of her beachwear business, Cass often longs for someone special to share her life.

Nursing the wounds of a failed marriage, Mick Roberts has finally accepted his ex has moved on with her life. Determined to avoid his daughter's attempts at matchmaking, he immerses himself in his whale-watching business.

When family sickness brings the two together, Cass wonders if her life is about to take a turn for the better. But with Mick's ex-wife also being Cass's best friend, a seed of doubt emerges.

This doubt intensifies when Cass's recently widowed ex arrives in town, determined to use any means to drive a wedge between Cass and Mick as he fights for a second chance.

Can Bellbird Bay work its magic again and provide a happy ever after for Cass and Mick, or are they destined to spend the rest of their lives alone?

You can order it here https://mybook.to/HEAinBellbirdBay

# From the Author

Dear Reader,

First, I'd like to thank you for choosing to read *Celebrations in Bellbird Bay*. I hope you've enjoyed this trip to Bellbird Bay as much as I've enjoyed writing it.

I'm really enjoying writing about my fictional town in the part of Queensland where I live and populating it with characters who I hope you will come to love. I'm thrilled at the number of my readers who tell me they want to live there. It's the eighth book in this series, but like the others, can be read as a standalone.

If you'd like to stay up to date with my new releases and special offers you can sign up to my reader's group.

You can sign up here

https://mailchi.mp/f5cbde96a5e6/maggiechristensensreadersgroup

I'll never share your email address, and you can unsubscribe at any time. You can also contact me via Facebook, Twitter or by email. I love hearing from my readers and will always reply.

Thanks again.

# Acknowledgements

As always, this book could not have been written without the help and advice of a number of people.

Firstly, my husband Jim for listening to my plotlines without complaint, for his patience and insights as I discuss my characters and storyline with him, for his patience and help with difficult passages and advice on my male dialogue, and for being there when I need him.

John Hudspith, editor extraordinaire for his ideas, suggestions, encouragement and attention to detail, and for helping me make this book better.

Jane Dixon-Smith for her patience and for working her magic on my beautiful cover and interior.

My thanks also to early readers of this book – Helen, Maggie and Louise for their helpful comments and advice.

And to all of my readers, reviewers and bloggers. Your support and comments make it all worthwhile.

# About the Author

After a career in education, Maggie Christensen began writing romantic women's fiction heartwarming stories of second chances in later life, proving it's never too late to fall in love. Her travels inspire her writing, be it her trips to visit family in Scotland, in Oregon, USA or her home on Queensland's beautiful Sunshine Coast. Maggie writes of mature heroines coming to terms with changes in their lives and the heroes worthy of them. Maggie has been called *the queen of mature age fiction* and her writing has been described by one reviewer as *like a nice warm cup of tea. It is warm, nourishing, comforting and embracing.*

From the small town in Scotland where she grew up, Maggie was lured to Australia by the call to 'Come and teach in the sun'. Once there, she worked as a primary school teacher, university lecturer and in educational management. Now living with her husband of over thirty years on Queensland's Sunshine Coast, she loves walking on the deserted beach in the early mornings and having coffee by the river on weekends. Her days are spent surrounded by books, either reading or writing them – her idea of heaven!

Maggie can be found on Facebook, Twitter, Goodreads, Instagram, Bookbub or on her website.

https://www.facebook.com/maggiechristensenauthor
https://twitter.com/MaggieChriste33
https://www.goodreads.com/author/show/8120020.Maggie_Christensen
https://www.instagram.com/maggiechriste33/
https://www.bookbub.com/profile/maggie-christensen?list=about
https://maggiechristensenauthor.com/